Books by Margaret Millar

The Devil Loves Me
The Weak-Eyed Bat
The Invisible Worm
Wall of Eyes
Fire Will Freeze
The Iron Gates
Experiment in Springtime
It's All in the Family
The Cannibal Heart
Do Evil in Return
Vanish in an Instant
Rose's Last Summer
Wives and Lovers
Beast in View
An Air That Kills
The Listening Walls
A Stranger in My Grave
How Like an Angel
The Fiend
The Birds and the Beasts Were There
Beyond This Point Are Monsters
Ask for Me Tomorrow

The Murder of Miranda

The Murder of Miranda

Margaret Millar

Random House: New York

Library of Congress Cataloging in Publication Data
Millar, Margaret.
   The murder of Miranda.
   I. Title.
PZ3.M5995Mu   [PS3563.I3725]   813'.5'4
ISBN 0-394-50509-3   78-21811

Manufactured in the United States of America
9 8 7 6 5 4 3 2
First Edition

To my grandson, Jim Pagnusat

The Murder of Miranda

Part I

Mr. Van Eyck had a great deal of money which he didn't want to spend, and a great deal of time which he didn't know how to spend. On sunny days he sat on the club terrace writing anonymous letters.

Bent over the glass and aluminum table he looked dedicated, intense. He might have been composing a poem about the waves that were crashing against the sea wall below him or about the gulls soaring high overhead reflected in the depths of the pool like languid white fish. But Mr. Van Eyck was oblivious to the sound of the ocean or the sight of birds. The more benign the weather, the more vicious the contents of his letters became. His pen glided and whirled across the paper like an expert skater across ice.

> . . . You miserable, contemptible old fraud. Everyone is on to what you do in the shower room . . .

His attention was not distracted by the new assistant lifeguard sitting on the mini-tower above the pool. She was a bony redhead whose biceps outmeasured her breasts and Van Eyck's taste still ran to blondes with more conventional anatomy. Nor was he paying, at the moment, any attention to the other club members, who dozed on chaises, gossiped in deck chairs, read under umbrellas, swam briefly in the pool. Wet or dry, they presented to the public a dull front.

3

Viewed from different, more personal angles they were far from dull. Van Eyck was in a position to know this. He had, in fact, made it his business as well as his hobby. He spent his time shuffling along the dimly lit corridors that led to the secluded cabanas. He wandered in and out of the sauna and massage department on the roof, the wine cellar in the basement, the boiler room and, if it wasn't locked, the office marked Private, Keep Out, which belonged to Henderson, the manager.

Locks and bolts and signs like Keep Out didn't bother Van Eyck, since he assumed they must be meant for other people, passing strangers, new members, crooked employees. As a result of this casual attitude, he had acquired a basic knowledge of vintage wines, therapeutic massage, Henderson's relationship with his bookie, the heating and chlorination of swimming pools and human nature in general.

   . . . You are weaving a tangled web and you will be caught in it, blundering spider that you are . . .

Van Eyck had another advantage in his pursuit of knowledge. He frequently pretended to be hard of hearing. He looked blank, shook his head sadly, cupped his ears: "Eh? What's that? Speak up!" So people spoke up, often saying highly interesting things both in front of and behind him. He grabbed at every morsel like a hungry squirrel and stored the lot of them away in the various hollows in his head. When he was bored he brought them out to chew and finally spit out on paper.

   . . . You must be incredibly stupid to think you can keep your evil ways hidden from an intelligent woman like me . . .

Van Eyck reread the sentence. Then, very lightly, he struck out woman and substituted man, leaving the original word easily legible. It was one of his favorite stratagems, to toss

4

in small false clues and allow the reader to lead himself astray, up and down blind alleys, far from the center of the maze where Van Eyck sat secure, anonymous, shrouded in mystery, like a Minotaur.

He leaned back and took off his glasses, wiped them on the sleeve of his Polynesian print shirt and smiled at the bony redhead across the pool. No one would ever suspect that such a kindly old man, hard of hearing and seeing, was a Minotaur.

"He's at it again," Walter Henderson told Ellen, his secretary. "Don't give him any more club stationery."

"How can I refuse?"

"Say no. Like in N-O."

"We haven't had any complaints. Whoever he addresses the letters to can't be club members or we'd have heard about it before this."

"Suppose he's sending threats to the President. On *our* stationery."

"Oh, he wouldn't. I mean, why should he?"

"Because he needs a keeper," Henderson said gloomily. "They *all* need keepers . . . Ellen, sane people like you and me don't belong in a place like this. I think we should run away together. Wouldn't that be fun?"

Ellen shook her head.

"You don't consider me a fun person, is that what you're trying to tell me? Very well. But bear in mind that you've seen me only in these non-fun circumstances. After five I can be awfully amusing . . . It's that lifeguard, Grady, isn't it? Ellen, Ellen, you're making a most grievous error. He's a creep . . . Now, what were we talking about?"

"Stationery."

"A very non-fun subject. However, let us proceed. In the future club stationery is to be used exclusively for club business."

"When members ask for some stationery it's hard to refuse," Ellen said. "It's their club, they pay my salary."

5

"When they joined they signed an agreement to abide by the rules."

"But we have no rule concerning stationery."

"Then make one and post it on the bulletin board."

"Don't you think it would be more appropriate if you made it, since you're the manager?"

"No. And remember to keep it simple, most of them can't read. Perhaps you should try to get the message across in pictures or sign language."

Ellen couldn't tell by looking at him whether he was serious or not. He wore Polaroid sunglasses which hid his eyes and reflected Ellen herself, twin Ellens that stared back at her in miniature as if from the wrong end of a telescope. Henderson's glasses needed cleaning, so that in addition to being miniature, the twin Ellens were fuzzy and indefinite, two vague pale faces with short brownish hair balanced on top like inverted baskets. Sometimes, deep inside, she felt quite interesting and vivacious and different. It was always a shock to run into her real self in Henderson's glasses.

"Why are you peering at me, Ellen?"

"I wasn't, sir. I was just thinking there isn't any room on the bulletin board since you put up all those pictures your nephew took of sunsets."

"What's the matter with sunsets?"

"Nothing."

"And by the way, I wish you'd stop calling me sir. I am forty-nine, hardly old enough to be called sir by a mature woman of—"

"Twenty-seven."

"I made it quite clear on my arrival how the various echelons are to address me. Let me repeat. To the maintenance men and busboys I am boss. Waiters and lifeguards are to call me sir, and the engineer and catering manager, Mr. Henderson. To you I am Walter, or perhaps some simple little endearment." He smiled dreadfully. "Sweetie-pie, love bunny, angelface, something on that order."

"Really, Mr. Henderson," Ellen said, but the reproof sounded mild. Henderson's lechery was, in fact, so faint-hearted and spasmodic that Ellen considered it one of the lesser burdens of the job. She didn't expect him to be around long anyway. He was the seventh club manager since she'd worked there, and though he was competent enough and had arrived with excellent references, his temperament seemed ill-suited to dealing with the wide variety of emergencies that came with the territory.

The current emergency involved the plumbing in the men's shower room.

One of the toilets had been plugged with a pair of sneakers and a T-shirt. All three objects, in spite of their prolonged soaking, were still clearly inked Frederic Quinn and the nine-year-old was confronted with the evidence. He was then locked in the first-aid room to ponder his crime by Grady, the head lifeguard.

Little Frederic, who went to an exclusive boys' school and knew obscenities in several languages, needed only one: "You can't keep me a prisoner, you pig frig, you didn't read me my rights."

"Okay, here are your rights," Grady said. "You've got a right to stay in there until hell freezes."

"There is no hell, everybody knows that."

"Or until a tidal wave washes away the club."

"The correct word is *tsunami,* not tidal wave."

"Or an earthquake destroys the entire city."

"Let me out, goddammit."

"Sorry, it's time for my lunch break."

"I'll tell everybody you beat me up."

But Grady was already on his way to his locker to get his sandwiches and Thermos.

Left to his own devices little Frederic poured a bottle of Mercurochrome over his head to simulate blood and painted himself two black eyes with burnt match tips. Once his creativity was activated, it was hard to stop. He added a mustache, a Vandyke beard, sideburns and a giant mole in the center of his forehead. Then he redirected his attention to the problem of getting out:

"Help! May Day! Police! Paramedics!"

If some of the members heard him, they paid no attention. There was a strong tradition of status quo at the club as well as the vaguely religious notion that somewhere, somehow, someone was taking care of things.

Miranda Shaw lay on a chaise beside the pool, shielded from the sun by a beach towel, a straw hat, an umbrella and several layers of an ointment imported for her from Mexico. She had no way of knowing that she was the subject of Mr. Van Eyck's current literary project.

> . . . What a fraud you are, acting so refined in public and doing all those you-know-what things in private. I can see behind those baby-blue eyes of yours. You ought to be ashamed. Poor Neville was a good husband to you and he is barely cold in his grave and already you're ogling young men like Grady. Grady is hardly more than a boy and you are an old bat who's had your face, fanny and boobs lifted. Now if you could only lift your morals . . .

Miranda was beginning to feel uncomfortable, and there seemed to be no particular reason why. The sound of the waves was soothing, the sun's rays were not too warm and the humidity registered forty percent, exactly right for the complexion. *It must be the new ointment working,* she thought, *rejuvenating the cells by stimulating the nerve endings. Oh God, I hope it doesn't hurt. I can't stand any more pain.*

She twitched, coughed, sat up.

Van Eyck was staring at her from the other side of the pool, smiling. At least she thought he was smiling. She had to put on her glasses to make sure. When she did, Van Eyck raised his free hand and waved at her. It was a lively gesture, youthful and mischievous compared to the rest of him, which had been sobered and slowed and soured by age. *He must be eighty; Neville was almost eighty when he died last spring—*

She gave her head a quick hard shake. She must stop thinking of age and death. Dr. Ortiz insisted that his patients should picture in their minds only pleasant gentle things like flowers and birds and happy children and swaying trees. Nothing too amusing. Laughter stretched the muscles around the eyes and mouth.

She attempted to picture happy children, but unfortunately little Frederic Quinn was screaming again.

Since his cries for help had gone unanswered, little Frederic was resorting to threats.

"My father's going to buy me a fifty-thousand-volt Taser stun gun and I'm going to point it at you and shock you right out of your pants. How will you like that, Grady you creep?"

"It'll be okay for starters," Grady said, finishing his second peanut butter and jelly sandwich. "Then what?"

"You'll fall motionless to the ground and go into convulsions."

"How about that."

"And maybe die."

"What if your father doesn't want you running around loose with a stun gun?"

"My brother Harold can get one for me," Frederic said. "He has Mafia connections at school."

"No kidding."

"I told you that before."

"Well, I didn't believe you before. Now I don't believe you again."

"It's true. Harold's best friend is Bingo Firenze whose uncle is a hit man. Bingo's teaching Harold a lot of things and Harold's going to teach me."

"You could probably teach both of them. And the uncle."

"What a heap of crap. I'm just a kid, an innocent little kid who was molested in the locker room by the head lifeguard. How will *that* sound to Henderson when I tell him?"

"Like music. He'll probably give me a medal."

"You're a mean bastard, Grady."

"You bet."

Happy children, swaying trees, birds, flowers—Miranda couldn't keep her mind on any of them. Her discomfort was increasing. The doctor had assured her that the new ointment wasn't just another peeling treatment, but it felt the same as the last time, like acid burning off the top layers of skin, dissolving away the wrinkles, the age spots, the keratoids. *He promised no pain. He said I'd hardly be aware of the stuff. Perhaps I used too much. Oh God, let me out of here. I must wash it off.*

She didn't allow her panic to show. She rose, draped the beach towel around her with careless elegance and headed toward the shower room. She walked the way the physical therapist at the clinic had taught her to walk, languidly, as if she were moving through water. The instruction manual advised clients to keep an aquarium and observe how even the ugliest fish was a model of grace in motion. Miranda had an aquarium installed in the master bedroom but Neville had complained that all that swimming around kept him awake. The fish solved the problem by dying off rather quickly, with, Miranda suspected, some help from Neville, because the water had begun to look murky and smell of Scotch.

She moved through an imagined aqueous world, a creature of grace. Past the lifeguard eating a peanut butter sandwich, past the young sisters squabbling over a magazine, and into the corridor, where she met Charles Van Eyck.

10

"Good morning, good morning, Mrs. Shaw. You are looking very beautiful today."

"Oh, Mr. Van Eyck, I'm not. Really I'm not."

"Have it your way," Van Eyck said and shuffled into the office to get some more stationery. It was fine sunny weather. His venomous juices were flowing like sap through a maple tree.

The episode left Miranda so shaken that she forgot all about fish and aquariums and broke into a run for the showers. Van Eyck watched her with the detachment of a veteran coach: Miranda was still frisky and the fanny surgeon had done a nice job.

"No, Mr. Van Eyck," Ellen said. "Absolutely no. It has the club letterhead on it and must be used only for official business."

"I can cut the letterhead off."

"It could still be identified."

"By whom?"

"The police."

"Now why would the police want to identify our club stationery?" Van Eyck said reasonably. "Has there been any embezzlement, murder, interesting stuff like that?"

"No."

"Then why should the police be concerned?" He peered at her over the top of his rimless half-glasses. "Aha. *Aha.* I'm catching on."

"If only you'd just take no for an answer, Mr. Van Eyck."

"When you crossed the terrace you peeked over my shoulder."

"Not really. And I couldn't help—"

"Yes really. And you could help. What did you *see*?"

"You. That's all. The word you."

"You and then what?"

"You—well, then maybe a couple of adjectives or so. Also, maybe a noun."

Van Eyck shook his head gravely. "I consider this a serious breech of club etiquette, Ellen. However, I will overlook it in exchange for a few sheets of notepaper. That's fair, isn't it?"

"Not for me. I have strict orders from Mr. Henderson. If I don't obey them I might get fired."

"Nonsense. You'll outlast a dozen Hendersons. Be a good girl and rustle me up that paper. Half a dozen sheets will do for the time being."

Little Frederic was trying a new ploy.

"Grady, sir, will you please unlock this door?"

"Can't. I swallowed the key."

"Hey man, that's great. You can sue the club and I'll act as your lawyer. We can gross maybe a couple—"

"No."

"Okay, just let me out of here and we'll press the flesh and forget the whole thing."

Grady peeled a banana and took a two-inch bite. "What whole thing?"

"You know. The toilet bit."

"Are you confessing, Quinn?"

"Hell no. Why would I pull a dumb trick like plug a toilet with my own clothes? I'm a smart kid. I was framed."

"If you're so smart," Grady said, "how come you're always being framed?"

"Someone is out to get me."

"I have news for you, Quinn. *Everybody* is out to get you."

"Tell them my father is buying me a stun gun."

"Okay, I'll spread the word right now."

"Where are you going?"

"To the office. They should be the first to know."

Before he left, Grady combed his hair in front of the mirror in the cubbyhole that served as the lifeguards' dressing room. He knew Ellen was interested in him and there was always a chance that some day he might get interested back. She was a nice sensible girl with a steady job and great-looking legs. He could do better but he'd often done a lot worse.

"We can't expel Frederic," Ellen said. "He's already expelled."

"Then how come he's here?"

"He must have climbed over the back fence."

"There are four rows of barbed wire on top."

"The engineer reported yesterday that his wire cutters were missing from the storage shed."

"The kid's a genius," Grady said. "I wish we could think of something constructive for him to be a genius at."

"You can handle him. Opinion among the members is that you're very good with children. They seem to like you—the children, I mean."

"What about the other people?"

"What other people?"

"The ones who aren't children."

"Oh, I'm sure everyone likes you."

"Does that include you?"

She fixed her eyes at a point on the wall just over his left shoulder. "It's against the rules for you to come into the office wearing only swim trunks. You're supposed to put on your warm-up suit."

"I'm not cold," Grady said. "Are you?"

"Stop the cute act."

"What kind of act would you like? I'm versatile."

"I bet you are. But don't waste any of it on me."

He sat on the edge of the desk swinging one leg and admiring the way the sun had tanned the skin while bleaching the hair to a reddish gold. Then he turned his attention back to Ellen. Under ordinary circumstances he wouldn't have bothered making a pass, but right now the pickings were poor. Club members were off limits, especially the teenagers who'd hung around him during the summer indicating their availability in ways that would have shocked their parents as thoroughly as little Frederic's projected stun gun. Anyway, it was fall and they were back in school. Ellen was still here.

He said, "You sure play hard to get. What's the point?"

"And speaking of rules, tell your girl friends not to phone here for you. Mr. Henderson doesn't approve of personal calls at the office."

"Hey, you're laying it on me pretty heavy. Lighten up, will you? I'm not your run-of-the-mill rapist."

"You could have fooled me."

"What are you so mad about, anyway?"

"I'm not mad, merely observant. I've watched you spreading the charm around for your fourteen-year-old groupies all summer and—"

"I like your eyes when you're mad, they're light bright green. Like emeralds. Or 7-Up bottles."

"Yours are gray. And strictly granite."

"I didn't know you were such a mean-type lady."

"I didn't know either." Ellen sounded a little surprised. "I guess it takes a mean-type man to bring it out in me."

"Okay, let's start over. I come into the office to report that I'm having some trouble with one of the kids. And you say we can't expel him because he's already expelled. Then I say—Oh hell, I forget what I said. You really do have pretty eyes, Ellen. They're emeralds. Forget the 7-Up bottles, I just tossed them in to make you laugh. Only you didn't."

"It wasn't funny."

"In fact, you never laugh at anything I say any more." The telephone rang and she was about to pick it up when he reached across the desk and stopped her by grabbing her arm. "I notice you kidding around with some of the members and the engineer and even Henderson. Why the sudden down on me?"

"It's not sudden. It's been coming on for some time."

"Why? I didn't do anything to you. I thought we were friends, you know, on the same side but cool."

14

"Is that your definition of friends, on the same side but cool?"

"What's the matter with it?"

"It seems to leave out a few essentials."

"Put them in and we're still friends. Aren't we?" The phone had stopped ringing. Neither of them noticed. Grady said again, "Aren't we?"

"No."

"Why not . . .? Oh hell, don't answer that. I wouldn't make much of a friend anyhow. Want to hear something funny? I must have had friends all along the line—I've got a lot going for me—but I don't remember them. I remember the places, none of them amounting to a hill of beans, but I forget the people. They walked away or I walked away. Same difference. They're gone like they died on me."

"This sounds like a pitch for sympathy."

"Sympathy? Why would I want sympathy? I'm on top of the world."

"Fine. How's the view?"

"Right now it's not so bad."

A woman was coming down the corridor toward the office and he liked the way she moved, kind of slow and waltzing like a bride walking down the aisle. She wore a long silky robe that clung to her thighs. Her blond hair had been twisted into a single braid that fell over one shoulder and was fastened with a pink flower. With every step she took, the pink flower brushed her left breast. This seemed guileless, but Grady knew enough about women to be pretty sure it wasn't.

He said, "Who's the lady?"

"Mrs. Shaw."

"She looks rich."

"I guess she is."

"Very rich?"

"I don't know. How do you tell the difference between rich and very rich?"

"Easy. The very rich count their money, then put it in a

bank and throw away the key. The rich spend theirs. They drive it, fly it, eat it, wear it, drink it."

"Mrs. Shaw put hers on her face."

"That's not a bad choice."

Ellen's voice was cold. "I can understand a glandular type like you getting excited about some teenage groupies. But a fifty-year-old widow, that's overdoing it a bit, isn't it? She's fifty-two, in fact. When her husband died a few months ago I had to look up their membership application to write an obit for the club bulletin. He was a very sweet old man nearly eighty."

"What's her first name?"

"Why?"

"I just want to know. You make it sound like a crime no matter what I say or do."

"Her name is Miranda. But you'd better stick to Mrs. Shaw if you know what's good for you."

"Can't I even ask a question without you getting all torqued up?"

"Mr. Henderson has a strict rule prohibiting fraternization between members and employees. You were warned about it several times last summer, remember? Frederic's sister April, the Peterson girl, Cindy Kellogg—"

"What's to remember? Nothing happened."

"Nothing?"

"Practically nothing."

"Sometime when I have a week to spare you'll have to tell me what 'practically nothing' covers."

He hesitated for a moment, then leaned across the desk and patted her lightly on the top of her head. Her hair was very soft, like the feathers of a baby duck he'd found on a creek bank when he was a boy. The duck had died in his hands. "Hey, stop fighting me. I'm not so bad. What's so bad about me?" For no reason that he could see or figure out, the duck had died in his hands. Maybe it was because he touched it. Maybe there were soft delicate things that should never be touched.

16

He straightened up, crossing his arms over his chest as through he was suddenly conscious of his nakedness. "I like the girls and the girls like me. Why would you want to change that? It's normal."

"So it's normal. Hurray."

"Don't you like normal?"

"I like normal."

"But not in me," Grady said. "I wish we were friends, Ellen, I honest to God do. You seem to be friends with everyone else around here. What's so bad about me?"

With the ointment washed off her face and replaced with moisturizer and makeup, Miranda felt a little calmer. But each minute had its own tiny nucleus of panic. There was a new brownish patch on her forehead, the mole on her neck appeared to be enlarging, and the first ominous ripples of cellulite were showing on her upper arms and thighs. She missed Neville to tell her that the mole and the brown patch were her special beauty spots and the ripples of cellulite existed only in her imagination. Not that she would have believed him. She knew they were real, that it was time to go back to the clinic in Mexico for more injections.

She couldn't leave immediately or even make a reservation. Her lawyer had advised her to stay in town until Neville's will was probated. When she asked for a reason he'd been evasive, as if he knew something she didn't and wouldn't want to. His attitude worried her, especially since there was a story going around that Neville's son by his first marriage was planning to contest the will. She would have liked to question Ellen about it—Ellen might know the truth, people were always confiding in her—but when Miranda went into the office the lifeguard was there and Ellen looked a little flustered.

Miranda said, "I'm expecting to hear from my lawyer, Mr. Smedler. Has he called?"

"No, Mrs. Shaw."

17

"When he does, have someone bring me the message, will you please? I'll be in the snack bar."

She hadn't looked at Grady yet, or even in his direction, but he was well aware that she'd seen him. She'd been watching him off and on all morning from under the floppy straw hat and behind the oversized amber sunglasses.

She turned toward him, taking off the glasses very slowly, like a professional stripper. "You're the lifeguard, aren't you?"

"Yes, ma'am. Grady."

"Pardon?"

"That's my name. Grady Keaton."

"Oh. Well, there seems to be a child screaming somewhere."

"Yes, ma'am. It's the Quinn kid, Frederic."

"Can you do something about it?"

"Probably not."

"You might at least try. It sounds as though he's suffering."

"He'd be suffering a lot more right now if his father didn't have ten million dollars. Or maybe twenty. After the first million who counts?"

Her smile was so faint it was hardly more than a softening of the expression in her eyes. "Everybody counts, Grady. You must be new around here if you haven't learned that."

"I'm a slow learner. I may need some private tutoring."

"Indeed. Well, I'm sure Ellen would be willing to acquaint you with some basics."

"Ellen and I don't agree on basics. That presents kind of a problem."

"Then perhaps you'd better concentrate on more immediate problems, like Frederic Quinn."

She meant to put him in his place by sounding severe, but she couldn't quite manage it. During the years of her marriage to Neville she'd never had occasion to use her voice to exert authority or raise it in anger. Everything was

18

arranged so she'd have no reason to feel dissatisfied or insecure. Her only bad times were at the clinic in Mexico when she'd screamed during the injections. Even then the screams had seemed to be coming from someone else, a shrill, undisciplined stranger, some poor scared old woman: *"Stop, you're killing me."* — *"The Señora will be young again!"* — *"For God's sake, please stop."* — *"The Señora will be twenty-five . . ."*

For the first she looked directly and carefully at Grady. He had a small golden mustache that matched his eyebrows, and a scar on his right cheek like a dimple. He was no more than twenty-five. She felt a sudden sharp pain between her breasts like a needle going through the skin and right into the bone. *"Stop, you're killing me."* — *"The Señora will be twenty-five."*

She took a deep breath. "You'd better attend to the boy."

"Yes, ma'am."

"I may be able to help. I haven't had much experience with children but I like them."

"I don't," Grady said.

"You must like some of them, surely."

"Not a damn one."

"They don't all act like Frederic."

"They would if their fathers had ten million dollars."

"So here we are back at the ten million. It's quite pervasive, isn't it, like a smell."

"Yes, ma'am. Like a smell."

"Well, the boy can't be allowed to suffer simply because his father has a great deal of money. That would hardly be fair. Come on, I'll go with you and help you quiet him down."

"That won't be necessary, Mrs. Shaw," Ellen said. "Grady can handle the situation himself."

"Of course he can. I'll just tag along to see how it's done . . . if Grady doesn't mind. Do you mind, Grady?"

Grady didn't mind at all.

19

Ellen stood and watched the two of them walk down the hall side by side. She wanted to turn and busy herself at her desk with her own work but she couldn't take her eyes off them. In an odd disturbing way they looked exactly right together, as if they'd been matched up in a toy store and sold as a pair.

Having secured his notepaper, Mr. Van Eyck decided to drop by Mr. Henderson's private office to thank him.

Henderson was glancing through a week-old *Wall Street Journal* while he ate his lunch, a pint of cottage cheese which he spooned into his mouth with dip chips. He preferred to read with his meals, on the theory that his gastric juices flowed more freely when they were not interrupted by the conversation of nincompoops.

What he read was not important, was not, in fact, even his own choice. After the swimming area of the club closed for the day he went around gathering up all the reading material that had been abandoned or forgotten—paperback books, newspapers, travel brochures, medical journals, airplane schedules, magazines, even the occasional briefcase with interesting contents like the top-secret financial report of an oil company, or complete plans for an air-sea attack on Mogadishu drawn up by retired Rear Admiral Cooper Young. Henderson had no idea where Mogadishu was, but it was reassuring to know that if and when such an attack proved necessary, Admiral Young would be ready to take care of the situation.

Economics, war, politics, porn, pathology—Henderson devoured them all while his gastric juices flowed on like some good old dependable river that never spilled or went dry. But even the best-behaved river could be dammed.

"Very decent of you, Henderson, to lend me this stuff," Van Eyck said.

"What?"

"The notepaper. If you hadn't lent it, I'd have pinched it of course, but this way is preferable." The old man cleared his throat. "You will be able to take credit for making some small contribution to the cause of world literature."

"What?"

"I'm writing a novel."

"On our club paper?"

"Oh, don't thank me yet, Henderson, it's a bit premature for that. But some day a single page of this stuff might be worth a fortune."

"What?"

"You keep repeating *what*. Is there something the matter with your hearing?"

Henderson dipped a chip in his cottage cheese but he couldn't swallow, his mouth was dry. The good old dependable river had stopped flowing at its source. "This writing you're doing on our club paper, you claim it will be worth a fortune?"

"Oh yes."

"To whom?"

"Posterity. All those people out there. In a figurative sense."

In a less figurative sense Henderson pictured all the people out there as a line of attorneys waiting to file suit against the club for libel, character assassination and malicious mischief. He went over to the water cooler and poured himself a drink. Perhaps he would buy a ticket to Mogadishu. If there was going to be a war there, he might be lucky enough to become one of the first casualties.

"By the way," Van Eyck said, "to facilitate my research you might tell me how the club got its name."

"The birds."

"What birds?"

"All those penguins out there diving for fish."

"Those are pelicans. The nearest penguin is ten thousand miles away. They're an antarctic species."

"There must be a penguin around here some place," Henderson said quickly. "How else did the club get its name?"

21

"My dear chap, that's what *I* asked *you*."

"Ten thousand miles?"

"Approximately."

"This puts me in an intolerable position. I've been telling everyone those little beasts are penguins, and now they aren't."

"They never were."

"You're sure?"

"Positive. But go on lying if you like. No law against it."

Van Eyck returned to his table on the terrace. There seemed little doubt that Henderson was getting peculiar, exactly like every other manager before him. In the next few weeks the same symptoms would emerge, a tendency to twitch, to smile at inappropriate moments, to mutter to himself. *A pity,* Van Eyck thought, taking up his pen. *He's not really a bad sort in spite of all that money he owes his bookie.*

Admiral Young's battle plans for Mogadishu were of no concern to his two daughters, who were busy conducting a war of their own in the snack bar. Their weapons were simple, their attacks direct. Cordelia hit Juliet over the head with a piece of celery, and as she was running for the door to avoid retaliation Juliet caught her on the ear with a ripe olive. The incident was reported to Ellen, who in turn telephoned Admiral Young and advised him to come and take the girls home.

Within a few minutes Young drove up in his vintage Rolls-Royce. Though he'd been retired for a number of years, he still moved like one of his own battleships, with a complete confidence that the way ahead was clear, and if the seas got rough the stabilizers were in operational order. His thick white hair was kept in the Annapolis crew cut of his youth, so that from a distance he looked like a bald man who'd been caught in a light flurry of snow.

He parked the Rolls-Royce in the No Parking zone outside the front door where his daughters were waiting with Ellen.

"Now, girls, what's this Ellen tells me about your fighting? Surely you're old enough to know better."

"*She* knows better," Juliet said. "She's older than I am."

"Only two years," Cordelia said.

"Which means you were talking and walking when I was born."

"Well, I *wasn't* learning *not* to fight."

"You should have been. Here you are all grown up and you haven't learned yet."

"Dear me," the Admiral said mildly. "Are you really all grown up, Cordelia?"

"You should know. Mrs. Young sent you a cable when I was born. You were in Hong Kong."

"I don't recall that it was Hong Kong."

"It was. She tried to get there but she had to stop off in Manila to have me. There were a lot of rats around the hospital."

"So one more wouldn't matter." Juliet laughed so hard at her own joke that her head, with its short brown hair, shook like a mop and she almost lost her balance.

"You mustn't tease your sister, Juliet," Admiral Young said mildly. "It's unkind."

"Well, she's unkinder than I am, she's had two more years of practice. I've got to catch up. It's only fair I should have a chance to catch up."

"Nobody has a guarantee that life will be fair, girls. We're lucky to get justice, let alone mercy."

"Oh, Pops, don't start throwing that bull at us," Cordelia said.

"Save it for the ensigns," Juliet added.

"Or second looies."

"We're *your* daughters."

"Serves you right, too."

"We're *your* fault."

"Think about it, Pops. If you hadn't—"

"But you *did*."

"So here we are."

And there they were, a problem not covered in the Navy rule book, yet to a certain extent a product of it.

They'd been brought up all over the world. At the language academy in Geneva they learned enough French and Italian to order a meal and summon a taxi or policeman. They attended finishing schools in London, Rome and Paris, with no visible results except to the teachers. At the music academy in Austria, during the periods set aside for Cordelia to practice the violin and Juliet the flute, they listened to Elvis Presley records in the basement and went to old Hollywood movies dubbed in German. At the American school in Singapore most of their time was spent tearing through the streets in a jeep, Cordelia having learned to drive somewhere between Sydney and Tokyo. The effect of this cosmopolitan background had been not to make them more sophisticated and at ease with people but to isolate them. While the real world expanded around them their personal world grew smaller and tighter. No matter who was present on social occasions, they talked to or at each other, as if they were surrounded by foreigners, interchangeable and of no importance. They had become immune to people as beekeepers do to stings.

"I never really liked this club," Cordelia said. "Did you?"

Juliet pursed her lips as though she were pondering the subject. There was no need to ponder, of course. If Cordelia didn't like the club, neither did she. "Never. Never ever."

"Let's go home."

"We'd better say goodbye to Ellen."

"Why?"

"Noblesse oblige."

"That's French. I don't recognize French rules in the U.S.A."

"Pops is giving us an executive look."

"Oh, all right. Goodbye, Ellen."

"Goodbye, Ellen."

"Goodbye, girls," Ellen said.

Nearly everyone called them girls. Cordelia was thirty-five, Juliet thirty-three.

From his carefully chosen position on the terrace Van Eyck had an unobstructed view of what was happening at the entrance to the club. With a kind of detached loathing he watched his brother-in-law, Admiral Young, drive off in the Rolls-Royce with the two girls.

Van Eyck had strong feelings about the military and for a number of years he'd been working out plans for bringing it under control. His ideas, though varying in emphasis from time to time, remained basically the same. Salaries must be immediately and drastically reduced, especially at the upper levels. Pensions should begin no earlier than age seventy and continue only for a prudent and reasonable time. The brass should not be encouraged to live longer than necessary at taxpayers' expense. Wars should be confined to countries with unpronounceable names and severe climates—the former would prevent television and newsmen from mentioning them, the latter would keep foreign correspondents to a minimum.

Most important of all, uniforms were to be abolished or simplified, with no more fancy hats or tailored jackets with gold braid and rows of ribbons.

If it hadn't been for the uniform, his sister Iris wouldn't have looked twice at Cooper Young. It was the second look that did it. Until then Iris was a nice intelligent girl, expected to marry a nice intelligent man who would put her fortune to good use and sire three or four sons to carry on with it. Instead she fell for a uniform, gave birth to two half-witted daughters and became a sour, sick old woman. Poor Iris. The crowning irony was that the Admiral retired and now wore his uniform only once a year at the Regimental Ball. Van Eyck didn't enjoy music or dancing, and he certainly didn't spend money lightly, but he never missed a Regimental Ball. Each one produced a yearly renewal of his anger against the military.

Van Eyck took up his pen and a sheet of the paper Ellen had given him.

> Secretary of Defense, The Pentagon, Washington, D.C.
> Sir:
> Overspend is overkill. Explore the following ways to cut your preposterous budget:—
> Reduce salaries.
> Begin pensions later, terminate sooner.
> Dispense with all uniforms.
> Eliminate commissaries and personnel, R & R stations, free transportation to and from battles.
> Avoid wars. If this is impossible, put them on a paying basis with TV and publishing rights, et cetera.
> Reform, retrench or resign, sir.
>
> John Q. Public

Van Eyck reread the letter, making only one change. He underlined *dispense with all uniforms* and added an exclamation point. Once uniforms were abolished, the other reforms would automatically occur sooner or later.

He heard someone yell Fire but he didn't bother looking around. If there was, in fact, a fire, it seemed silly to yell about it instead of calling the fire department.

There was, in fact, a fire.

Little Frederic Quinn, acting on the advice of his older brother Harold, who was taking the advice of his best friend Bingo Firenze whose uncle was a hit man for the Mafia, always carried a packet of matches even though he had given up smoking when he was seven. Bingo had figured it out. Fire was the best attention-getter in the world and no matter where you were something was flammable, not merely the more obvious things like paper and wood, but stuff like Grady's polyester warm-up suit hanging on a hook in the first-aid room. It took nearly all the matches in the packet before the warm-up suit finally ignited.

"Ha ha, Grady," Frederic said just before he passed out from smoke inhalation.

In the excitement following the discovery of the fire nobody could find the key to the first-aid room. Grady tried to pick the lock with a nail file. When that failed, the engineer pried the door open with a hatchet and put out the fire by tossing Grady's warm-up suit into the pool.

Frederic was given artificial respiration, and in a few minutes he was conscious again and coughing up the pizza, doughnuts and potato chips he'd had for breakfast.

Miranda Shaw knelt beside him and pressed a wet towel to his forehead. "Poor child, what happened? Are you all right?"

"I want a chocolate malted cherry Coke."

"A glass of milk would be more—"

"I want a chocolate malted cherry Coke."

"Of course, dear. Stay quiet and someone will bring you one. How did the fire start?"

"I don't know," Frederic said. "I got amnesty."

"What's that?"

"I can't remember."

"The little bastard set it himself," Grady said. "And I'm going to kick his butt in as soon as his pulse is normal. Give me the rest of the matches, Frederic."

"What matches? I don't remember any matches. I got amnesty."

"You're going to need amnesty, kid, if you don't hand over the evidence."

"I want a lawyer."

"A lawyer?" Miranda repeated. "Why would a child want a lawyer?"

"I'm pleading not guilty and taking the Fifth."

"A fifth of what, dear? I don't understand."

"Hey, Grady, this is a far-out chick."

Miranda stood up, looking helplessly at Grady and holding the wet towel at arm's length as if it had turned into a snake. "He seems to be acting so strangely. Do you suppose he could be delirious?"

"No, ma'am. He always acts like this."

"When I get my lawyer," Frederic said, "I'm going to sue you both for libel."

Miranda's silk robe was stained with smoke as well as the remains of Frederic's breakfast, and the flower had fallen out of her hair. Grady picked it up. Some of the petals came loose in his hand and drifted down on the tile floor. He hadn't realized until then that the flower was genuine and perishable. He thought of the baby duck that had died in his hands and all the soft delicate things that shouldn't be touched.

"I'm sorry," Grady said. "I didn't mean to wreck it like that."

"It's not your fault."

"I thought the thing was—oh, plastic or something you can't wreck."

"Forget about it, please. It simply happened."

"Like the fire," Frederic said. "Honest to God, Grady, one minute I was sitting there doing my transcendental meditation and the next minute I was surrounded by leaping flames."

"There were no leaping flames."

"*I* saw leaping flames. I must have been delirious."

"No flames, no delirium. Just a little creep with some matches, and a smoldering warm-up suit which will cost the club twenty-five bucks to replace. A new door lock will bring the tab to two hundred, and cleaning and painting, fifty extra. Maybe I should add ten bucks for my medical services. I saved your life."

"Who asked you to?"

"Nobody. People were on their knees begging me to let you croak. But I have a kind heart."

"Yeah? Well, bring me a chocolate malted cherry Coke, double whipped cream."

"Get it yourself," Grady said.

"I can't."

"Try."

"I bet you want me to split so you can come on with the chick. Well, ha ha, I'm not going."

"You just changed your mind, Frederic." Grady grabbed him under the arms and jerked him to his feet. "Ha ha, you're going."

"All right, I'm going, I'm going. Only don't pull any of the mucho macho stuff till I get back, will you? It's time I started my education. The kids depend on me for info."

Miranda leaned against the wall, watching Frederic skip down the corridor toward the snack bar. Her braid was half-unraveled and her face had already started to sunburn.

"He's a very strange little boy," she repeated. "I find it difficult to understand what he's talking about, don't you?"

"No, I don't."

"What did he mean when he called me a chick?"

"A girl."

"A *girl*." Involuntarily she reached up and touched her face, as if to cover the tiny scars left by the last knife. "How nice. Though I'm afraid it's not very accurate."

"Accurate enough."

"You're kidding me."

Sure I am, lady. But that's the way you want it.

"Let me get this straight, Ellen." Mr. Henderson closed his eyes and pressed his fingertips very tightly together. This was supposed to set up a magnetic current which had soothing and curative powers. "The door to the first-aid room has been burned."

"Yes, Mr. Henderson."

"Perhaps you mean singed or scorched, requiring a few touches of paint here and there?"

"Burned," Ellen said. "Also, the lock's broken."

"I don't understand, it doesn't make sense, how such peculiar things happen to *me*."

"Frederic Quinn was playing with matches."

"In the first-aid room?"

"Yes."

"Why?"

"Grady had locked him in there to teach him not to plug toilets."

"And while he was being taught not to plug toilets he was learning how to set fire to things."

"He already knew. Last year it was a bunch of towels on the beach. He was cremating a dead gull."

Henderson loosened his fingers, which were beginning to ache. No magnetic current had manifested itself, certainly not one that was soothing or curative. He felt the same vague pervasive dissatisfaction. A little here, a little there, life was letting him down. There were plus factors—he had a pleasant apartment and a job with some prestige, his ex-wife had given up her alimony by remarrying, he picked an occasional long shot at the track—but the minuses were increasing. The long shots were getting longer and the neighbors complained about his new stereo system. There were aggravations at work, members with overdue bar bills, Van Eyck's anonymous letters, and Frederic's parents, whose passionate quarrels and no less passionate reconciliations—Frederic, Harold, Foster, April and Caroline—posed daily and debilitating problems.

"Obviously Grady showed poor judgment in locking the boy up," Henderson said. "He should have sent him to me."

"He sent him to you last week. You sent him back. You told him he should handle situations like that by himself. How can you blame him?"

"Easy. *I* didn't lock the little bastard in a closet."

"I heard you give Grady orders to use his own judgment in the future. Well, the future arrived and he did. Maybe the results weren't too good, but he tried."

"You are becoming," Henderson said, "increasingly transparent. Do you know what I mean, Ellen?"

"No."

30

"Let us have a moment's silence while you think about it."

Henderson's office was decorated with pictures of airplanes left over from an aeronautical engineers' convention. Henderson had hung them himself. He had no interest in planes or engines of any kind. But he liked the pictures because they were non-human. He didn't have to wonder what the expression in an eye meant, or what a mouth might have been on the verge of saying, or what a pair of ears had heard. Nobody had to wonder what an airplane had done or was going to do next. It went up and came down again.

"Transparent as glass," Henderson said. "I have been in what you might call the people business for twenty-five years. I know them. So let me give you some advice, Ellen. Don't waste your time on Grady. He has no character, no staying power. Not much of a future, in fact, unless he hits it lucky, and that's a longer shot than any I've ever hit on."

"Why are you telling me? I don't—"

"You do. All the girls do. Getting a crush on the lifeguard is part of growing up. But you're already grown up ... Ah well, I suppose it's too late, isn't it? Advice usually is."

In the parking lot south of the club Miranda couldn't get her car started, and she sent one of the gardeners to bring someone out to help her.

The car, a gift from Neville on her last birthday, bore special license plates, U R 52, and it was as black and cumbersome as the joke itself. She hated it and intended to get rid of it at the first opportunity. But like the house and furniture of the condominium in Palm Springs, the car was considered part of the estate and couldn't be sold until Neville's will was probated. "You will be provided with a small widow's allowance," Smedler, the lawyer, had said. "In the meantime everything must be kept intact. Shall I explain to you what frozen assets are, Mrs. Shaw?" "No, thank you, Mr. Smedler. I know . . ." She knew very well. Hers had been frozen for years.

Grady came out the back door of the club, barefooted but wearing jeans over his swim trunks and a T-shirt with a picture of a surfer printed on it. He seemed surprised to see her. Perhaps this was where his girl friends waited for him and he was expecting one of them. Or two or a dozen.

"Oh, it's you, Mrs. Shaw." He smiled, showing teeth that were small and even but not very clean. "The gardener told me some lady wanted to see me. He was right, You are some lady."

"I didn't want to—to see you."

"Oh. Sorry."

"I mean, not personally. It's simply that I can't start this engine."

The car was parked in full sun, and its black paint and black leather upholstery had absorbed the heat and turned the interior into a furnace. *"I really wanted a light-colored car, Neville, they're so much cooler."* — *"Black has more dignity, Miranda."*

She sat, faint with heat and dignity.

"Are you all right, Mrs. Shaw?"

"I—it's very warm in here."

"Get out and stand in the shade. Come on, I'll help you."

"I can manage, thank you."

"Leave the key in the ignition."

She got out and he took her place behind the wheel. The engine turned over on his second attempt. He liked the sound of it, soft, powerful, steady.

"Here you are, all set to go, Mrs. Shaw."

"What was wrong?"

"You probably flooded it. If it happens again, push the accelerator to the floorboard and let it up slowly. Or if you're not in a hurry, wait a few minutes."

"I'm never in a hurry. I have nothing to do."

She didn't know why she said it. Neither did he, obviously. He looked puzzled and a little embarrassed, as though she'd made a very personal remark and he wasn't sure how to respond.

"I meant nothing important," she added. "The way you have, with your job."

"There's nothing important about my job. I put in time, I get paid. That's all."

"You save lives. You saved Frederic's only half an hour ago."

"He'd have come around eventually. Don't blame me for saving his life . . . And as far as the pool is concerned, there hasn't been a near-drowning, or even a nearly near, since I was hired. Which is fine with me, since I'm not even sure what I'd do if somebody yelled for help. Maybe I'd walk away and let him drown."

"You mustn't say that. Someone might take it seriously."

"Don't you?"

"Of course not."

"I hope you're a good swimmer."

They'd been talking above the noise of the engine. He reached over and switched it off. Then he got out, wiping the sweat from his forehead with the back of his hand. "Okay. It's all yours, Mrs. Shaw."

"Why didn't you leave the engine running?"

"Causes pollution, wastes gas. You can start it again when you're ready to leave."

They stood beside the long black car, almost touching but not looking at each other, like strangers at a funeral.

She said, "It's a very ugly car, don't you agree? Such a lot of bulk and horsepower merely to take someone like me from the house to the club to the market and back to the house. My husband gave it to me on my last birthday. Did you see the license plate?"

"Not well enough to remember."

"It's U R 52. Neville did it as a joke so I couldn't lie about my age. He didn't mean to be cruel, he adored me, he would never have been deliberately cruel. He simply considered it funny."

"Next year when you're fifty-three the laugh will be on

him. Hang on to the car for ten or fifteen years and you can have yourself a real chuckle."

"No," she said sharply. "I'm going to get rid of it as soon as they give me permission."

"They?"

"The lawyers who are handling my husband's estate. Of course, if something *happened* to the car they'd have to give me permission, wouldn't they?"

"Happened like what?"

"I don't know exactly, but there are lots of stories in the newspapers about people having paint sprayed all over their cars or their windows damaged or their tires slashed."

"If that's what you want," Grady said, "maybe I can arrange it for you. I've got some rough pals."

"Do you? Have rough pals, I mean."

"I know a lot of crummy people."

She glanced up at him with an anxious little smile. "You mustn't take it seriously, what I said about something happening to the car. It was pretty crazy. I can't understand why I suddenly had such a wild idea. I'm not a violent person."

"You don't look it."

"Honestly I'm not."

"I believe you, I believe you."

"Why do you say it twice like that? It makes it sound as if you don't really believe me." She crossed her arms over her breasts as if for protection. Her skin was very white, and the veins so close to the surface they looked like routes of rivers on a map. "How can you think I'm a violent person?"

"Oh, come on now, Mrs. Shaw," Grady said. "You're having a bad day. Go home and pour yourself a drink."

"I can't drink alone."

"Then take a couple of aspirins. Or don't you do that alone either?"

She lowered her head as if it had suddenly become too heavy for her neck to support. "That wasn't a kind thing to

34

say. You may be right about yourself, Grady. Perhaps if someone were drowning, you'd just walk away."

"Now wait a minute. What's the matter with you, anyway?"

"I'm drowning," she said. "You're not a very good lifeguard if you can't tell when people are drowning."

Little Frederic Quinn was hiding behind a eucalyptus tree in the middle of the parking lot. So far the conversation had been dumb and the action nil, so he decided to liven things up by revealing his presence.

He stepped out from his cover. The burnt-match Deco work had been scrubbed off his face but most of the Mercurochrome remained, leaving his hair streaked pink and his skin interestingly diseased-looking.

"Hey, Grady, how're you doing?"

"Beat it, you little bastard," Grady said.

"Using foul language in front of a lady, that's a misdemeanor."

"What is it when a kid is hacked to pieces and thrown off the wharf to feed the sharks?"

"Why are you so torqued up? Lost the old macho magic? Wait till I tell the kids, ha ha."

"You didn't hear me, Quinn. I said beat it."

"All right."

"Now."

"All right. I'm going, I'm going. I'm on my way. I'm— Help! Police! May Day! May Day!"

Admiral Cooper Young was returning to the club to pick up the handbag Cordelia had left in the snack bar. It was such a pleasant day he'd rolled one window down, though his wife, Iris, would be sure to notice the dust on the dashboard and complain about it. As he passed the parking lot he heard the May Day call.

"I do believe I hear someone crying for help."

"Then shut the window," Juliet said.

"Just because a person is crying for help," Cordelia added reasonably, "is no reason why you should listen. You're not in the Navy any more. Besides, we have to hurry. There's a one-hundred-dollar-bill in my handbag."

The Admiral's grip on the steering wheel tightened perceptibly. "Now where did you get a one-hundred-dollar bill, Cordelia?"

"Mrs. Young. Your wife."

"Why did she give it to you?"

"Bribery."

"She gave me one too," Juliet said, "though I wouldn't call it bribery exactly, Cordelia."

"I would. It was. Her instructions were to stay away from the house until the club closed because she was going to take a backgammon lesson."

The May Day calls had ceased.

"I didn't know your mother played backgammon," the Admiral said.

"She doesn't," Cordelia said. "Yet. She's taking a course."

"I see."

The Admiral did indeed see. There'd been other courses, dozens, but none of them seemed to satisfy his poor Iris. She'd been cheated and she was unable to think of any way to cheat back.

The crisis in the parking lot was altered by the sudden appearance of Mr. Tolliver, headmaster of the school Frederic more or less attended. Having learned during lunch hour that the surf was up, Mr. Tolliver shrewdly connected this information with the large number of absentees that morning. As a result he was patrolling the beach areas, armed with a pair of well-used binoculars and an officer's swagger stick left over from his Canadian army days.

Frederic Quinn was his first trophy. The boy was given a swat on the behind with the swagger stick and the promise of two hundred demerits. He was then locked in what the students called the cop cage, the rear of the school station wagon separated from the driver's seat by heavy canvas webbing.

Frederic proved a docile prisoner. He was tired, for one thing, and consequently, running short of ideas. For another, the new batch of demerits put him one hundred and fifteen ahead of Bingo Firenze for the current school championship. This was not a paltry achievement, in view of Bingo's superior age and connections with the Mafia, and Frederic leaned back smiling in anticipation of a hero's welcome.

Mr. Tolliver peered at his trophy through the canvas webbing. "Well, Quinn, what have you got to say for yourself?"

"Mea culpa."

"So you are admitting your guilt."

"Nolo contendere," Frederic said. "It doesn't matter anyway. I've already been punished."

"That's what *you* think, kiddo."

The hundred-dollar bill was still in Cordelia's handbag, much to her disappointment. She didn't need the money as much as she needed the attention she would have gotten if the bill had been missing. She thought of all the excitement, cops arriving at the club with sirens wailing, Henderson rounding up the employees for questioning, newsmen, photographers, maybe even an ambulance if she could have managed to faint . . .

"Oh hell, it's right where I left it."

Cordelia climbed into the back seat of the Rolls-Royce for the second time that day while her father said his second courteous farewells to Mr. Henderson and Ellen. He also wished them a Happy Thanksgiving, adding a little joke about turkeys which Ellen didn't understand and Henderson didn't hear.

"Thanksgiving is more than a month away," Henderson said as the Rolls moved majestically into the street. "Was he being sarcastic, do you suppose? If he was, I should have countered with something about Pearl Harbor. 'Happy Pearl Harbor to you, Admiral.' *That's* what I should have said . . . Speaking of turkeys, which I hadn't planned on doing and don't want to, you'd better have the catering manager come to the office to discuss the Thanksgiving menu. Thanksgiving. My God, I'm still recuperating from Labor Day and the Fourth of July. Will I make it to Christmas? Will I, Ellen?"

"I don't know," Ellen said.

"And you don't care, either. I hear it in your voice, that I-don't-care note. It's cruel."

"Sorry. But there've been so many managers, Mr. Henderson. I'd have been done in years ago if I'd allowed myself to care. I must maintain the proper emotional distance."

"Don't give me that crap."

"You asked for it."

Admiral Cooper Young lived with his wife, Iris, and the girls in a massive stone house on what had once been the most fashionable street in town.

The ride home was short and silent. It was only toward the end that Cordelia spoke in an uncharacteristically gloomy voice: "Mrs. Young's not going to like this. She might even force us to give the money back to her."

"She can't if we won't," Juliet said. "And let's not. Let's stand fast."

"She'll think of something. You know the mean way she stops payment on checks."

"This isn't like that. It's hard cash. Good as gold. Coin of the realm. And we can hide it in our bras."

"Even so . . . Pops, we don't really have to go home yet, do we?"

"Yes, girls, I think we do." The Admiral cleared his throat. "You see, your exclusion from the club was intended to teach you a lesson, and you can't be taught a lesson without suffering a bit."

"Oh, I hate suffering," Juliet said passionately. "It makes me throw up. If I throw up in the car, plus we arrive home three hours early, Mrs. Young will be *really* mad."

"Now, now, now. Don't borrow trouble, girls. Your mother will be just as glad to see you as she usually is."

And she was.

"I told you two to stay at the club until five o'clock," Iris Young said. "What happened?"

Cordelia answered first. "We got bounced."

"Dishonorably discharged," Juliet added.

"For conduct unbecoming."

Iris banged her cane on the floor. A tall athletic woman in her younger days, she was now stooped and misshapen. Her broad sallow face seldom changed expression and the hump she carried between her shoulder blades was a backpack of resentments that grew heavier each year.

She looked at her husband not in order to see him but to make sure he was seeing her and her displeasure. "You didn't have to bring them home, Cooper. You could have dropped them off at the zoo."

"We were at the zoo yesterday," Juliet said. "What's so great about being stared at by a bunch of animals?"

"The object of going to a zoo is to stare *at* the animals."

"You taught us not to stare because it's impolite. We never ever stare, do we, Cordelia?"

"Oh God," Iris said, but as usual He wasn't paying any attention.

The girls finally went out to the kitchen to make some butterscotch coconut pecan cookies and Iris was left alone with her husband in the small bright room she used both as an office and a refuge.

Here Iris spent most of her time with her books and stereo, a tiny champagne-colored poodle, Alouette, and an assortment of miniature chess sets. She played chess by mail with people she'd met in other parts of the world: a diplomat's wife in Bogotá, a medical missionary assigned to a hospital in Jakarta, a professor at the University of Tokyo, a petroleum engineer in Tabriz. She wasn't completely crippled and could have gone places if she'd wanted to, but she'd already been everywhere and her increasing deafness made communication with strangers difficult.

She sat by the window with the elderly poodle in her lap, leaning toward the sun as if its rays could rejuvenate both of them.

"Cooper."

"Yes, Iris."

"The girls aren't improving."

"I don't believe they are."

"Can't we do something, anything? I've been reading in the newspapers and magazines about vitamin E. Do you suppose if we put some in their food—?"

"No."

"We could give it a try, couldn't we?"

"No, I think not."

The little dog began to whimper in his sleep. Iris patted his woolly head and whispered in his ear, "Wake up, Alouette. Nothing's wrong, it's only a dream."

Cooper listened, sighing, wishing nothing was wrong, it was only a dream. Even the dog wasn't fooled. He woke up with a snort and cast a melancholy look around the room. He had eyes like bitter chocolate.

"Did you say something, Cooper?"

"No."

"I thought I heard—"

"No."

"We hardly ever talk these days."

"It's difficult to find anything new to say." And to say it loudly enough and enunciate clearly enough. "Iris, you promised me you'd ask the doctor about a hearing aid. I hate to press the point."

"Then don't."

He didn't. Besides the fact that he knew further argument would be useless, the Admiral was not combative on a person-to-person level. When his wife and the girls started fighting he got as far away as he could, usually withdrawing to his tiny hideaway in the bell tower, reached by a ladder which Iris couldn't climb and filled with squeals and scurryings which intimidated the girls. Here, where a century ago there had been a bell to proclaim peace and good will, the Admiral sat and planned wars.

They were not the ordinary kind found in history books. They were small interesting gentlemen's wars played under the old rules, captain against captain, plane against plane. And when they ended they left no poverty or desolation or bitterness. Everyone simply rallied round and got ready for the next one. A few people had to die, of course, but when they did, it was bravely, almost apologetically: "Sorry to let you down, old chap. I must—go—now—"

He didn't tell his wife about these private little wars. She was too serious. A mere look from her could cripple a tank or send a platoon into disorderly retreat or bring down a plane. Iris would be no fun in battle—she would insist on winning.

"Are you paying attention to me, Cooper?"

"Certainly, certainly I am."

"My brother Charles called to wish you a happy birthday. Is it your birthday?"

"No."

"Good. I didn't buy you anything . . . Charles must have had some reason for calling. Perhaps it's *his* birthday and this was a subtle way of reminding me. Would you check the birthday book in the top drawer of my desk?"

The desk, like the other furniture in the room, was an antique. Iris had no real interest in antiques. She'd bought the house furnished when Cooper retired because she and Cooper had never lived more than a couple of years in one place and it pleased her to own a house that looked and felt and even smelled ancestral.

Cooper said, "Is Charles listed under Charles or Van Eyck?"

"Van Eyck."

"Yes. Here it is. His birthday's next week, he'll be seventy-five."

"So I was right. He meant the phone call as a hint. Well,

perhaps we should celebrate in some way, since he probably won't be around much longer. What do you think of a small dinner party?"

Cooper thought nothing at all of it but he didn't say so. He knew perfectly well that his opinion was not being asked, Iris was merely talking to herself.

"The trouble with a dinner party is that we'll have to invite some woman for Charles to escort. He's alienated so many people, I wonder who's left. Remember Mrs. Roffman who inherited all that meat money? I haven't heard of her dying, have you?"

"No."

"Then she's probably still alive. We could try her."

"Mrs. Roffman is nearly eighty. Charles prefers younger women."

"She used to be quite beautiful."

"I doubt that he'd take that into consideration."

"If you're just going to be negative about the whole thing, forget it."

"I'm not being negative, Iris. I want you to enjoy yourself."

"*Enjoy* myself?" The little dog jumped off her lap and darted across the room to hide under the desk. "*Enjoy* myself? Are you insane? Look at me, stuck here day after day, hardly able to move, worrying myself sick over the girls, wondering what will become of them, of me, of—"

"A small dinner party would be very nice," Cooper said. "Very nice. As for a partner for Charles, what about Neville's widow?"

"Who?"

"Miranda Shaw. I had a glimpse of her today at the club, so she's obviously over her period of mourning. She might be pleased to get back in circulation even if it means sitting next to Charles."

"I've never really liked Miranda Shaw," Iris said, "but I can't think of anyone else offhand."

Part II

It was only the second time since he'd worked for Smedler's law firm that Tom Aragon had been summoned by Smedler himself up to the penthouse office.

The penthouse wasn't far in terms of distance. The city of Santa Felicia had a building code limiting the height of buildings, so Smedler's office was in fact only three stories from the sidewalk. But in terms of accessibility it might as well have been a mile. It was serviced by an elevator whose movements could be controlled by Smedler through a circuit breaker beside his desk. There were, of course, little buttons in the elevator for clients to press, giving them the comfortable feeling of being in command of the situation, but a few minutes trapped between floors, or behind a door that wouldn't open, left them with reasonable doubts.

Smedler's secretary, Charity Nelson, wearing her orange wig slightly askew, was gluing on her fingernails for the day. She said, without looking up, "Aragon, you're late."

"Sorry."

"We expect our junior employees to be like the Boy Scouts, trustworthy, loyal, helpful, friendly, punctual—"

"Punctual is not part of the Boy Scout creed."

"Let's add it right now. Punctual."

"I couldn't get the elevator moving," Aragon said. "It happens all the time. The air conditioners and electric machines still function and the lights are on, but the elevator won't work."

"Electricity is a very mysterious thing."

43

"Not all that mysterious. I was the assistant manager of an apartment house when I want to law school. If I could take a look at the transformer—"

"Well, you're not the assistant manager here, so mind your own business. Sit down. Smedler's on the phone." Charity filed the glue and the rest of the fingernails under B for bite. "Did he tell you what he wanted?"

"No."

"Maybe he asked for you specifically because you did such a bang-up job on the Lockwood case. By the way, we're still waiting for Mrs. Lockwood to pay up. But that's a mere trifle, forget it. We can't have you worrying your pretty little head about anything as crass as money, can we? No indeedy."

Aragon sat down in a leather swivel chair facing Charity's desk. Though it was late October and only ten-thirty in the morning, the room was uncomfortably warm and humid. Charity had turned off the air conditioner to protect her house plants, massed like a bonsai jungle in the east corner of the room. The plants didn't like air conditioning, and she felt the same maternal obligation to them that she would have to a child or pet, rejoicing in their growth and good health and fighting off their enemies like aphids and mealybugs and red spider mites.

Aragon looked at one of the plants, wondering if Charity talked to it, and if she did, why it hadn't shriveled up and blown away.

"You want to know why I believe you'll make it as a lawyer, Aragon?"

"Not particularly."

"You look dumb. Not dumb dumb, more innocent-like dumb. Any judge or jury would feel sorry for you seeing those calf eyes peering from behind those horn-rimmed glasses. Juries hate a smart-looking lawyer who dresses well."

"Do you talk to your plants, Miss Nelson?"

"No."

"I thought not."

44

"I'm not a loony. What in hell would I say to a plant?"

"Oh, something soothing, pleasant, complimentary—you know, the way you talk to the new employees."

"I don't talk like that to *any* employees. You trying to come on funny, junior? Better think twice."

Aragon thought twice and changed the subject. "What does Smedler want?"

"What he always wants, *everything.*"

"I meant from me."

"The file sent up was from Probate, so don't expect any fun and games like last time. Probates are ho hum." A light flashed on the intercom. "Okay, he's off the phone. You can go in."

Even on Monday morning Smedler looked fit and vigorous. Though office rumors had him spending every weekend fighting with his third wife at the country club, he showed no signs of injury, physical or mental. He wore a vested pin-striped suit, a Dartmouth tie and a small permanent smile unrelated to anything he happened to be saying. His admirers, mostly female, thought this smile made him look inscrutable and they were always disappointed to find out how scrutable he actually was.

"This matter is more of a nuisance than a problem," Smedler said. "So far, anyway. The reason I called you in is because I hear you get along well with women. Is this correct?"

"It depends on the circ—"

"Yes. Well, anyway, to get down to business, I have some probate papers that must be signed. An elderly man, Neville Shaw, died last spring, leaving his wife, Miranda, as the administrator and sole beneficiary of his estate. I made it clear to Mrs. Shaw that probate was often long and involved and that she'd better keep in touch with me, since there'd be matters coming up from time to time which would require her notarized signature. Well, matters have come up, a lot of them, but the past week I haven't been able to contact her. There's no answer when I call her house, she doesn't respond to messages left at her club, and two registered letters have been returned to the office undelivered. Even with her full cooperation, probate may drag on for months. So find her."

"I'll try."

"You shouldn't have much trouble. I'm sure this isn't a deliberate evasion on her part—she's a nice little woman, a good deal younger than her husband, well-bred, pretty, not too bright, always acts somewhat scared. In this case she has damned good reason to be scared."

There was a long pause, which Aragon recognized as a standard courtroom tactic: dangling question, delayed answer. He said nothing.

Smedler looked annoyed. "Don't you want to know *why*?"

"I figured you'd tell me."

"Of course I'll tell you. The problem is how much. It's important not to start any more rumors about Neville Shaw's will. There are enough already. He was nearly eighty when he died, and the fact is the estate should have had a conservator for the last few years of his life. He was getting senile, making a lot of crazy purchases and investments, highly speculative stocks, foreign currency, real estate syndicates. He even put up his house as down payment on a stud farm in Kentucky. I didn't know any of this was happening—and merely acted as his attorney when he made his will a dozen years ago—but I found out in a hurry. When the routine notice to creditors was published, they began coming out of the woodwork: brokers, bankers, developers, even the real estate hustler who'd handled the Kentucky transaction. To put it briefly, the creditors outnumber the credits. Shaw died broke."

"And Mrs. Shaw doesn't know this?"

"No."

"That seems peculiar for this day and age."

"The Shaws didn't live in this day and age."

"When are you going to bring her up to date?"

"The first step is yours, Aragon. Now, here's the address and phone number of her residence and her club. When you contact her, inform her firmly that she must come to my office to sign some papers. After that, I'll—well, I'll simply tell her that she's not quite as rich as she was at one time and that she'll have to make substantial reductions in her standard of living."

"Maybe you'd better tell her the truth, that she's broke."

"You don't tell women the truth," Smedler said. "Not all at once anyway, and certainly not a woman like Mrs. Shaw who's been protected and insulated from the world. My God, she might scream or cry or faint. She might even shoot me."

"If Mrs. Shaw is as insulated from the world as you claim she is, why would she be carrying a gun?"

"I only meant there's no way of predicting how a woman will act when she's *in extremis.* And believe me, that's what she is going to be. If nothing else does it, the stud farm in Kentucky will."

"It's a nice Freudian touch."

Smedler went over to the water cooler and poured himself a drink in a clear plastic cup. The water looked slightly murky and when he drank it he winced. "Ever taste this stuff, Aragon? It's lethal. I often suspect my secretary of trying to poison me. The only reason I survive is because I've gradually built up an immunity. Have some?"

"No, thank you."

"Better start working on your immunity. The water situation is not likely to improve. In fact, I predict that some day the world will dry up and blow away. There'll be no nonsense about floods and arks, just a whole lot of dust. Think about it."

"Yes, sir." Aragon thought about it and concluded that Smedler's weekend bash with his wife must have been worse than usual.

Smedler returned to his desk. "I was your age, Aragon,

when I passed my bar exams and assumed I was about to enter the practice of law. What I actually entered was the practice of people. To put it another way, anyone can memorize the criminal code, but what's important is the code of criminals."

"That's very good, sir."

"I know. I've used it in a dozen speeches. Well, you have work to do, I won't keep you."

The Penguin Club was a long blue one-and-a-half-story building built on a narrow strip of land between the road and the sea. To passers-by it presented a windowless front except for a series of shuttered air ducts that peeked out from beneath the roof like half-closed eyes. In spite of the club's reputation as a gathering place for the very rich, the cars in the parking lot were the same size and brand as the ones found outside a supermarket or a laundromat. The only difference was that there were fewer of them—less than a quarter of the slots were occupied. In a time and place of abundance, space was the only real luxury left.

Tom Aragon hadn't been inside the Penguin Club since the night he and some of his high school friends had come up from the beach to scale the back fence and swim in the pool. Before they even hit the water the lights went on, every light in the place—at the entrance and inside the office, along the corridors and the terrace, under the water and from the depths of shrubbery, the tops of palm trees, the interiors of cabanas. A uniformed security guard appeared, his gun drawn. "Back to the barrio, you bobos!"

This time he was ten years older and went to the front entrance. For the first few seconds he felt nervous, as if the same security guard was going to be on duty and might recognize him.

The fancy gold lettering on the door didn't soften its message: Members and Guests Only. No Trespassing. Dress Code Enforced. He went inside. No one recognized him or even noticed him. In the office, on the other side of the waist-high counter, only one person was visible, a young woman sitting at a desk with a pencil behind her ear. She didn't seem to be doing anything except possibly thinking.

Aragon was the first to speak. "Miss?"

She removed the pencil and came over to the counter. She was tall and on the verge of being pretty, with dark hair and serious green eyes. The lids were pink, as if, not too long ago, she'd been crying. He wondered why, estimating his chance of finding out as very slight.

"May I help you?" The hoarseness of her voice tied in with the pink eyelids. "I'm Miss Brewster, the club secretary."

He gave her one of his business cards: Tomas Aragon, Attorney, Smedler, Downs, Castleberg, McFee, Powell. "I'm trying to locate one of our clients, Mrs. Miranda Shaw. I understand she's a member of this club."

"Yes."

"There are some important papers for her to sign and Mr. Smedler hasn't been able to contact her at her house. He thought she might be here."

"I haven't seen her."

"Does that mean she's not here?"

"Not necessarily. She might have come in while I was on my coffee break or before I arrived. I was late this morning. My car wouldn't start and I had to ride my bicycle."

"What kind of bicycle?"

"What difference does it make what *kind* of bicycle?"

"No difference. I was merely putting in time until you decide to tell me about Mrs. Shaw."

She took a deep breath. It seemed to hurt her. She began coughing, holding on hard to her throat.

He waited, looking toward the pool. A couple of swimmers were doing laps and half a dozen women were taking part in an exercise class at the shallow end. On the terrace an elderly man wearing a tennis visor sat at a table, writing. Most of the deck chairs on the opposite side of the pool were empty.

The lifeguard tower interested Aragon most. It was occupied by a red-haired boy about eight or nine looking through a pair of outsized binoculars. Aragon had the impression that they were focused on him. To test this he smiled and waved, and immediately the binoculars were lowered and the boy climbed down from the tower and disappeared.

The young woman had finished coughing. "We're not allowed to give out information about our members. It's in the rule book. Practically everything is, including fraternization." She gave the word a certain bitter emphasis which he didn't understand. "I— Look, I'm having a bad morning. You'd better talk to the manager, Mr. Henderson. Wait here and I'll see if he's busy."

"Sure. Sorry about the bad morning. By noon things may be better."

"Or worse."

"Or worse," Aragon said. There was no point in wasting happy talk on Miss Brewster. She wasn't in a receptive mood.

Neither was Mr. Henderson.

Henderson had been going over the delinquent-dues list, trying to decide whether to take the drastic step of posting it on the main bulletin board or merely to keep a copy in strategic areas like the card and game room. There was the added decision of which names should be removed.

Each case had to be judged on its individual merits, or lack of them. The Whipples, for example, were traveling in the Orient and probably hadn't received the notice that the rent on their cabana was overdue. Billy Parr Davis had run up a two-thousand-dollar bill at his sixtieth birthday party, but it was only a matter of time before his mother sent a check to cover it as usual. The Redferns were in the throes of a divorce and custody of the club membership hadn't yet been determined, so it was unreasonable to expect payment from either of them. Mr. and Mrs. Quinn were protesting the charges for damages little Frederic had done to the first-aid station and the plumbing in the men's locker room. Mrs. Guinevere had gone to a fat farm to lose fifty pounds and her bill would be paid when the remaining two hundred returned.

There were, of course, the usual deadbeats, some, like Charles Van Eyck, very wealthy and intent on staying that way, others obviously having a hard time keeping up with inflation and the Joneses. Henderson was checking the list a final time when Ellen opened the door of his office.

He looked up, frowning. "You didn't knock. I've told you—"

"Sorry. Knock knock."

"Come in and be brief."

"Yes, sir. There's a Tomas Aragon here. He's a lawyer. I think you'd better talk to him."

"Is he applying for membership?"

"No. He wants some information about Mrs. Shaw."

"That's a funny coincidence." Henderson sounded uneasy. He didn't like coincidences. Through some obscure mechanism they usually ended up working against him. "I was just going to ask you about her myself. Her name's been crossed off the delinquent list."

"She paid up," Ellen said. "In cash."

"Her bill's been outstanding for some time. I haven't pressed the matter because I wanted to give her a chance to get over the loss of her husband."

"Well, I guess she got over it."

"Why cash, I wonder. Nobody around here pays cash. It's a dirty word . . . This lawyer, Aragon, what sort of information is he after?"

"He's trying to find Mrs. Shaw so she can sign some legal papers."

"That sounds plausible to me," Henderson said. "What's he like?"

"Young, dark-haired, horn-rimmed glasses, rather appealing."

"I meant inside."

"I can't see his inside. Outside he looks honest enough."

"Then there's no reason to be secretive about it. Tell him Mrs. Shaw is not here. Unless, of course, she is?"

"I haven't seen her."

"Neither have I. Odd, she was coming every day for a while. Mr. Van Eyck used to stare at her across the pool. I sensed a possible romance between two lonely people. That would have been good for the club—we could have held a lovely wedding reception in the ballroom, with white cymbidiums and silver ribbon and podocarpus instead of ferns. Ferns are common . . . When's the last time you saw Mrs. Shaw at the club?"

"I don't remember exactly," Ellen said. She did, though. Exactly, to the minute. *"Goodbye, Ellen. Hasn't it been lovely weather? I must fly now. See you tomorrow."*

She went back into the corridor. On one of the rattan settees placed at intervals along the wall Admiral Young's two daughters sat in identical postures. They looked so stiff and self-conscious that Ellen knew they'd been eavesdropping. Cordelia's face was sallow, as usual, but Juliet's cheeks and chin and the tip of her nose were pink with suppressed excitement.

Ellen tried to brush past them but they rose simultaneously and blocked her way.

"Sorry, girls, I haven't time to talk to you right now."

"You were talking to *him*," Cordelia said.

"And that other him," Juliet added. "We think something's wrong. I smelled disaster the instant I heard Miranda Shaw's name."

"Juliet's no magna cum laude," her sister explained. "But she has very keen senses."

Juliet lowered her eyes modestly. "I really do, don't I, Cordelia?"

"I already said so. Now get on with the story."

"Why don't *you* tell it if you're in such a bloody hurry?"

"No. You tell, I'll edit."

"Oh, I hate being edited," Juliet cried. "Oh God, I hate it, it makes me throw up."

Cordelia did her Rhett Butler imitation, *Frankly, my dear, I don't give a damn,* which put Juliet in a good mood again and she was able to continue her narrative: "This year Mrs. Young had the peculiar idea of giving her brother, our Uncle Charley Van Eyck, a birthday party."

"Why you didn't smell *that* disaster, I'd like to know."

"Heavens to horehound, I can't smell them all . . . The trouble with Mrs. Young's idea was fixing Uncle Charley up with a dinner partner because he's such a weirdo. She decided to try Miranda Shaw, probably because Miranda doesn't know Uncle Charley very well. Mrs. Young kept phoning and phoning, and when she couldn't get an answer she gave us the job of coming down here every day to keep an eye out for Miranda so we could pass along the invitation when she showed up. Only she never did and the party was last week."

Cordelia started to describe the party, how Uncle Charley got drunk and dressed up in one of the Admiral's old uniforms and sang "Anchors Aweigh" with dirty lyrics, but Ellen interrupted.

"Thank you for your information, girls. Don't worry about Mrs. Shaw, I'm sure she's quite all right."

"You are very unworldly, Ellen," Cordelia said. "Things *happen* to women."

Juliet nodded. "Even to us. Once in Singapore we were escorted by—"

"Shut up. The Singapore incident is nobody's business."

"Well, you told everybody at the time. You could hardly wait to spread it around the yacht club."

"This isn't Singapore and Mrs. Shaw wasn't accosted," Ellen said. *And if she was, she accosted right back.* "Mrs. Shaw probably decided to take a vacation."

She told Aragon the same thing, while the girls stood in the background listening, Cordelia rolling her eyes in a pantomime of disbelief, Juliet waving one hand back and forth across her face as if fanning away a bad smell.

Aragon said, "Mrs. Shaw didn't actually mention taking a vacation?"

"No. Some of our members talk about their trips for six months in advance and six months afterwards, but Mrs. Shaw is the quiet type."

"I see. Well, if you happen to hear from her, please let me know. You have my card."

"Yes." She had thrown the card away immediately, without even stopping to think about it. "I'm terribly sorry I couldn't be of more help."

As he went out the door Aragon wondered why someone who was so terribly sorry didn't look even a little bit sorry.

In the parking lot he found his car already occupied. Sitting behind the wheel was the red-haired boy he'd seen on the lifeguard's tower. He wore a T-shirt with a picture of a surfer on it and the advice Make Waves, but he looked as if he didn't need the advice.

He slid across the seat to make room for Aragon. "You should lock your heap, man. These old-model Chevs are very big."

"Thanks for telling me."

"I *showed* you, man, I didn't tell you. Nobody learns by being told."

"All right, thanks for showing me."

"No sweat. It's because of the ignition."

"What is?"

"The reason the old Chevs are being ripped off. They're easy to start without a key. Let me show you."

"Don't bother," Aragon said. "I have a key."

"Yeah, but suppose you lose it and—"

"The only thing I ever lose is my temper."

The boy studied his fingernails, found them uninteresting, jammed his hands into the rear pockets of his jeans. The resulting posture made him look as though he'd been strapped in a strait jacket. "I suppose you're wondering who I am."

"It crossed my mind."

"I am Frederic Marshall Quinn the Third, *número tres.*"

"I figure you're also a smart-ass *número uno.*"

Frederic acknowledged the compliment with a worldly little shrug. "Sure, man. Why not? I got to survive."

"Haven't you heard, Freddy? Smart-asses are the first to go."

"In your day, maybe. Times have changed." His hands came out of his pockets and his fingernails were reexamined. "I heard you talking about Mrs. Shaw. You a lawyer?"

"Yes."

"I may need a lawyer some day so I thought I'd do you a favor, then you'll owe me one. Right?"

"I'll consider it," Aragon said.

"That's not good enough. Let's make it a real deal here and now. We're both in the same boat, see, on account of I'm looking for somebody too."

"Sure you are."

"Honest. There's this lifeguard, Grady. He's okay. I mean, he's kind of like my friend. I've been learning about macho from him so I can pass the info to some of the kids at school. Only just when I was catching on to a few tricks he split. Didn't say goodbye or where he was going or when he'd be back, didn't even wait for his paycheck."

"How do you know all this?"

"I heard Ellen talking to Henderson about it, wondering where to send Grady's paycheck. She got mad because it would screw up the bookkeeping if Grady didn't cash his check. She was even crying about it. She cries easy. Really gross."

"Who was Grady practicing his macho on?"

"That's the favor I'm doing you, man. Her, Mrs. Shaw. She was his new chick."

Aragon watched in silence as a fat brown bird landed on the hood of his car, hopped over to the windshield and picked a bug off one of the wipers. "You wouldn't make up a story like that, would you?"

"Sure I would, but I didn't. It was right here in the parking lot that I first saw them together. Grady was using a different technique, high class, no hands, lots of talk and eye contact. Then they drove off in her car, a custom-job black Lincoln Continental. What about our deal?"

"It's on. I owe you one. When you need my services, give me a call. Here's my card."

Frederic shook his head. "I already got your card. I picked it out of the wastebasket where Ellen threw it."

"All right, Frederic, now I owe you two."

"Two? How come?"

"It's a personal thing."

"I like personal things."

"So do I," Aragon said. *But not this one. She threw it in the wastebasket because she had no intention of telling me anything. The conversation was a cover-up, hocus pocus.* "The girl in the front office, Ellen you called her, what's she like?"

"She loses her cool and chews me out about once a day, but she's not on my H list."

"What's your H list, Frederic?"

"H for hate."

"Is this a real list or do you merely keep it in your head?"

"Real, man. Lots of people on it, too. I added one today, that old creep Van Eyck. He told me he was going to string me up by my thumbs in the boiler room. Imagine saying that to a kid."

"I'm trying to imagine what the kid said first."

"I only asked him if he was queen of the fairies."

"That's not an endearing question, Frederic."

56

Frederic looked up into the sun, squinting. "How am I going to learn things without asking? If he isn't queen of the fairies, he could have answered no. And if he is, well, we live in an enlightened society."

"Don't bet your thumbs on it, kid."

"It wasn't even my idea in the first place. The two flakies, those sisters that are always hanging around, they were talking about it. You know, hormones. They decided if the old man's trouble was hormones it could be corrected, but if it was genes it couldn't and they were stuck with it. Would you care to know what *I* think?"

"I don't believe I would, no."

"Van Eyck has blue genes." The boy doubled up with laughter and his tomato-red face looked ready to burst its skin. "That's a joke I heard at school. Blue genes, see? Hey, man, don't you have a sense of humor?"

"It's been temporarily deactivated," Aragon said. "Now let's leave it at that and you go back to school and I'll go back to the office."

"No. No, you can't. You have to look for Grady. I got everything figured out for you—find Mrs. Shaw and Grady will be with her. They're probably just shacked up in her house making macho and not answering the phone."

"How many times have you called there, Frederic?"

"Six, seven. Why shouldn't I? I mean, Grady and me, we're like friends almost. When he's not around I don't have anyone to talk to."

"You could attend classes once in a while. They have people there you can talk to called teachers."

"Don't lecture me, man. Every time I go near a grownup I get a lecture. Except Grady."

"And what do you get from Grady?"

"Action. Anyway, he can't afford to give me a lecture. He dropped out of the tenth grade and has been maxing it ever since."

"Maxing?"

"Living up to his maximum potential, like doing what he wants to without being caught."

Aragon watched the brown bird hop across the hood and down to the ground, thinking that Mrs. Shaw was an unlikely choice for Grady's maxing. "Listen, Frederic, are you sure Mrs. Shaw is Grady's new chick? She's an older woman, a widow with a refined background—"

"Where have you been all these years? Backgrounds don't matter any more unless they're real special like Bingo Firenze's. His uncle is a hit man for the Mafia. Now *that* matters . . . Are you going to find Grady for me?"

"I'm going to keep looking for Mrs. Shaw. If Grady's with her, fine. I can't guarantee anything beyond that."

"Why are you after Mrs. Shaw, anyway?"

"There are some probate papers for her to sign. Know what probate means?"

"Sure," Frederic said. "It's when a person dies and everybody's fighting for the money that's left and a judge decides who gets it."

"Close enough."

"I hope Mrs. Shaw gets the money. Grady needs it. He's always scrounging. Last month he borrowed twenty dollars from my sister April just before they sent her away to riding school in Arizona. Grady doesn't know it yet but April gave me the IOU so I could collect. I'm saving it to use sort of like blackmail when I need a very important favor."

"Bingo Firenze's uncle would be proud of you, kid."

"Sure." Frederic opened the car door. "Listen, when you see Grady don't tell him it was me who sent you. I wouldn't want him to think I care what he does, or anything like that. Deal?"

"Deal."

They shook hands. It was a solemn occasion: Aragon had acquired his first private client.

Leaving the parking lot, he drove past the front entrance of the club. The two sisters were standing outside the door looking as though they were expecting something or someone. He hoped he wasn't it.

•   •   •

"That's him, all right," Cordelia said. "Did you notice how he stepped on the accelerator the instant he spotted us? Very odd, don't you think?"

"Well, a lot of people do it," Juliet said wistfully.

"A lot of people have reason to because they know us. But this young man doesn't know us, so *that* can't be the reason."

"He has rather a pleasant face."

"You gullible idiot, they're the worst kind. Believe me, he's up to no good. You mustn't be taken in by appearances, Juliet."

"I'll try not."

"They mean nothing."

"I know. But wouldn't it be nice to be pretty, Cordelia? Just for a little while, even a few days?"

"Oh, shut up." Cordelia gave her sister a warning pinch on the arm. "We are us and that's that. Don't go dreaming."

"I won't. Still, it would be nice, just for a few—"

"All right, it would be nice. But it's not going to happen, never ever, so forget it."

Juliet's eyes were moist, partly from the pinch, partly from the *never ever,* which was even more final than plain *never.* Through the moisture, however, she could see the Admiral's Rolls-Royce approaching, as slow and steady as a ship nearing port. "Here comes Pops."

"Maybe we should tell him."

"What about?"

"The disaster," Cordelia said, frowning. "You told Ellen you distinctly smelled disaster the instant you heard Miranda Shaw's name."

"I did smell it, I really did. Unless it was my depilatory."

"Oh, for God's sakes, there you go ruining things again."

"I can't help it. I only this minute remembered using the depilatory, which has a peculiar odor, kind of sulphurous, like hellfire. I'm sorry, Cordelia."

"You damn well should be, blowing the whole bit like this."

"It's still very *possible* that something awful happened to her. We saw her and that lifeguard looking at each other and it was *that kind* of look, like in Singapore."

The mention of Singapore inspired Cordelia to new heights. It was her opinion that Grady had lured Mrs. Shaw up into the mountains, stripped her of her clothes, virtue, cash and jewels, probably in that order, and left her there to perish.

Juliet contemplated this in silence for a moment. Then she said cheerfully, "So it wasn't my depilatory after all."

The Admiral had agreed, after a somewhat one-sided discussion with his wife, Iris, to forgo the football game on TV and take the girls downtown for lunch at a cafeteria. They both loved cafeterias and selected so many things to eat that they had to use an extra tray to hold the desserts. After consuming as much as they could, they packed the rest into doggy bags and took them down to the bird refuge to feed the geese and gulls and coots. The gulls and coots ate anything, but the geese were choosy, preferring mixed green salad and apple pie.

The Admiral parked the Rolls, then moved to the rear to open the door for his daughters like a salaried chauffeur. "Are you ready for lunch?"

"I guess," Juliet said.

"You *guess*? Dear me, that doesn't sound like one of my girls talking. What about you, Cordelia?"

Cordelia didn't waste time on amenities. "Pops, did you ever know anyone who was murdered?"

"Now that depends on your definition of murder. During the Second World War and the Korean conflict I saw many of my—"

"Oh, not that kind of murder, it's so ordinary. I meant the real thing, with real motives and everything."

"What's the point of such a question, Cordelia?"

"Miranda Shaw has disappeared."

"Vanished," Juliet added.

"We think she's been murdered."

"Done in."

"Come, come," the Admiral said mildly. "Miranda Shaw isn't the kind of person who gets murdered. She's a fine lady with many womanly virtues."

"Ah so," Cordelia said. "And what are womanly virtues, Pops?"

"My dear, I should have thought your mother would have told you by this time."

"Maybe nobody told *her.*"

"Yes, I see. Well, I can't speak for all men, of course, but among the traits I consider desirable in a woman are kindness, gentleness, loving patience."

They both stared at him for a few seconds before Cordelia spoke again. "Then what made you pick Mrs. Young?"

"That's a very rude question, Cordelia. I shall do my best to forget it was ever asked."

"Oh bull. You always say that when you don't know the answer to something."

"Most likely," Juliet said, "he didn't pick her, she picked him. Ten to one it happened like that. Didn't it, Pops?"

The Admiral cleared his throat. "I wish you girls could manage to show more respect towards your parents."

"We're trying, Pops."

"But remember, you're not in the Navy any more," Cordelia said briskly. "We're not ensigns or junior looies. Are we, Juliet?"

"Not on your poop deck," Juliet said.

Aragon left his car on the street at the bottom of the Shaws' driveway.

It was an area of huge old houses build on large multiple acreages when land was cheap, and surrounded by tall iron or stone fences constructed when labor was cheap. Most of the residences had gatehouses, some not much larger than the gondolas of a ski lift, others obviously intended as living quarters for servants. The Shaws' gatehouse had venetian blinds on the largest window and a well-used broom propped outside the front door.

Aragon pressed the button that was supposed to activate the squawk box connecting the gate to the main residence. Nothing happened. The squawk box was either out of order or disconnected. He waited several minutes, trying to decide what to do next. The gate was iron grillwork ten feet high. It would be possible to scale it, as he'd once scaled the Penguin Club fence, but the results might be more severe—a couple of police cars instead of a lone security guard.

He was turning to leave when he noticed that two slats of the blind on the gatehouse window had been parted and a pair of eyes was staring at him. They were small and dark and liquid, like drops of strong coffee.

"Hello," Aragon said. "Are you in charge here?"

"Nobody in charge. Nobody home. All gone, gone away." The man's accent sounded Mexican but there were Oriental inflections in his voice. "Maybe *you* are in charge?"

"No. I just want to see Mrs. Shaw."

"Me too. I need my truck."

"Mrs. Shaw took your truck?"

"You bet not. I have the keys. How could the Missus take my truck?"

"All right, let's start over. And it might make it easier if we didn't have to talk through the window. Why don't you come out?"

"Sure." The door of the gatehouse opened and a tiny man stepped out, moving briskly in spite of his age. He was so shriveled and hairless that he looked as though he'd fallen into a tanning vat and emerged a leather doll. "See, I can go in and out, out and in, easy for me. But for my truck to go in and out, out and in, I need to use the gate, and it won't work."

"Why not?"

"It is an electric gate and there is no electric."

"Why is there no electric?"

"Missus forgot to pay, I guess. A man came and shut it off. I said you can't do that, Missus is important rich lady. He said, the hell I can't. And he did."

"That's too bad."

"Very bad, yes. He wouldn't wait for me to get my truck onto the driveway, so it is still up there behind the garage with all my tools in it. I can't earn a living without my truck and tools. Here, see who I am." The old man showed Aragon his business card, so dirty and dilapidated that the printing was scarcely legible: Mitsu Hippollomia, Tree Care, Clean Up, Hauling, Reasonable Rates. "I can't leave without my truck, so I stay here in the gatehouse waiting for the electric and keeping my eye out for truck thieves."

"How long have you been living in the gatehouse?"

Hippollomia, having no clock or calendar, didn't know for sure. Nor did he care much. He was enjoying the closest thing to a holiday he'd ever had, with plenty of rest and food. He went to bed when it was dark and got up when it was light. He ate the avocados and persimmons that were ripening on the trees, and tomatoes reddening on the vines. From the storage room beside the main kitchen he had canned goods and preserves off the shelves, and melted ice cream out of the freezer. Besides such physical luxuries, he had the satisfaction of knowing he was doing an important job, protecting his livelihood.

Aragon said, "Do you mind if I come in and take a look around the property?"

"Why do you want to do that?"

"I work for Mrs. Shaw's attorney. There are some papers for her to sign and he hasn't been able to get in touch with her."

"She's not here."

"Have you been inside the house?"

"Not so much."

"How much is that?"

"Only in the storage room off the kitchen. I take a little food now and then."

"How do you get in?"

"There are a whole bunch of keys on nails in the garage," the old man said. "But I didn't need any of them. Missus isn't too careful about locking the house because the electric gate keeps strangers out."

"You found the back door open, Mr. Hippollomia?"

"Not open, unlocked."

"And it's unlocked now?"

"Yes."

"Would you have any objection to my going in?"

"It's not my house. I have no say-so."

"You're the only one on the premises," Aragon said. "That more or less puts you in charge."

The old man's shoulders twitched inside his oversized work shirt. "You go when you want, you do whatever, I'm out of it. I wait here."

"I'd like to make sure Mrs. Shaw left the house of her own free will. By the way, do you work for her on a regular basis?"

"Yes."

"Every day?"

"No. Twice a week I clip hedges and mow the lawn and haul away clippings."

"Are there live-in servants?"

"No more. The fat lady who cooks, the college girl who vacuums and cleans, the handyman living in the room over the garage, I don't see them for a long time. What do you think?"

"I think," Aragon said, "Missus forgot to pay."

The size and beauty of the place made its neglect more apparent. There was a sixty-foot white-tiled pool with a Jacuzzi at one end, but the water had turned green with algae and the weir was clogged with leaves and a dead gopher. Across a corner of the patio a dripping faucet had left a trail of rust like last year's blood. A marble birdbath was filled with the needles and sheathed pods of cypress. Pollen from the jellicoe trees had sifted the flour over the glass-topped tables and latticed chairs.

Inside, the house was dusty but very neat. Two living rooms, a library and a formal dining room all had fireplaces scrubbed as clean as the ovens in the kitchen. Upstairs there was a sitting room and half a dozen bedrooms, the largest of which was obviously Miranda Shaw's. It was here that Aragon found the only disorder in the house. The covers of the canopy bed had been pulled up over the pillows but the blue velvet spread was still draped across a matching chaise. Clothes were bulging out of one of the sliding doors of the closet. Beside the picture window a plant that looked like a refined cousin of marijuana was dying from lack of water. Some of its leaves had turned black and were curled up like charred Christmas ribbons.

In the adjoining bathroom used towels had been thrown into the pink porcelain tub. The chrome toothbrush holder was empty. So was the monogrammed silver tray made to hold a conventional hairbrush-comb-hand-mirror set.

Hippollomia was waiting at the kitchen door where Aragon had left him.

"Missus has taken a trip?"

"It looks that way."

"I hope she comes back soon and pays the electric. I want to go home. All the ice cream is gone."

"When I get back to my office I'll call the company and see if I can arrange to have your truck released."

"Why?"

"Because I feel that an injustice was done, probably due to a misunderstanding between you and the man who—"

"Misunderstanding," Hippollomia said. "I laugh. Ha ha."

It was noon when Aragon returned to the office. Smedler was busy on the phone, so Aragon made his report to Smedler's secretary, Charity Nelson.

65

She didn't like it. "What do you mean Mrs. Shaw went away?"

"Like in sayonara, auf Wiedersehen, adios."

"Where did you get your information?"

"Various sources. First, a kid told me."

"A what?"

"A child," Aragon said. "And an old man, a Filipino, I think."

Charity leaned back in her swivel chair, so that her orange-colored wig slid forward on her head and she had to peer out at Aragon through a fringe of bangs that looked like shredded pumpkin. "Smedler's not going to like this, one of his attorneys prying information out of children and old men."

"I didn't pry and it wasn't an ordinary child. It wasn't an ordinary old man either. He's waiting to get his truck out of Mrs. Shaw's driveway. I promised to help him, so if you don't mind I'd like to use your phone."

"I mind."

"Don't you want to help an old man?"

"How old?"

"About seventy or seventy-five."

"Sorry, I don't help anyone under eighty," Charity said pleasantly. "It's one of my rules."

Smedler came out of his office straightening his tie and smoothing his hair like a man who'd just been in a scuffle. He stared at Aragon the way he usually did, as though he wasn't quite sure of his identity. "Did you arrange for Mrs. Shaw to come in and sign the papers?"

"No, sir. I couldn't find her."

"Why not?"

"She wasn't where I looked."

"That answer will be stricken from the record as frivolous and non-responsive. Better try again."

Aragon tried again. "She left town."

"Go after her."

"I'm not even sure which direction she went, let alone—"

66

"Mrs. Shaw is not one of these modern flyaway women you find hanging around bars in San Francisco or blackjack tables in Las Vegas. If she left town she's probably visiting some elderly relative in Pasadena. Miss Nelson, check and see if Mrs. Shaw has an elderly relative in Pasadena or thereabouts."

"She ran off with a lifeguard," Aragon said.

"This seems to be your day for making funnies . . . It *is* a funny, of course?

"No, sir. His name's Grady and he's broke. That's about all I can tell you. I'm not even sure whether Grady's a first or last name."

"Find out and go after him."

"The staff at the Penguin Club aren't eager to give out information, especially the girl in the front office."

"So make yourself charming."

"That wasn't part of my contract with you, Mr. Smedler."

"It is now," Smedler said and went back into his office.

The conversation, which seemed to depress Smedler, had the opposite effect on his secretary. Her normally flat eyes looked round as marbles.

"A lifeguard yet," Charity said. "I wonder if she had to fake a drowning in order to make contact."

"Probably not. Lifeguards are usually quite accessible."

"Were you ever a lifeguard, Aragon?"

"No."

"Too bad. I bet you'd look cute in one of those teeny-weeny Mark Spitz numbers."

"Irresistible."

"What a shame you're married. I could arrange marvelous little office romances. I could anyway, of course, since your wife lives in San Francisco and you live here. That's a terribly funny arrangement, by the way."

"I'm glad it amuses you."

"Don't you get, well, you know?"

"I get you know," Aragon said. "But San Francisco is where my wife was offered a residency in pediatrics and she took it like a nice sensible girl. Like a nice sensible guy I approved."

Charity frowned. "I hate all that much sense. Takes the fun out of life . . . This Grady, I suppose he's years younger that Miranda Shaw. She's over fifty and there aren't many fifty-year-old lifeguards around. By that time they're gone on to better things."

"Or worse."

"Whatever. Actually, Mrs. Shaw looks marvelous for her age. In a nice dark restaurant she could pass for thirty-five. It can be done if you've got the money, the time, the motivation, the right doctor and lots of luck."

"That's a heap of ifs."

"I know. I've only got one of them, motivation. But I wouldn't want to spend the rest of my life sitting around dark restaurants anyway." Charity glanced toward Smedler's door as if to confirm that it was closed. "I heard a rumor about Miranda Shaw which I would like to repeat, I really would."

"Force yourself."

"Okay. I heard she gets injections made from the glands of unborn goats."

"Where does she get these injections?"

"In the butt, probably."

"No, no. I meant, does she go to a local doctor, a hospital, a clinic?"

"The rumor didn't cover details, but it doesn't sound like the sort of thing you could have done locally. Santa Felicia is a conservative city. Unborn goats get born, not injected."

"Where did you hear this about Mrs. Shaw?"

"Smedler. His wife picked it up at the country club. The injections are supposed to start working right away. You know, I wouldn't mind having a face lift if it didn't hurt too much and the results were guaranteed. But goat glands, that's positively obscene. Though if I had to keep up with a young lifeguard, maybe I wouldn't think so." Charity was sixty. In a nice dark restaurant she could pass for fifty-nine. "What's your opinion?"

68

"My opinion," Aragon said, "is that you are a fund of information and I'd like to take you to lunch."

Her eyebrows climbed up and hid briefly under her bangs. "Yeah? When?"

"Now."

"Have you flipped? You can't afford it on your salary."

"We can go to some simple little place. Do you like chili burgers?"

"No."

"Tacos? Burritos? Enchiladas?"

"No, no and no. I'm not a fun date at lunch anyway," Charity added. "I have an ulcer."

From his shoebox-sized office in the basement Aragon called the electric company and arranged to have Hippollomia's truck released. Then he phoned the Penguin Club and was told Ellen Brewster had gone into town on an errand and was expected back about two o'clock. He didn't leave a name, number or message; anticipating another visit from him probably wouldn't improve Miss Brewster's attitude.

He picked up a burger and fries at a fast food and ate them on his way to the public library.

The young woman on duty at the reference desk looked surprised when he asked for material on current methods of rejuvenation. "Starting early, aren't you?"

"A stitch in time."

"If we don't have the information you need, you might try the medical library at Castle Hospital."

"I just want a general idea of what's being done in the field."

"Okay. Be right back."

She disappeared in the stacks and emerged a few minutes later carrying a magazine. "You're in luck. The subject was researched a couple of months ago by one of the women's magazines. It's sketchy but it looks like the straight dope."

"Thanks."

"I get paid."

"Not enough."

"Now how did you know that?"

"A wild guess," Aragon said, wondering if he would ever meet anyone who admitted being paid enough.

During the next half-hour he learned some of the hard facts and fiction about growing old and how to prevent it.

At the Institute of Geriatrics in Bucharest a drug called KH-3 was administered to cure heart disease, arthritis, impotence, wrinkles and gray hair.

In Switzerland injections of live lamb embryo glands were available to revitalize the body and prevent disease by slowing down the aging process.

A villa outside Rome offered tours of the countryside alternating with periods of deep sleep induced by a narcotic banned in the United States.

A Viennese clinic guaranteed loss of ugly cellulite, and not so ugly money, by means of hypnotherapy and massive doses of vitamins.

In the Bahamas the Center for Study and Application of Revitalization Therapies promised to help the mature individual counteract the pressures of contemporary life, and overcome sleeplessness, fatigue, loss of vigor, frigidity, impotence, poor muscle and skin tone, problems of weight, anxiety and premature aging. Many different techniques were used, including lamb-cell therapy, but here the cells were freeze-dried.

At an experimental lab in New York volunteer patients underwent plasmaphoresis, a process in which a quantity of their blood was removed, the plasma taken out and the blood put back. The fresh new plasma which the body then created was the stuff of youth and supposed to make the patients look better, feel stronger and heal faster.

Nowhere in the article was there any mention of goats.

Aragon called Charity Nelson from the pay phone beside the checkout desk.

She wasn't thrilled. "Oh, it's you."

"Listen, that rumor you heard about Mrs. Shaw, are you sure it was goats?"

"It was goats. What difference does it make? Where are you, anyway?"

"The library."

"Wise up. You're not going to find Mrs. Shaw at any library. She's not the type."

"I'm working on a hunch."

"Well, don't tell Smedler. He lost two grand playing one last week. Hunches won't be popular around here until he figures out a way to deduct it from his income tax."

"Will he?"

"Bet on it, junior."

He reached the parking lot of the Penguin Club as Ellen Brewster was getting out of her car. It was a fairly new Volkswagen but it already had a couple of body dents that were beginning to rust in the sea air.

She didn't notice, or at least acknowledge, his presence until he spoke.

"I see you got your car started."

"Yes. The garage man came out and charged the battery."

"Good."

"Yes."

"It could have been something more serious."

"I suppose." She pushed her hair back from her forehead with an impatient gesture. She had nice features. He wondered why they didn't add up to make her a pretty woman. "Are you coming or going, Mr. Aragon?"

"A question I often ask myself."

"Try answering."

"I'm arriving. Is that all right with you, Miss Brewster?"

"It depends on what you want. If it's the same thing you wanted this morning, I really can't help you now any more than I could then. Really I can't."

"That's one too many reallys."

"It's a speech habit I picked up from all the teenagers around this summer. You know, like you know."

"I went to Mrs. Shaw's house," Aragon said. "It seems she took off in a hurry, didn't even bother to lock the doors. What concerns my boss is that she was aware of the important papers she had to sign but she made no attempt to do it. Naturally there's some question of whether she left voluntarily."

"That's a joke."

"Is it private or do I get to laugh too?"

"The question is not whether *she* left voluntarily but whether *he* did."

The afternoon wind had begun blowing in from the sea, carrying the smell of tar from the underwater oil wells. It was a faint pervasive smell like a hint of doomsday.

"Forget I said that," she added. "I'm not supposed to gossip about the members."

"This ranks as a little more than gossip, Miss Brewster. I learned the man's name this morning. Grady. He's a friend of yours, isn't he?"

"Did you learn that this morning too?"

"Yes."

"You were misinformed. He's no friend of mine."

She turned and walked away. He followed her. She was almost as tall as he was and their steps exactly matched, so they looked as though they were marching in single file.

"Miss Brewster."

"If you already know so much, why did you come back here?"

"What's his full name?"

"Grady Keaton."

"Has he worked at the club long?"

"About six months."

"Can you tell me something of his background?"

"He didn't talk much about himself. Not to me anyway. Maybe to fifty other women."

"Why fifty?"

"Why not? One thing I can tell you about Grady is his philosophy—*why not?*"

They had reached the front door of the club but neither of them made any move to open it. They stood facing each other, almost eye to eye. Hers were green and very solemn. His were obscured by horn-rimmed glasses which needed cleaning.

Aragon said, "A minute ago you made it sound as though Mrs. Shaw had kidnapped an innocent lad. Now he's not such a lad and not so innocent, and Mrs. Shaw had to take a number and wait in line. Which version are you sticking with?"

"Are you going to make trouble for him?"

"I might. It's not my main objective, though. All I really want is Mrs. Shaw's signature on some legal documents."

"Why keep coming back here?"

"This is where she's known, where her friends are."

"I'm not sure she has friends at the club. She and her husband sort of dropped out of things when he began showing signs of senility, and after his death she didn't come around for ages. When she finally did she talked to me more than anyone else, mostly chitchat about the weather, food, clothes. Nothing heavy or even interesting."

"What makes you dislike her?"

"That's pretty strong. Let's just say I disapprove."

"Of what?"

"Her vanity," Ellen said. "She probably had reason to be vain some time ago. But at her age she should be able to pass a mirror without stopping to adore herself."

"Or criticize herself?"

"Whatever she's doing, the key word is *herself.* No matter how big the universe is it has to have a center, and Miranda decided long ago that she's it."

"Do you call her by her first name?"

"She asked me to. I don't, though. Mr. Henderson wouldn't like it."

"She must consider you a friend."

"I—well, I'm not. It's part of my job to act friendly toward the members and I do it. But when some of them expect or demand too much, that's their problem. I couldn't help them even if I wanted to. Mr. Henderson has rules about the staff becoming involved with any of the members."

"Evidently Mrs. Shaw wasn't aware of the rules."

"Grady was. But then, rules aren't exactly his strong suit."

A small plane passed very low along the edge of the sea as though it was searching for something washed up by the tide. She shielded her eyes to watch it until it disappeared behind a row of eucalyptus trees.

"You'd better come into the office," she said. "If people see us talking outside like this, some of them might think I'm carrying on an illicit affair. That wouldn't bother me but I don't suppose your wife would approve. You *are* married, of course."

"How did you know?"

"Intuition. Extrasensory perception."

"I don't buy those."

"Okay. How about research? The City Directory lists a Tomas Aragon, 203 Ramitas Road. Occupation, attorney. Wife, Laurie MacGregor, M.D."

"No age, weight, political party?"

"I'll have to guess about those. Twenty-seven, a hundred and eighty pounds, and a Democrat."

"You're very good, Miss Brewster. I wish you were on my side."

"I might be when I figure out what game we're playing."

The door opened and a tall elderly woman came out, leaning heavily on a cane. In her free hand she carried a small red leather case with a snap fastener. She had short thick gray hair and colorless lips so thin they looked glued together.They came apart only slightly when she spoke. "There you are, Ellen. I've been asking for you."

"Sorry, Mrs. Young. I had to—"

"My daughter Juliet has been complaining of burning eyes after swimming, so I brought over my own testing kit. It turns out Juliet is not imagining things, as she often does. Your chlorine registers too high and your pH too low."

"I'll tell the engineer."

"He'll deny it, of course, but I have the evidence." She shook the red leather case vigorously. "Considering the dues we pay, I should think the club would be able to afford a competent engineer."

"We try."

For the first time Iris Young acknowledged Aragon's presence with a brief glance. Then she turned back to Ellen. "Who's he?"

"Mr. Aragon is a lawyer."

"I hope he's not applying for membership."

"I don't think so, Mrs. Young."

"Good. The club has too many lawyers as it is, sitting around encouraging people to sue each other. By the way, I expected to find the girls here. The Admiral brought them down this morning before his golf game."

"They left some time ago," Ellen said. "The Ingersolls gave them a lift into town."

"I've instructed them not to accept rides from strangers."

"The Ingersolls aren't exactly stra—"

"Too late to fuss now. The whole problem will be resolved as soon as Cordelia gets her driver's license back and I can buy her a new car, something more conventional. That Jaguar she had was a bad influence. It practically demanded to be driven at excessive speeds. It was too stimulating."

"A Jaguar would certainly stimulate me."

"I'm glad you agree."

Ellen wasn't entirely sure what she'd agreed about, but Mrs. Young seemed satisfied.

She crossed the road to her own car, a chauffeur-driven Mercedes, walking as if every step was painful. The chauffeur helped her into the back seat and put a blanket over her legs.

In Ellen's absence Mr. Henderson had taken charge of the office, a job he despised, since it nearly always involved complaints ranging from errors in billing to the fat content of the hamburgers in the snack bar. Neither of these extremes, and very little in between, interested him. He thought of himself as creative, a man of ideas. His latest idea, closing the club one day a week in order to conduct a bus tour to Santa Anita, Hollywood Park or Agua Caliente, had been poorly received by the membership. It was noted in the club newsletter that plans for a weekly Racing Revel had been indefinitely postponed. So were plans for a Blackjack Bash, which violated a local ordinance, and a Saturday Cinema for Stags, sabotaged by does, who outnumbered stags four to one.

Henderson kept right on trying. When Ellen entered he was, in fact, sketching out in his mind a Garden of Eden Ball.

People were tired of costume parties and the main attraction of the ball was certain to be its lack of costumes— except a figleaf or three. There would be some opposition, of course, from the elderly and fat, but in the long run the ball seemed destined to be a rousing success, the stuff of memories.

Ellen said, "Mr. Henderson."

He kept his eyes fixed on the ceiling and the future. The waitresses and busboys would be dressed as serpents, and from the chandeliers, just out of reach, would hang huge red paper apples. When the more athletic merrymakers succeeded in breaking the apples, confetti would come flying out with sinful abandon. Beautiful, beautiful.

"Mr. Henderson."

Henderson dragged himself rather irritably out of the Garden of Eden. "Welcome back, Miss Brewster. Did you have a nice vacation?"

"I was only gone for two hours."

"Two hours can be an eternity in this madhouse. The Admiral's wife was just in here complaining that we have too much chlorine in the pool and not enough pH. What the hell is pH? When you find out, buy some and pour it in."

"Mr. Henderson, this is Mr. Aragon."

"I can't help that. My God, people expect me to solve all their problems."

"I don't expect you to do anything about mine," Aragon said.

"You don't. Good. Stout fella. Now if you'll pardon me, I have important work to do, pH and all that."

"I understand."

"Of course, of course you do. Very understanding face you have there. Not many of them around these days."

Henderson departed, wondering why he was always meeting such odd people. Perhaps it was a family curse.

"We keep two files on each member," Ellen told Aragon. "One is for regular office use: address, phone number, occupation, names of family members, and so on. The other is private, to be used only by Mr. Henderson and the executive committee. It contains each member's original application for membership and the names and comments of their sponsors, letters of resignation and reinstatement, pertinent financial records, lists of other clubs they belong to. Some of this is useful, but mainly the file is a hodgepodge that should be cleaned out or updated."

"What's your definition of hodgepodge?"

"Oh, complaints from one person about another person, perhaps one or both of them long since dead, old newspaper clippings covering social events, divorces, scandals and the like; cards from members traveling abroad; photographs, many of them unidentified and unidentifiable."

"Apparently you have access to the file."

"Only when Mr. Henderson wants me to look something up," Ellen said. "He keeps the key."

"But you can ask him for it any time."

"Yes."

"Will you?"

"I'm supposed to have a good reason."

"Mrs. Shaw skipped town under unusual circumstances. That good enough?"

"We'll see if Mr. Henderson thinks so."

While she went to get the key Aragon stood at the door and watched the people. There were about twice as many of them as there had been during the morning. Several small groups were having late lunch on the terrace and most of the chaises on the opposite side of the pool were occupied. The water of the pool itself was being churned up by half a dozen earnest swimmers doing laps to a pace clock. On the lifeguard tower an ivory-haired young man was picking absently at his chest, peeling away the dead skin of his latest sunburn.

The elderly man in shorts and tennis visor was still busy writing but he had changed his position from the terrace to a chair under a cypress tree at the corner of the fence. The tree was bent and twisted by the wind and salt air. It seemed a good place for him.

Ellen came back carrying the key and looking a little embarrassed, as though Henderson might have given her a reprimand or a warning.

Her voice was subdued. "Listen, I'm sorry I said some of those things about Mrs. Shaw and Grady."

"Why?"

"Because I don't know for sure whether they're together or not. They both left at approximately the same time but that may be only a coincidence. She takes trips every now and then, cruises and stuff like that. As for Grady, lifeguards come and go around here like the tides. It's a boring job and the salary's lousy, that's why we mostly have to hire college kids who are subsidized by their families. Grady isn't a kid and he has no family. We all knew he wouldn't last."

"It's funny he didn't last long enough to pick up his paycheck."

"Where—how did you find that out?"

"Frederic told me."

"What else did he tell you?"

"He had the idea," Aragon said carefully, "that Mrs. Shaw was, in his words, Grady's new chick."

She looked down at the key in her hands, turning it over and over as if she was trying to remember what lock it fitted. "So even the kids were talking about it."

"Or kid. And he's not exactly typical."

"They probably all knew before I did, everyone in the club. What a prize cluck that makes me. I never even suspected her because she's so much older, and that day in the office they both pretended to be meeting for the first time."

"Some first meetings can be quite electric," Aragon said. The word reminded him of Hippollomia and his truck trapped behind Mrs. Shaw's locked gate. *"There is no electric . . . Missus forgot to pay."*

She said, "Afterward I watched them walk down the corridor together. There was something about them, something inevitable, fated. I couldn't describe it but I knew Grady was walking out of my life before he was even in it." She turned away with a shrug. "So scratch one lifeguard. He won't be back."

"Not even for his paycheck?"

"He won't need it. Miranda Shaw is a very wealthy woman."

He didn't correct her.

The files took up half the width of one wall of the office. They were painted pastel blues and pinks and mauves to help conceal their purpose. They still looked like files. Ellen unlocked the blue one.

The material on the Shaws was sparse. Attached to an application form dated twenty years previously were enthusiastic comments from the Shaws' sponsors, Mr. and Mrs. Edgar Godwit, and their seconders, Dr. Franklin Spitz and Mrs. Ada Cottam, and a card with a single word printed on it and underlined: *OIL*. Whether it was the *OIL* or the enthusiastic support, the Shaws were admitted to membership in the Penguin Club the following month, paid the initiation fee and a year's dues in advance and rented cabana number 22. Neville Shaw's other affiliations included the University Forum, the Greenhills Country Club, Turf and Tanbark, Rancheros Felicianos and the Yale Club.

An old letter from Shaw addressed to the manager and the Executive Committee deplored the kind of music played at the New Year's Eve Ball. A later one canceled the rental of cabana number 22, citing excessive noise from 21 and 23. To the bottom of this someone had added a brief comment in ink: Party Pooper!

There were only two recent items in the file, a copy of a delinquent-dues notice signed by Walter Henderson, and a greeting card bearing an indecipherable postmark and addressed to Miss Ellen Brewster, c/o Penguin Club, Santa Felicia, California.

"Go ahead, read it," Ellen said. "It's not personal. She wrote cards like that to a lot of people. I think she was homesick, she didn't enjoy traveling, especially in Mexico."

"Where was she in Mexico when she wrote this?"

"Pasoloma."

He had never heard of it.

Dear Ellen: Heavenly weather, blue sea, blue sky. Only fly in ointment is more like a mosquito or flea, what the tourists call no-see-ums. My husband is off on a 3-week fishing trip but I get seasick so I'm here on the beach, *scratching*. By the way, a mistake must have been in our last billing. I'm sure my husband paid it promptly as usual. Regards, Miranda Shaw

"She didn't like Pasoloma," Ellen said. "There's nothing to do except surf and fish, she told me. Yet she kept going back."

"Did her husband always go with her?"

"As far as Pasoloma. Then he'd charter a fishing boat for two or three weeks and do his thing while she did hers."

"That doesn't sound like the sort of vacation a rich beautiful woman would plan for herself."

"Not unless she liked surfing. Or surfers. Anyway, she went."

"When she came back," Aragon said, "did she look like a woman who'd just spent a couple of weeks lying on a beach?"

"No. She avoids the sun and salt water because they dry the skin. Even when she sits on the terrace here she hides under an umbrella and a wide-brimmed hat and a robe big enough for three Arabs and a camel."

"You're sure about the camel?"

She smiled faintly. "All right, scratch the camel and one Arab. The general picture remains the same."

"Where is Pasoloma?"

"I looked for it on the map once and couldn't find it. But I think it's fairly close to the border because they always took their car and Mr. Shaw refused to drive long distances."

He figured that would put it somewhere in the northern part of Baja California. During the Lockwood case he'd covered the area by car and he couldn't recall even a small village by that name. Either Ellen Brewster had made a mistake—which seemed unlikely—or else Pasoloma wasn't a geographical location at all but merely the name of a resort where people went to swim in the surf or lie on the beach or charter a boat for deep-sea fishing. If so, it was a peculiar choice for a woman who didn't like any of those things. Maybe Pasoloma offered other enticements Mrs. Shaw hadn't mentioned to anyone at the Penguin Club.

Aragon said, "Is there a phone booth around?"

"At the south end of the corridor. But you can use the phone on my desk if it's for a local call."

"It's not."

"Oh. Well." She looked slightly annoyed, as though she

considered listening to other people's talk a privilege that came with her territory.

"I am going to call my wife," Aragon said. "She works at a hospital in San Francisco and the call will be put through a switchboard. The operators all know my voice and are certain to monitor the conversation, so it won't be very interesting."

"Why tell me?"

"I wouldn't want you to think you're missing anything."

The switchboard operator at the hospital recognized his voice.

"Dr. MacGregor's on Ward C right now, Mr. Aragon. You want me to page her?"

"Please."

"Hold on. Won't take a minute."

The minute dragged out to three. He put in four more quarters, and as the last one clanked into its slot he heard Laurie's voice.

"Tom?"

"Hi."

There was a silence, the kind there often was at the beginning of their calls, as if they were trying to bridge the distance between them and it seemed, for a time, impossible.

Then, "Laurie, are you there?"

"Yes."

"Can we talk?"

"Business-type stuff only. I'm on duty."

"This is a business call."

"Really?"

"You've just been appointed my special assistant in charge of regenerative processes."

"What's the salary?"

"It's a purely honorary position."

"I figured it would be," she said. "You're a terrible tightwad."

82

"Of course, if you're not interested, there's a roster of beautiful blondes whose qualifications I've been studying."

"Tell them to get lost. Now, what exactly do you mean by regenerative processes?"

"I've been doing a rundown on rejuvenation clinics. Most of them operate outside the country because they use illegal drugs or unorthodox methods, shots of KH-3, monkey and lamb embryo glands, hypnotherapy, plasmaphoresis, deep sleep, et cetera."

"So?"

He hesitated. "I'd like you to find out if there's one that uses goat glands."

"Goat glands? *Now* what have you got yourself into?"

"The story's kind of long and I'm running out of change. Will you do it?"

"I guess so. How do you know such a place exists?"

"Smedler's wife heard about it at the country club. Do you think you can find out by tonight? I'll be at the apartment from six—"

There was a sudden click and the long-distance operator's voice: "Your time is up. Please deposit another twenty-five cents."

"All I've got is two dimes. Will you—?" She wouldn't. The line went dead. He spoke into it anyway. "Hey Laurie, I forgot to tell you I love you."

The Admiral's daughters came charging through the front door, pursued by the dust devils that were whirling down the road behind them.

Neither wind nor sun had affected Cordelia's face, which remained as sallow and somber as usual, but Juliet had turned pink from her forehead all the way down to the pearl choker that emphasized the neckline of her favorite thrift-shop dress. Everything about her seemed to be in motion at the same time, as though one of the dust devils had caught her and infected her with frenzy. She shook her head and giggled and moved her arms around so that her bracelets kept jangling, clank, clank, clank. Cordelia didn't have on as many bracelets but she wore a ruby and silver necklace, jade earrings, a pair of ruby-eyed owl pins, a diamond-studded pendant watch, a gold wristwatch and half a dozen rings.

Cordelia gave her sister a kick on the ankle to calm her down and said to Ellen, "We are back. Notice anything different about us?"

"Your mother was here," Ellen said. "She left half an hour ago."

"You're avoiding the subject. Besides, she never comes to this place any more. She hates it."

"Considers it gross," Juliet added. "Hoi polloi."

"You must notice *something* different about us. If you don't, you're not trying. Concentrate. Use your eyes."

"And ears. That's a clue. Use your ears. Listen."

Ellen listened and heard clank, clank, clank, clank. "The bracelets? Has it anything to do with the bracelets?"

"Not just the bracelets," Cordelia said sharply. "Everything. We've changed our image."

"Cordelia read about it in a magazine."

"I thought about it before I ever read it in a magazine. That was merely the clincher, an article on How to Change Your Image in Twenty-Four Hours. So we went down to the bank this morning and took our jewelry out of the safe-deposit box and we're going to wear it from now on, everywhere we go, night and day, even in bed. We are sick of being *plain*."

"*No more plain.*"

"You are looking at the new us."

"The new us." Beneath the excitement there was a note of anxiety in Juliet's voice. "In *bed*, Cordelia? My earrings hurt already and I'm not even lying down yet."

"Stop fussing. Nobody gets a new image for nothing."

"Well, I don't see why it has to hurt. Are you sure the article specified in *bed*?"

"It did."

"I'm going to hate that part. It's fine for you, you sleep

flat on your back like you're on an operating table having your gall bladder out. But I'm a side sleeper."

"You'll have to change. That's what this is all about, change. You're the new you now, so act like it."

The new Juliet nodded. The old Juliet simply decided to cheat. Instead of wearing the earrings at night, she would keep them on her bedside table so that in case of an earthquake or fire she could put them on in a hurry. No one would be any the wiser, unless Cordelia got scared by a strange noise and came barging into her room in the middle of the night. Anyway, the new Cordelia might not be scared of strange noises.

Cordelia fingered the ruby and silver necklace. "You don't recognize this, do you, Ellen? Ha, I knew you wouldn't. You're not a noticer the way I am."

"And I," Juliet said. "I'm a noticer too. In fact, *I* recognized it first. She wore it to the club's open house at Christmas with a green dress. Red and green, it looked very Christmasy."

"Are you telling this, Juliet, or am I?"

"You are, Cordelia."

"Then let me proceed. We went to an auction last week and saw this necklace with a matching bracelet that was to be sold as a set. I wanted both, but there's a limit on my charge card so I bought the necklace and Juliet bought the bracelet."

"Wait a minute," Ellen said. "*Who* wore it at the Christmas open house?"

"Mrs. Shaw," Cordelia said.

"She looked very Christmasy," Juliet said.

Ellen caught up with Aragon in the corridor. "Admiral Young's daughters are here. They have some information which may or may not be accurate, but I think you should talk to them."

The two girls were half hidden behind the door of Ellen's office like children ready to pop out and say boo when a grownup came along. Aragon smiled at them in a friendly way but they didn't respond.

"Why, it's him," Cordelia said. "The man who was staring at us this morning. Like in Singapore, that kind of stare."

"Singapore? I'm sure you're mistaken." But Juliet glanced nervously around the room as though planning an escape if one proved necessary. Cordelia was very frequently right. "Why, this is our very own club and we're just as safe here as—"

"Pops had two ensigns following us around Singapore, and what good did that do?"

Juliet couldn't remember the ensigns and had only the vaguest recollection of ever being in Singapore, let alone of what had actually happened. But she was too sensible to admit this to Cordelia, who would merely take it as additional proof of Juliet's inferiority.

"Stop this nonsense, girls," Ellen said briskly. "I want you to tell Mr. Aragon what you told me."

Cordelia came out from behind the door, her arms crossed on her chest in a defensive posture. "Why does he want to know?"

"He's a lawyer."

"We are not talking to any lawyer unless our lawyer is also present. Everybody who watches television knows that."

"Oh, Cordelia," Juliet said with a touch of sadness. "We don't have a lawyer."

"We'll get one immediately."

"Very well, you get one, but I refuse to pay for my half of him. He'll be entirely on your charge card."

"Wait a minute," Aragon said. "We should be able to settle this quite simply. You hire me and I'll waive the fee for my services."

"What does that mean?"

"I'm free."

"Bull," Cordelia said.

"No bull."

"I never heard of a free lawyer."

"There aren't many of us around. Business is good but the pay's lousy."

"The arrangement seems rather loose, but it's not costing us anything, so all right, you're hired."

Aragon congratulated himself. Not every young lawyer could afford to acquire in a single day such clients as the Admiral's daughters and little Frederic Quinn. If the trend continued, it would be very handy, probably downright necessary, to have a working wife.

The girls had a whispered conference behind the door, punctuated by the clank of Juliet's bracelets and the bronchial wheeze she developed when she became excited. Then Cordelia approached Aragon, licking her thin pale lips.

"No one could possibly connect us with Miranda Shaw's disappearance. We didn't get hold of her necklace and bracelet until a week ago when we spotted them at an auction. It wasn't a regular auction, more of a small estate sale where the prices are set ahead of time. There's this nice quiet young man who sells valuables other people want to get rid of for one reason or another."

"We think he's a fence," Juliet said.

Cordelia silenced her sister with a jab in the ribs. "He seems to be a perfectly legitimate businessman who conducts auctions, the refined low-key kind. Most auctioneers are such screamers. Mr. Tannenbaum never raises his voice. Every now and then when we're downtown we pop into his establishment to see what's available."

"Sometimes we buy, sometimes we spy," Juliet said.

"We don't actually spy, we just look around with our eyes wide open. I mean, you can never be *sure,* can you, Mr. Aragon?"

Aragon agreed that you could never be sure, at the same time feeling a twinge of sympathy for the unfortunate Tannenbaum. It was not an enviable fate, being the target of the girls' suspicions, the recipient of their pop-ins, the focus of their wide-opens. He hoped the occasional sale recompensed Tannenbaum to some degree.

He said, "Was the jewelry expensive?"

"It's crude to ask the price of things," Cordelia reminded him.

"Yes. However—"

"A mark of ill-breeding."

"Right. But I'd still like to know. It may be important."

Juliet let out an anxious little wheeze. "You hear that, Cordelia? He said—"

"I heard him."

"We've never done anything the least bit important in our whole lives."

"Oh, we have so. We were born, weren't we? And Mrs. Young's often told us how much it changed her life. That's important, changing someone's life."

"She didn't *mean* it nice."

"Important things aren't necessarily nice."

"I still don't see what harm would come from answering the man's question about the jewelry."

"Mind your own business, sister."

"It's half my business," Juliet said. "The bracelet was put on *my* charge card. If I want to tell someone what's on my own charge card, I can. It's a free country."

"You shut up."

"Fifteen hundred dollars. So there, ha ha! Fifteen hundred dollars."

Tannenbaum's place of business was on Estero Street in the lower part of the city. Two blocks to the east was the barrio where Aragon had been born and raised and gone to schools where English was in reality, if not in theory, a second language. The barrio was gradually filling up with the debris of poverty: pieces of abandoned cars, tires and doors and twisted bumpers, broken wine jugs and baby strollers, fallen branches of half-dead trees, disemboweled sofas and dismembered chairs.

Estero Street, at one time almost part of the barrio, had been salvaged by a downtown rehabilitation plan. Its two- and three-story redwood houses, built before the turn of the century, had been carefully restored and painted. Yards were tended, hedges clipped, lawns raked and clusters of birds-of-paradise and lilies-of-the-Nile bloomed under neat little windmill palms. The upper floors of the houses had been made into apartments, and the ground floors into small offices occupied by a travel agent, a chiropractor, a realtor, a bail bondsman, an attorney, an art dealer, a watch repairman.

In the window of what had once been somebody's parlor was a small discreet sign: R. Tannenbaum, Estate Sales and Appraisals. An old-fashioned bell above the front door announced Aragon's entrance. He found himself in a hall whose walls were hung with tapestries, some large enough to be used as rugs, some so small they were framed under glass. In a single spotlighted display case a collection of miniature musical instruments was arranged in a semicircle on a red velvet stage: a golden harp, an ivory grand piano, violins and cellos with silver strings fine as spider silk, trumpets and French horns carved from amethyst and woodwinds from tourmaline. No prices were shown. Tannenbaum's merchandise—if the tapestries and miniatures were typical—was not that of an ordinary fence doing business in a small city like Santa Felicia. Fences gravitated south to Los Angeles and San Diego or north to San Francisco.

A large black and brown mongrel came loping down the hall like an official greeter, and behind him, Tannenbaum himself. He was a tall angular man about forty, wearing a beard and rimless glasses and formally dressed in a dark vested suit and tie, white shirt with cuff links and carefully polished black oxfords.

Putting his hand on the dog's head, he said, "My partner, Rupert, likes you."

"Tell Rupert I like him back."

"He knows. In our profession we develop a sixth sense

about people. At least in my case it's sixth, in Rupert's it's probably first. Perhaps a very long time ago it was our first, too, and our initial reaction to the approach of a stranger was, is this a friend or an enemy? It remains a good question. You are—" Tannenbaum narrowed his eyes to concentrate their focus—"I'd guess somewhere in between, leaning a bit towards friend, right?"

"Well . . . "

"I see you were admiring my miniatures. Or perhaps admire isn't quite the word. I don't care for miniatures myself, life is small and meager enough. A sculpture by Henry Moore, that's what I covet, though my mean little hall here is hardly the place for one."

Tannenbaum had a soft pleasant voice which made what he had to say seem more interesting than it actually was. He went on to describe the particular Henry Moore he would have liked to own, now in a private collection in Paris. Evidently Rupert had heard it all before. He went back to his rug at the rear of the hall, leaving the practical end of the business to his partner.

The dog's action seemed to remind Tannenbaum of his duties. He said, "What can I do for you?"

Aragon presented his card, which Tannenbaum glanced at briefly before putting it in his inside breast pocket. The pocket was already bulging, Aragon noticed, as if Tannenbaum's collections were not confined to valuables like tapestries and miniatures.

"Are you buying or selling, Mr. Aragon?"

"I'm asking."

"You want information?"

"Yes."

"My profit on information will never buy me a Henry Moore. However, in the interests of good will and that sort of thing, I'll try to oblige. What's on your mind?"

"Our office is holding some important legal documents which must be signed by one of our clients. I have cause to believe she's also one of yours, Miranda Shaw, Mrs. Neville Shaw."

"So?"

"Mrs. Shaw has, for all practical purposes, disappeared."

"Well, I haven't got her," Tannenbaum said reasonably. "My partner wouldn't approve. Rupert took an immediate dislike to her. Probably her perfume—too much and too musky. Rupert has such a sensitive nose it sometimes affects his judgment. I myself found her attractive, though a bit over the hill, wouldn't you say?"

"I might, but the fact is I've never met her."

"You should."

"My boss thinks I should too, and the sooner the better."

Tannenbaum brushed a piece of lint off one of the tapestries. His movements were quick and precise, as if even the least important of them was thought out in advance for maximum efficiency. "Mrs. Shaw is not one of my regular customers. She came in about three weeks ago with a number of things she wanted to sell me then and there. I explained to her that my business is usually done on consignment and there would be a delay in payment. Some of the stuff might go immediately—for example, I've had a buyer waiting a long time for a coin collection like Shaw's. But other items, like the antique silver chess set and the jewelry, would have to wait for the right buyers. Mrs. Shaw was anxious to avoid a delay, so she offered to take whatever I was willing to pay her on the spot. I gave her what I believed to be a fair price considering the financial risk I was assuming. Actually, the deal's turning out better than I expected—some of the jewelry has been sold already. I included it in an estate auction which I conducted last week and the right buyers came along."

"Admiral Young's daughters."

"Why, yes. You know them?"

"Slightly," Aragon said. Even slightly seemed like a lot.

"The girls come in here quite often looking for a bargain. They never find any, of course—it's my business to see that people don't get bargains—but they think they do, so they make a purchase now and then, usually a rather small one. The ruby necklace and bracelet set was more expensive than anything they'd previously bought. They took a fancy to it for some reason."

"Juliet recognized it as Mrs. Shaw's."

"I see." Tannenbaum took off his glasses and rubbed the bridge of his nose where the frame had carved a red arc. "Or rather, I don't see. Surely you can't believe they bought the set for sentimental reasons?"

"It's possible."

"Oh, come now, Mr. Aragon. The Admiral's daughters aren't given to sentiment. Behind all that moronic conversation they're as hard-headed and hard-nosed as a pair of old Navy chiefs."

"I think they're pathetic."

"Are they clients of yours?"

"Yes."

"Wait till they try to beat you out of your fee. They won't seem quite so pathetic."

"The fee's already been settled."

"Well. You must have a way with you."

Aragon resisted the urge to tell the truth. Smedler wouldn't be too happy if word got out that one of his employees had, twice in the same day, offered his services free. "It's a gift," he said, more or less accurately. "What can you tell me about Mrs. Shaw?"

Tannenbaum replaced his glasses and looked toward the rear of the hall as if seeking the advice of his partner. Rupert was asleep and snoring. "She puzzled me, that much I can tell you. Many of my first-time customers act the way she did, nervous and ill-at-ease, but there was something contradictory about her, an air of excitement I couldn't figure out. It was the watch that clued me in."

"What kind of watch?"

"A man's wristwatch, a gold Swiss Jubilee. Very sophisticated and classy, with a face that shows the time only when viewed from a certain angle. I picked it up to examine it for an on-the-spot appraisal, but she asked for it back, said she'd changed her mind and wanted to hold on

92

to it as a memento of her late husband. This is a common enough practice, for a bereaved person to hold on to a watch and keep it running and ticking like a heartbeat. I didn't believe her, though. Still don't."

"What do you believe?"

"A watch like that," Tannenbaum said, "would make a very nice gift."

Aragon was eating dinner, a barely warm pizza with mozzarella that clung in strings to the roof of his mouth and had to be dislodged with beer. He'd placed the phone on the table in front of him and every now and then he stared at it as though it was a stubborn little beast that needed to be urged into action. It rang, finally, shortly after seven-thirty and he answered on the first ring.

"Hello, Laurie."

"Tom." She sounded pleased. "How did you know it was me?"

"Just a lucky guess."

"What a liar you are. You were thinking about me."

"Yes."

"Good things?"

"The best."

"Me too. Listen, Tom, we'll see each other at Thanksgiving. That's not too far away and I get three whole days off."

"The last time you had three whole days off you slept two and a half of them."

"I remember the other half-day very well," Laurie said. "Do you?"

"Vaguely. I may have to refresh my memory at Thanksgiving."

"That's a lovely idea."

"I hope so. It's the only one I have at the moment."

"Oh, *Tom*." There was a silence. "We'd better change the subject. This one is getting us nowhere and costing twenty-four cents a minute. Let's talk about goats."

"I don't want to talk about goats."

"Yes, you do. You appointed me your assistant in charge of regenerative process, goat division . . . Well, I found out from a geriatric specialist at the County Medical Association that there are a couple of places where people can get injections of goat embryo glands to stay young. One is in Hungary, and that's the extent of the information I could get on it. The other's in Mexico, run by a Dr. Manuel Ortiz. Ortiz doesn't advertise, but the word has spread around youth-oriented places like Beverly Hills. His clinic's main attractions seem to be that it guarantees immediate results and costs a lot of money."

"That's the attraction?"

"It is for wealthy people who have only one thing left to spend their money on, turning back the clock."

"Where does this Dr. Ortiz turn back the clock?"

"The clinic is a converted ranch in a small seaside village south of Ensenada."

"Pasoloma."

"That's it. How did you know?"

"Just another lucky guess."

"Come on, tell me."

"It's kind of complicated," Aragon said. "And as you mentioned a while ago, this conversation is costing twenty-four cents a minute. I figure we should save our money so that when you're old and gray we'll be able to send you down to Pasoloma for some of Dr. Ortiz's goat glands."

"How thoughtful of you."

"I come from a long line of thinkers."

"Tom, you're not going to tell me a thing, are you?"

"Just the usual. I love you."

"Well, I love you too, but it doesn't prevent me from wondering why you're suddenly interested in rejuvenation. Did Smedler put you on a case involving Pasoloma?"

"I don't know yet," he said. "Honest."

"The last time you went to Mexico you got in all kinds of trouble."

"Other people got in trouble. I didn't."

"The Mexican police aren't normally interested in such fine distinctions."

"Laurie, dear, I can't tell you any more than I already have because I don't know any more. I'm working on a hunch and it may be miles off the track. You've been a great help finding out about Dr. Ortiz. Tomorrow morning I'll get Smedler's secretary to call Ortiz's clinic and see if our client is there. If she is, I'll take the papers down to her for her signature and come home, mission accomplished. If she isn't there, I'll start thinking up another angle."

It sounded logical, straightforward, easy. He wondered why he didn't feel better about it.

Aragon arrived at the office shortly before nine o'clock and took up a strategic position at the door of Smedler's private elevator. He was beginning to know Charity Nelson's weaknesses and strengths, and one of them was punctuality. The bell in the City Hall tower across the street was striking the hour when she came in. In addition to her handbag, she was carrying a large canvas tote fully packed and showing a number of interesting lumps and bumps. Her wig had been anchored with a scarf tied so tightly under her jaw that her lips could scarcely move when she spoke: "Whatever you want, no."

"I wasn't asking for anything," Aragon said. "I'm just reporting in."

"Like on what?"

"Mrs. Shaw."

"You found her."

"No."

"Then there's nothing to report."

"There may be."

"Listen, junior, this isn't the best time to mess around. Smedler spent the night in his office because he had a fight with his wife and he'd like her to believe he killed himself, which may not be such a bad idea, but who am I to suggest

it. In here"—she indicated the canvas tote—"is his breakfast. Also mine. One thing Smedler and I have in common,
we don't like problems before breakfast, so bug off."

Charity pressed the button and the little iron-grilled elevator came down from the top floor with the majestic dignity of a vehicle intended only for royalty.

When the door opened Charity said, "You'd better not
come up yet, junior."

"That canvas bag looks heavy. Let me carry it for you."

"Okay. But don't say I didn't warn you."

Once in her office Charity untied the scarf anchoring her
wig and filled the glass coffeepot from the water cooler.
Then she began unpacking the canvas tote Aragon had put
on her desk: cans of tomato juice, some fresh pears and
oranges, a bag from a local doughnut shop, a plastic container of plant food, a bottle of leaf polish and a jar of
instant coffee.

"I have to make a long-distance call to a place in Mexico," Aragon said. "I thought you'd want me to do it from
here."

"Why should I?"

"Because it involves Mrs. Shaw."

He explained. In spite of the early hour and lack of
breakfast, she was pleased with his theory. It fitted not only
the rumors she'd heard but also her own picture of Miranda Shaw as the kind of vain, stupid woman who would go
to a clinic in Mexico to buy back her youth. Charity didn't
consider her own youth worth buying back.

She put the call in herself. Whether it was her crisp voice
or just plain luck, the call was relayed through Tijuana to
Pasoloma within five minutes. Almost immediately a
woman answered in Spanish, switching to heavily accented
English in response to Charity's question. Yes, this was the
Clinica Pasoloma but no Mrs. Shaw was registered.

Charity held her hand over the mouthpiece. "The lady
says Mrs. Shaw is not there. That blows your theory, junior."

"Let me talk to her." He took over the phone and spoke in Spanish. But Mrs. Shaw wasn't there in Spanish any more than she'd been in English.

The clinic, in fact, did not give out names or any other information over the telephone except to the proper authorities. Though Aragon tried to convince her that he was, as Mrs. Shaw's lawyer, a proper authority, she didn't wait for him to finish.

"You struck out," Charity said. "Admit it."

"Not yet. The woman was just following orders, no names over the telephone."

"So?"

"Suppose I go down to the clinic and ask her in person."

"Why don't you take no for an answer, junior? You had a nice little idea that died. Bury it."

Smedler came out of his office. He showed no signs of having spent a night involving any physical or emotional discomfort. He was freshly shaved and impeccably groomed. Even the frown he aimed at his secretary was normal for the time of day.

"I tried to use the phone, Miss Nelson, and it was tied up by a bunch of foreigners."

"Sorry," Aragon said. "I was one of them."

Smedler ignored him. "I don't like foreign languages spoken on my telephone, Miss Nelson. What if the CIA is listening? They might think I'm selling secrets to Cuba or something."

"We don't have any secrets to sell to Cuba, Mr. Smedler."

"You and I know that but *they* don't . . . Did you get the kind of doughnuts I asked for?"

"With jelly inside," Charity said. "Mr. Aragon has a theory about Mrs. Shaw's disappearance."

"Cherry?"

"Yes, sir. It's an interesting theory."

"The strawberry ones have those irritating little things in them."

97

"Seeds. Shall I authorize him to pursue it?"

"Use your judgment, Miss Nelson. You've shown excellent judgment in the past. Nothing has happened to warp it, surely? Then carry on."

Smedler disappeared with the bag of doughnuts, two fresh pears and a can of tomato juice.

Aragon said, "Well, has it?"

"Has what?"

"Anything happened to warp your judgment?"

"It gets warped every hour on the hour," Charity said with a kind of grim satisfaction. "What's on your calendar for the next few days?"

"Nothing I can't clean up by this afternoon or push off on someone else."

"Will your car make it as far as Pasoloma?"

"Probably."

"Then a couple of hundred dollars should do it."

"Make it three."

"The plants you see growing around here are not money trees, junior."

"Okay, I'll settle for two. If I run short I can always sell a few secrets to Cuba."

"This is highway robbery," Charity said and made out a check for three hundred dollars. "And listen, junior, you'd better get going first thing tomorrow morning before Smedler finds out how really warped my judgment has become."

Part III

The highway was known on both sides of the border as Numero Uno.

The border with its twenty-four gates was the busiest in the world, but most of the cars and vans and buses going into Mexico stopped at Tijuana or some sixty miles further south at Ensenada. Beyond Ensenada the speed and volume of traffic decreased and Aragon was able to slow down enough to decipher an occasional weather-beaten sign along the road. Dr. Ortiz evidently didn't believe in encouraging visitors. The word Pasoloma and an arrow pointing west toward the sea was painted on a shingle nailed to the prostrate trunk of an elephant tree.

Aragon turned right on a narrow dirt road oiled just enough to settle the top layer of dust and coat the sides of his old Chevy with a kind of black glue. The road ended abruptly on a curve with the Pacific Ocean about twenty yards ahead, and Aragon realized he'd arrived in Pasoloma. What Laurie had described on the telephone as a small seaside village was in fact a gas pump, some dilapidated wooden shacks and a dozen kids accompanied by some dogs, chickens and a burro. One of the chickens flew up and landed on the burro's back and the reluctant host was trying to dislodge it with a series of kicks. It was the only activity in the entire village.

The clinic itself was at the top of a newly surfaced driveway curving up a hill between boulders and paloverde trees—the original ranchhouse now serving, according to a sign on the door, as the main office; a number of outbuildings remodeled as staff residences; a cluster of modern cottages with attached carports, most of them occupied by large American cars. In addition to the cottages, two other structures were new—a rectangular one with small high windows obviously meant to discourage sightseers and another that looked like a small hospital, with a late-model station wagon and a jeep parked outside. Both vehicles were identified by the lettering on their sides as belonging to Dr. Manuel Ortiz, Clinica Pasoloma.

It was early afternoon, siesta time. Hardly anyone was in sight. A nurse in uniform was walking slowly toward the hospital, a gardener was clipping a mangy-looking hedge, leaf by leaf, and half a dozen people sat around the swimming pool. Only one was in the pool, an enormously fat man lying on his back with his belly protruding from the water like the carcass of a sea lion bloated with decomposing gases.

Aragon parked his car in front of the ranchhouse and went into the door marked *Oficio.*

A middle-aged woman sat behind the reception desk reading a newspaper. She had Indian features, eyes flat and expressionless as pennies, straight black hair and lips that moved only enough to permit limited conversation. Though her language was Spanish, she used no exaggerated gestures or inflections.

"The office is closed."

"Oh, sorry," Aragon said. "I didn't see any sign to that effect."

"Something happened to it."

"Perhaps you could answer one simple question?"

She looked him over carefully. His youth pegged him as a non-customer, his accent as American, his car as poor. There was no use wasting energy on him.

"The office is closed until three o'clock."

"It's two now. Let's pretend we're on daylight-saving time, that way we wouldn't be breaking any rules, would we?"

"I think yes, we would." She folded the newspaper and put it on the desk. "Dr. Ortiz is my sister's son-in-law. We make the rules together, the whole family, and we keep them together."

"I'm sure you do. You look like the kind of person who would make a good rule and stick to it."

"This is a family enterprise."

"And very successful, I hear."

"Where do you hear that?"

"Santa Felicia, California," Aragon said. "I just drove down today to see Mrs. Shaw."

"Who?"

"Miranda Shaw. Mrs. Neville Shaw. Or perhaps Mrs. Grady Keaton."

"Why do you want to see somebody whose name you don't even know?"

"I represent her lawyer."

"Our patients are not allowed to have visitors," said Dr. Ortiz's mother-in-law's sister. "We make that very clear in the instructions they're sent before they arrive for treatment. The only exceptions permitted are that a wife may bring her husband, or vice versa, if they choose to rent one of our cottages."

He asked the price of a cottage and she mentioned a figure that would have rented half a hotel in Santa Felicia.

"It is the sea," she added, observing his shock. "One must pay for the sound of waves and the bracing salt air."

Aragon went down to the beach for a free trial of the waves and the bracing salt air. There was a south swell with sets of eight to ten feet and almost no wind to rough them. In California on such a day, at Hammond's Reef, Malibu, Zuma, Huntington Beach, the water would be swarming with surfers in wet suits maneuvering for position or sitting on their boards like rows of cormorants. At Pasoloma there were only three surfers, young men wearing swim trunks instead of wet suits because the water was still summer-warm.

A purple van carrying Oregon license plates was parked nearby on a patch of sea daisies, its roof draped with jeans and T-shirts drying in the sun. Beside the van a blond girl lay on her back, nude, sleeping.

Aragon said, tentatively, "Hello?"

She twitched as though an insect had buzzed her ear. Aragon repeated the greeting a little louder and this time she opened one eye. It was blue and bored. "What?"

"I said hello."

"So hello. If you're from the Federales, we're not carrying any grass. Cross my heart. In fact, you can search me if you like, as long as Mike doesn't see you. He's the jealous type and I'm his lady."

"You could have fooled me."

She sat up, shaking the sand out of her hair. "If you're such a gentleman, stop looking."

Aragon tried. "Is that Mike out there?"

"Him and his friend, Carl."

"There are three of them."

"The other one's just a guy wo was on the beach when we got here."

"Does he have a name?"

"I didn't ask him. Names don't matter any more. I mean, nobody cares. My old lady had a neat system, she called all her guys the same name. Ed."

"Why Ed?"

"Why not? What's wrong with Ed?"

Aragon had never before argued the merits of the name Ed with a naked girl and it seemed a poor time to start. Besides, she had already lost interest. Her mind was on food.

"Is there any place around here where I could get a hamburger? We've had nothing to eat but fish all the way down the coast. I'm afraid my face will start to break out. Have you heard that too much fish will make your face break out?"

"I haven't heard that, no."

"Maybe it's not true. I hope not. It wouldn't be fair to have your face break out for eating something you don't even like . . . Mike's watching us. I better put some clothes on. Oh Christ, he's coming in."

All three surfers were heading for shore. The waves were still high but they'd started breaking too fast, so that ebb and flow met at an impasse in a wall of water. The girl had pulled a pair of jeans and a T-shirt off the roof of the van and was putting them on. The jeans fitted like hand-me-ups from a younger, thinner sister and the front of the white flimsy T-shirt was somewhat inaccurately labeled Out of Sight.

"Mike believes in nudity," the girl explained. "But not mine. He wants I should be bundled up like an Eskimo all the time."

"Maybe you should."

"Really? I look that good?"

"I think so. The trouble is, the Federales might think so too, which could cause problems. Officially, they're pretty stuffy about women wearing enough clothing. Unofficially—well, you'd better be more careful."

"No kidding, I look that good? Wait'll I tell Mike. He'll freak out."

The three men emerged from the surf. Aragon picked Grady out immediately. The other two were younger, not yet out of their teens, and they'd had their hair cut for the trip across the border, so that their foreheads and the backs of their necks were several shades lighter than the rest of their bodies. Grady was deep brown all over except for the permanent sun scars across his cheekbones and the bridge of his nose.

Mike escorted his lady into the van in spite of her protests—"Every girl's got two of those and one of them, so what's the big deal?"—and his friend Carl took the hint and began jogging up the beach.

Grady sat down in the sand, shaking his head to get the water out of his ears and off his hair. His movements were violent, as if he were trying to rid himself of something more adhesive than water.

Aragon said, "Are you Grady Keaton?"

"Good question." The gaze he directed at Aragon was without interest and his eyes had a frosted look like starboard lights seen through fog. "I used to be."

"What changed you?"

"I came here. In these parts I'm addressed as Mr. Shaw on account of the lady I'm with is Mrs. Shaw and the Mexicans are very very square. The real Mr. Shaw doesn't give a damn because he's dead. He died of old age, which is not something I expect to do. How about you?"

"I haven't thought about it."

"Sure you have. Everybody thinks about dying. It's the normal thing. Or is it? What the hell, who elected me judge of normal?" He transferred his gaze to the sea. "Every wave is different, did you know that? I mean every single one of them. Like if an experienced surfer sees a photograph of a wave in a magazine, he can usually tell where the photograph was taken—Pismo, Hollister, Huntington, any top spot on the coast."

"I've heard that but never believed it."

"It's true."

"So Miranda Shaw is with you."

"No."

"You said—"

"I said *I* was with her. There are a few small differences, like who's picking up the tab, who invited who, who gives the orders and makes the decisions. I never even heard of this place until I was on my way. And the kind of salary I make I couldn't afford to stay here for a day. I wouldn't want to, anyway. The surfing's nothing special and I'm usually the only one in the water, so what's the fun? Surfing isn't just riding waves on a board, it's a whole way of life, like those kids in the van surfing from Oregon to Le Paz. If I had the money—and I might someday, free money, no strings attached—that's what I'd do. Except I'd start further north at Vancouver and go down to San Lucas and take the ferry that runs over to Puerto Vallarta."

"It doesn't sound like the kind of trip she'd enjoy."

"Who?"

"Miranda Shaw."

"I wasn't thinking of inviting her."

Up to this point Aragon had been standing, shifting his weight from one foot to another until both his shoes were filled with sand. He sat down and removed them and his socks and finally his shirt. The sun struck his chest like a branding iron and he put the shirt back on.

"I'm Tom Aragon, an attorney from Santa Felicia. I was sent to find Miranda Shaw."

"I figured you weren't here on my account."

"In a way I am. I bring greetings from a young friend of yours in Santa Felicia, Frederic Quinn. He asked me to look you up. You're one of his heroes."

"So is Bingo Firenze's uncle, hit man for the Mafia, so I'm not exactly flattered . . . Why do you want to see Miranda?"

"It concerns her husband's will."

"I thought that had all been settled. Shaw left everything to her, didn't he?"

"The question is, what's everything?"

"What's everything? What in hell would it be? It's stocks, bonds, real estate, cars, bank accounts, jewelry, the works. He was a very rich man. Wasn't he?"

"Yes." It was true enough. Shaw was once a very rich man and he left everything to his wife. Aragon didn't consider it his duty to explain that everything was not only bank accounts and stocks and bonds and real estate, it was also debts.

"Something's funny the way you're talking," Grady said. "Was he or wasn't he a rich man?"

"I repeat, he was."

"And he willed his estate to Miranda?"

"She's his sole beneficiary."

"Then what's this about?"

"Shaw's will hasn't gone through probate yet. There are some papers which have to be signed by Mrs. Shaw."

"Well, that's easy." For a moment Grady looked almost friendly. "She's over in the cottage lying down. She sleeps a lot. They all do around here, the place is like a morgue."

The fatigue which Dr. Ortiz claimed was normal for people under treatment semed to spread from the point of injection throughout her entire body, leaving her simultaneously light-headed and lead-footed. She had giddy spells, and once she had fallen when Grady wasn't there and she couldn't even recall the incident until the soreness of her wrist and the bruises on her arm reminded her. Grady thought she'd been drinking and she let him think it.

She lay drowsy-eyed on the bed, wearing the white chiffon nightgown she'd purchased at a bride boutique in San Diego. She didn't feel like a bride. The injections weren't as painful as they'd been in previous years because Dr. Ortiz had added what he described as a secret new ingredient, but the numbness was almost worse than pain. She'd expected a surge of vitality and youth. Instead she felt shriveled, as though she were gradually being mummified. She had no appetite, for food or life or even Grady.

"Go and surf, dear."

"But you said—"

"Run along without me. I'll come down later and watch you."

Then suddenly it was later and Grady was back.

"Where were you, Miranda?"

"I must have dozed off."

"It's six o'clock."

"I'm sorry, dear. I meant to—"

"There wasn't a soul in sight the whole damn afternoon."

"I thought that's what you wanted, a beach where you didn't have to fight for every good wave."

"Well, I got it, I sure as hell got it."

Always, after one of her long sleeps, she was jittery. "Go and tell Dr. Ortiz I don't feel well. I need something to calm me."

"You've started pill-popping, you know that? Pills and booze and goat glands—Christ, what a combo."

"Please, Grady. I'm quite nervous."

"Let's get out of here, Miranda. Pack your stuff right now and we'll take off."

"I can't. Dr. Ortiz warned me that I must complete the course of treatments or the effect will be lost."

"What effect?"

"Don't I look . . . younger, Grady?"

"You look okay. You looked okay before."

"I feel younger. I really do." She giggled. It was a terrible effort.

The room was like that in any second-/or third-rate motel back home. The furnishings were new but already showing signs of wear—a double bed with a forty-watt lamp on each bedside table, a bureau topped by a mirror and a small electric fan, a desk scarred by cigarette burns, a standing ashtray advertising Tio's Tequila, a dressing alcove behind a wooden screen, a shoebox-sized kitchenette off the bathroom. An air-conditioning unit bore a sign *Fuero de Servicio,* Out of Order, and the atmosphere was hot and humid.

Insects droned and buzzed and whirred and ate each other and ate Miranda too when they discovered a way into the room through a hole in a screen. Her thin delicate skin was easy to penetrate, and the scent of her perfume was irresistible to bees in the daytime and mosquitoes at night, and to fleas and no-see-ums at any hour. There were clusters of fleabites across her abdomen and under her breasts. Her feet and ankles were covered with tiny red lumps like miniature pimples, which sometimes itched so terribly she scratched them until they bled. On her head, hidden by her hair, were curious welts oozing a colorless liquid that crystallized. When the fragile crystals broke under her comb, the oozing started all over again.

She dreamed of being consumed, of calling to Grady for help, and he came knocking at the door.

"Miranda?"

She opened her eyes.

"Are you awake, Miranda?"

She said, "No," not to be funny but because it was the truth. She was not awake, not hungry, not thirsty, not cold or hot, not in pain, not even itchy from the insect bites.

"Miranda, someone's here to see you from Santa Felicia."

She sat up on the bed, suddenly and fully awake. "I am not receiving visitors this afternoon. Who—who is it?"

"A lawyer named Aragon. Some legal technicality has come up and you've got to sign a few papers."

"Wait a minute, please."

She put on the robe that matched her gown and ran a brush quickly through her hair. With the blinds drawn, the room was nearly dark. When she passed the mirror on her way to the door her image was a white shadow, like the ectoplasm of a bride.

"Hey, Miranda, hurry up."

"All right."

She unbolted the door. Grady came in with a towel wrapped around his waist and immediately turned on the fan and began opening blinds and windows. The fan whined and whirred like a superinsect, scattering its inferiors across the room, muffling their sounds of protest.

Miranda shielded her eyes from the sudden sun. For a whole minute she could see nothing but a moving red blaze. Then gradually the stranger emerged from the blaze, a young man wearing college-style cords and a Hawaiian shirt and horn-rimmed glasses that gave him a rather shy look. He carried a briefcase.

"Mrs. Shaw? I'm Tom Aragon."

108

"I don't believe we've met."

"No, we haven't. I work for Mr. Smedler."

"Smedler." She repeated the name as if she was honestly trying to remember the man who went with it. "I can't quite . . ."

"Smedler, Downs, Castleberg, McFee, Powell."

"Oh, of course. That's the firm handling my husband's estate."

Or lack of it. He resisted an impulse to say the words, though he was pretty sure they wouldn't have shocked her. She didn't fit Smedler's description of her as a nice well-bred little woman who'd been insulated and protected from the world.

"I'm afraid this is not a very good place to entertain," she said carefully. "Or to do business, Mr. Aragon. There's a café in the main building but it's closed during the afternoon."

"I won't take much of your time."

"It will seem long to Grady. He's easily bored . . . Grady, would you mind? This promises to be a very dull session and you might as well be doing something interesting. Go and surf, dear."

Grady minded. "I surfed already."

"It's a private matter, Grady."

"We're not supposed to have secrets from each other," Grady said.

"Well, we do. Hundreds."

"He knows we're here as man and wife. I don't see what's to hide. I've got a right to be in on—"

"We'll discuss it later." *Go and surf, you bastard.*

As soon as he'd gone Miranda switched off the fan.

"I prefer the heat to the noise, if you have no objection, Mr. Aragon."

"None at all."

"Please sit down."

"Thank you."

He took one of the green vinyl chairs. It had a broken

spring in the middle of the seat. He couldn't avoid it, so he tried to sit as lightly as he could, keeping some of his weight on his thigh, a posture that made him look as if he were waiting for the starting gun of a race. He thought about what kind of race it would turn out to be—low or high hurdles, quarter-mile, marathon—and how he wasn't ready for any of them.

She sat in the other vinyl chair. If it had a broken spring, she showed no sign of it. She seemed composed, almost regal, a great lady willing to donate time to the problems of the little people, even in her nightclothes in a hot dingy little room in a foreign country.

"I find these circumstances quite extraordinary, Mr. Aragon. To begin with, no one is supposed to know where I am."

"Someone guessed."

"Smedler, I presume. It's rather bad form for him to send someone after me like this. One would think that he, of all people, would understand, since he's been married three times and heaven knows what else how many times. This is an affair of the heart."

"It is also an affair of the California judiciary."

"The California judiciary can wait. *I've* certainly been kept waiting long enough. Neville died last spring, leaving a legal and uncomplicated will which should have been settled months ago."

"Probate is often a long procedure," Aragon said. "You could have shortened it somewhat by cooperating with Smedler. Why these delaying tactics, Mrs. Shaw?"

"I was in a hurry. Some things can't be postponed. I was due for another treatment at the clinic and Grady needed a holiday. I thought it was possible to combine the two."

"And was it?"

The slight movement of her head didn't indicate yes or no.

"In practical terms, Mrs. Shaw, all you've gained is a couple of weeks and the money Tannenbaum paid you."

"How did you find that out?"

110

He told her about the Admiral's daughters and the ruby necklace and bracelet. As she listened her eyes narrowed and her jaw tightened as though she was resisting the idea of Juliet and Cordelia wearing her jewelry.

He added, "Disposing of items belonging to a frozen estate is against the law."

"The jewelry belonged to me and was not part of the estate."

"What about the other things you sold?"

"I'm the sole beneficiary, so they were mine too."

"Unfortunately, you're legally obliged to share them with Mr. Shaw's creditors . . . You knew about the creditors, of course."

Again the slight noncommittal movement of her head. "I didn't *know*."

"You suspected."

"I was aware of odd things happening, phone calls at all hours, strangers at the door. And Neville acted so different, secretive one minute, talking a blue streak the next, never letting me open the mail. I didn't understand what was happening."

"Do you understand now?"

"I'm beginning to," she said with a grim little smile. "He was making sure I didn't inherit anything. If he changed his will, I could fight it in court. If he simply left me nothing but debts, it would be legal and I'd be safe from fortune hunters. He kept referring to fortune hunters as though there was one behind every tree. He took it for granted that I was too stupid to protect myself so he had to do it. Well, he protected me all right. From fortune hunters, if not from anything else."

"He wasn't acting rationally, whatever his motives. Smedler believes you should have demanded a conservator for the estate."

"I'm not the kind of woman who demands. I guess I'm not sure enough of myself to tell other people what to do."

"You seem to me to be quite sure of yourself, Mrs. Shaw.

You've made some bold decisions in the past three weeks."

"Yes."

"Perhaps too bold."

She shrugged and turned away. Her movements were graceful but a little contrived, as though they'd been practiced for years in front of mirrors. "If I broke the law and a few conventions, I suppose I'll be sorry eventually. Right now I'm not, I'd do the same thing again. It's going to sound very silly coming from a grown woman, but I couldn't help myself. I fell in love. It never happened to me before, even when I was young. The other girls at school were continually in love, they took it for granted as an everyday thing. For me it was a miracle and still is . . . You look impatient. Am I boring you?"

"No."

"But you would prefer not to hear it."

"Happy beginnings are a dime a dozen. I like happy endings."

"There'll be a happy ending, I intend it that way."

He almost believed her. She seemed to be putting it all together, the strength and power she'd never used, the will she'd never exerted, the determination she'd been afraid to show.

"Fine," he said. "Great. Now let's get the business over with and I can leave." He opened the briefcase and took out a sheaf of papers. "I'll need your initials at the bottom of each page—after you've read it, of course—and your signature at the conclusion."

"I'm not signing."

"You'd better think this through, Mrs. Shaw."

"I already have. If Neville could play his little game, I can play mine."

Aragon sat with the briefcase across his lap. The blinding sun had given him a headache, the heat was unbearable, the broken spring of the chair was sticking into his flesh like a spur. "I told you I liked happy endings, Mrs. Shaw. Especially my own. I am, as Smedler's secretary keeps reminding me, a junior junior employee of the firm. It's not a secure position. Neither is yours. Whatever you got from Mr. Tannenbaum isn't going to last, so you have to consider the possibility that Grady and the money might run out simultaneously."

"I'm buying time, Mr. Aragon."

"Time can't be bought, it can only be spent."

"You don't understand. Grady is starting to love me, really *love* me. I'm becoming indispensable to him. When you're indispensable to someone he *has* to love you."

"My wife is indispensable to me, but so is my auto mechanic and him I'm not too crazy about."

"You're not even trying to understand."

"Look, Mrs. Shaw, sign the papers and I'll get out of here and you can tell Grady only whatever you think he'll believe."

"He'll believe anything I say. He's a beautiful person."

"Glad to hear it. In my line of work I don't meet too many beautiful persons."

She got up suddenly, and forgetting all the lessons she'd learned in mirrors, flung herself down on the bed and began to weep. She wept silently, barely moving a muscle of her face. It was a half-comic, half-sinister sight, like a wax-museum figure rigged to spout tears at the press of a button.

Aragon looked away from her, toward the sea. The purple van was gone and the wide stretch of beach was empty. In the water a solitary swimmer who had to be Grady was heading free-style straight out to sea as if his life depended on it. The next land in that direction was Hawaii, but maybe Grady figured it was worth a try.

"I mustn't cry," she said in a whisper. "Dr. Ortiz won't allow it."

"He's not here, so go right ahead."

"No. It's not good for me. Dr. Ortiz says I have to avoid bad emotions. I must think only of pleasant things."

"I hope he remembers that when he's making out his bill."

"You're a cruel, cynical man."

"I'm an errand boy for Smedler, Downs, Castleberg, McFee, Powell. This isn't a personal matter between you and me, so let's not get nasty."

As he spoke he saw the swimmer turn suddenly, as if he'd heard his name called, and head back for shore. *You should have kept going, Grady.*

Miranda was dabbing away tears with the sleeve of her robe, but new ones kept coming and her eyes were starting to turn red. "I need something to calm me."

Aragon wasn't sure what she meant but he hoped it was pharmaceutical. "I have some aspirin in my car. If you like, I can—"

"Aspirin. Aspirin, for God's sake. I'm dying and you offer me aspirin."

"It's all I've got."

"Call Grady. He can tell Dr. Ortiz to come and give me a shot."

"Grady went for a swim."

"Swim, that's the only thing he ever does, the only thing he ever thinks about."

"Beautiful persons need a lot of exercise," Aragon said.

When Grady returned to the cottage he stopped for a minute at the carport to admire the Porsche that was parked inside. It was a yellow Carrera with gold mag wheels and beige glove-leather seats. Every time he looked at it he felt a little light-headed, he had to convince himself that it was really his and Miranda was going to give him the pink ownership slip as soon as it arrived from the Department of Motor Vehicles. He called it Goldfinger, not out loud in front of anybody, but very softly and secretly as part of a pact between him and the car.

It was the only perfect thing he had ever owned and he felt personally insulted when Miranda criticized it: "Why can't we simply get in it and go? Why do we have to sit here for half an hour with the engine running?" "Not half an hour," he told her. "Just five minutes." For her it was ugly time, full of noise and smell and vibration. He loved every minute of it, it was like waiting for an orgasm.

He entered the cottage without knocking and went into the alcove behind the wooden screen to dress. A white T-shirt, a pair of shorts, the wristwatch Miranda had given him before they left Santa Felicia, the huaraches he'd picked up in Tijuana.

Nobody said anything. The loudest sounds in the room were insects humming and Grady slapping the sand off his legs with a towel. He began to whistle the song "Goldfinger" but stopped almost immediately because he was afraid someone might recognize it and guess it was the name he'd given the Porsche. He felt that in some crazy way this could ruin things. He didn't know how, he only knew things ruined easy.

He came out from behind the screen, still holding the sandy towel. "It's four o'clock, the café should be open by now. I'm going over for a can of beer. Anyone care to join me?"

No one did.

Miranda was sitting at the desk and there were a lot of papers spread out in front of her. She wore a pair of half-glasses he'd never seen before, and when she peered at him over the top of them she looked like an old woman.

"Hey, what is this, Halloween? Take those things off."

"I can't read the fine print without them."

"Fine print. Okay, I get it. This is private business and you want me to split."

"No, I think you should stay." She began gathering up the papers and putting them in numerical order. She moved slowly, as she always did, but Grady saw that this was a different kind of slowness, clumsy and reluctant. "Mr. Aragon has brought us some bad news, Grady. Nothing we can't handle, the two of us together, but—"

"It's about the will," Grady said.

"Yes."

"He didn't leave you everything, after all."

"Yes, he did."

"Then why is the news bad?"

" 'Everything' includes his mistakes. Neville made some reckless financial deals during the last year or two of his life."

"How reckless?"

"I'd rather not go into it now, Grady. I don't feel very well. My head—"

"How reckless?"

"Very," she said. "Very reckless."

"So he didn't leave you any money?"

"No."

"But there's the house."

"It has three mortgages on it. Among other things, Neville bought a stud farm in Kentucky."

Aragon, putting the papers back in his briefcase, wondered how she'd found out about the stud farm in Kentucky. If Shaw had told her that, he'd probably told her a lot of other things she'd been pretending not to know. Whatever her reason for the pretense, she had gained nothing from it but a small delay. *I'm buying time, Mr. Aragon . . . Grady is starting to love me, really love me. I'm becoming indispensable to him.*

"What about the car?" Grady said, "My Porsche."

"It's paid for, if that's what you mean. I traded in the Continental and the Mercury." She took off her glasses and hid them away in a needlepoint case. The fine print had been read, all of it bad. "It's really *our* car, isn't it, Grady?"

"Sure. Naturally. I call it mine because you promised to give me the pink slip on it—"

"Whatever is left of the estate we'll share, the two of us. We don't need a fortune to be happy together."

"—and because I do all the driving. You can't even shift gears."

"Shut up," she said. "Shut up about that stupid car."

"Stupid car? Now wait a minute, you can't talk like that about a turbo Carrera."

"I can if I paid for it."

"That's a bitchy remark."

"I have more of the same if you care to hear them."

"Say, what's the matter with you, anyway? I never saw you like this before."

"I have had bad news, terrible news, and all you can do is stand there blabbering about a car while I . . . while my whole world falls apart."

"Since we're supposed to be sharing everything, let's call it *our* world," Grady said. "So *our* world is falling apart. You're right, that's terrible news. But what I want to know is how new is this news?"

"What do you mean?"

"When did you find out?"

"Just now, from Mr. Aragon. He told me about the—the stud farm in Kentucky. And other things."

Aragon didn't deny it, but he glanced toward the door as though he wished he were on the other side of it.

"I had no idea Neville liked horses," she said. "He never let me keep any pets, not even goldfish." She thought of the aquarium in their bedroom at home, the dead fish floating in the murky water that smelled of Scotch. "I would have liked a dog, someone to talk to. Everything was always so quiet. I used to look forward to the gardener cutting the grass or clipping the hedges. He was a funny little man. I forget his name, or perhaps I never knew it. His lawn mower sounded very loud, worse than the Porsche. I have this— this awful headache, Grady. Could you get something for me from Dr. Ortiz?"

"No."

"But I hurt, I hurt all over."

"Sure you hurt. A needle in the butt every morning and a bunch of goats surging around in your bloodstream, what the hell do you expect?"

"I'm only doing it for you, Grady."

"Crap. You've been here two or three times before. Who were you doing it for then?"

"You're cruel, you're so cruel to me."

"I've never lied." He threw the towel into a corner as if he were trying to discard a piece of the past. It lay in a dirty heap. "You must have known Neville had blown away every bill he owned. Why didn't you tell me?"

"I didn't know. Ask Mr. Aragon."

In spite of the mention of his name, neither of them turned to look at Aragon. He picked up his briefcase and took a step toward the door. When this didn't attract attention he took several more steps until he was close enough to put his hand on the doorknob. *Goodbye, Miranda. Nice meeting you. Once.*

Miranda had started crying again. Her tears dropped on the burn-scarred desk, little crystal bombs iridescing in the sun for a moment before they exploded into words: people were cruel to her, they accused her of things, they picked on her. She hated Grady, Smedler, Aragon, all lawyers, lifeguards, nurses, doctors and the California judiciary. She was innocent, her butt hurt and she was going to throw up. She also had a terrible headache but nobody cared, nobody cared about anything except their damned Porsches and everyone should get the hell out of there.

"I was just leaving," Aragon said.

"Take Grady with you. He can show you his turbo Carrera."

Grady stood with his arms crossed on his chest, motionless, expressionless, like a cut-rate Midas turned to bronze instead of gold.

"Do you hear me, Grady? I want you to leave."

"Everybody hears you," Grady said. "You're screaming."

"Not yet. I'm working up to it, though."

"You're making an ass of yourself, Miranda."

"Get out of here."

"All right, all right. Like the man said, I was just leaving."

The café had been opened only a few minutes before and none of the tables was occupied. Two waiters were more or less on duty, an elderly man sitting on a stool picking his teeth and a teenager who bore a strong resemblance to the woman who'd greeted Aragon at the reception desk in the office, thin straight lips and nose, eyes cool as coins. When he saw Grady his face seemed to splinter with excitement.

"Mr. Shaw, Mr. Shaw, sir . . ."

"Bring us a couple of beers, Pedro."

"What kind?"

"You've only got one kind."

"My uncle says to ask. It sounds good."

"I'm buying," Grady told Aragon. "Or rather, Miranda's buying. All I do is write the magic name Shaw on the bill and everything is taken care of."

"Was taken care of."

"That's definite, is it? I mean you weren't trying to scare her to force her to economize, or something along those lines?"

"No."

Grady rubbed his eyes. The pupils were red from the salt water and sand and sun. "She conned me."

"Maybe you con easy."

"It's not just the money I'm talking about. It's the whole deal. I didn't go *after* her, man. She was *there*, I couldn't get past her. So I thought, why not? I was figuring on a little fling, a couple of months, three at the most, and I thought that's what she wanted too. But then she began using words like commitment and marriage and forever. Forever. Can you beat that? I'm not a forever guy."

Pedro returned, swinging a bottle of beer in each hand.

"Mr. Shaw, sir, I'm ready."

"So am I," Grady said. "What are we ready for?"

"The ride. Tomorrow."

"Oh. Sure."

"Very early before the traffic. How about seven o'clock?"

"You like seven o'clock, Pedro?"

"You bet."

"I don't like seven o'clock. But then, I don't like six or eight o'clock either, so let's make it seven. We'll race the wind, you and me."

"You and me will win. You bet?"

"I bet," Grady said. After the boy left he poured the beer himself. It gushed out over the tops of the bottles like used soapsuds and he sat staring at the foam as though he saw his fortune in it, brief as bubbles and a little dirty. "Here's to Miranda."

"To Miranda."

"Long may she live. Alone."

The beer was too warm and too sweet.

"Christ, I need something stronger than this," Grady said. "You don't have grass on you, do you?"

"No."

"Those kids in the van had some, I could smell it, but they weren't sharing . . . Listen, about Miranda and me, it wasn't working. It wouldn't have worked even if you hadn't shown up with the news about the money."

"I'm glad I didn't ruin anything good."

"Maybe she thinks so. I don't. Like I said, I'm not a forever guy. I feel trapped half the time and guilty the rest. She's so dependent. When I do some perfectly innocent little thing like taking the kid for a ride in my Porsche, she makes out like I abandoned her. It's kind of crazy anyone being dependent on me. Nobody ever was before. It gives me the creeps."

"About the Porsche," Aragon said. "I gather you don't have the pink slip for it."

"The car's mine, She gave it to me. I'm not conceited enough to claim I earned it, but it's *mine*. Hell, she can't even drive it, she doesn't know how to shift gears."

"All that has no bearing on the ownership of the car. As of now it may be the only thing she has left."

"Then how could she afford to come to an expensive place like this?"

"She sold some of her jewelry and other things to a dealer in Santa Felicia."

"Then she's honest-to-God broke."

"Yes."

"And it's a whole new ball game, with me stuck out here in left field."

"She's out there with you. She didn't plan it that way, it's not her fault."

"She shouldn't have lied to me."

"There are people who lie," Aragon said, "and people who want to be lied to. They're often the same people."

Grady drained his glass and put it down on the multicolored tile table. The tiles looked handmade. None of them matched and none of them came out even at the corners. Aragon wondered which of Dr. Ortiz's relatives had worked on it, perhaps a third-cousin-by-marriage who was considered too artistic for one of the menial jobs like Pedro's.

Without being asked, Pedro brought two more beers, wiped off the table with the hem of his apron and reminded Grady of their date to race the wind at seven in the morning.

"The essential thing now," Aragon said, "is to get her back home under the care of her own doctor. She looks pretty spaced-out. What kind of stuff has Ortiz been giving her?"

"It's powerful, I can tell you that much. Knocks her for a loop. Also, she's beginning to ask for it too damn often. She uses the slightest excuse to send me over to get a capsule from Ortiz. He won't let her have more than one at a time."

"How long is she scheduled to stay here?"

"Another two weeks."

"I don't think that would be wise."

"Then you tell her," Grady said. "I already have, for all the good it did. Every time I try to tell her anything she gets a pain in her stomach, her head, her appendix, her butt, you name it. Then she takes one of Ortiz's capsules and conks out. When she wakes up she can't remember what I told her. Half the time I can't either. She has me confused. She always makes me feel I'm in the wrong even when there's no right or wrong involved, just ordinary things."

"Equal alternatives."

"Yeah, that's it, equal alternatives. I'm beginning to think she's a little crazy. She even talked once about having a child. It was grotesque. She's fifty-two. She admitted it, but I knew anyway. Ellen Brewster, the secretary of the club, told me, she looked it up in the files."

"Why would Ellen do that?"

"She wanted to clue me in. For my own good."

"That was kind of Ellen as far as you're concerned. Miranda might feel somewhat different about it."

"It was the truth. I had the right to be told the truth."

"Knowing the truth obviously didn't alter your course of action."

"It never has." Grady's voice was somber. "Maybe I'm crazier than she is. Give me your honest opinion, do you think it's possible?"

"Lots of things are," Aragon said. He didn't give the rest of his honest opinion, that this was more possible than most.

It was after seven and almost dark when Aragon reached the outskirts of Tijuana. He had intended, if all went well, to stay on the freeway and drive right through to Santa Felicia, reaching there about midnight. But he was getting tired and the afternoon had been depressing. He checked in at an American franchise motel, had tostadas and beer at a nearby café and returned to his room.

He closed the windows to block out the noises of the street, which was just coming alive for the night. Then he called Charity Nelson at her apartment and told her he wouldn't be in the office the next morning.

"Where are you, junior?"

"Tijuana."

"What are you doing there?"

"Nothing."

"Nobody does nothing in Tijuana."

"Okay, I'm boozing it up with a couple of hookers."

"That's more like," Charity said. "Did you find Mrs. Shaw?"

"Yes."

"Can't you say anything more than plain ordinary *yes*?"

"I can but you might not want to hear it."

"Try me."

"She's at Dr. Ortiz's rejuvenation clinic in Pasoloma with her friend Grady Keaton."

"The lifeguard?"

"Yes."

"Is he cute?"

"What do you mean by cute?"

"Cute is cute. You know, like Robert Redford."

"He is not like Robert Redford."

"Oh. I wonder what she sees in him, then. To me Robert Redford is—"

"You can tell me about your fantasy life some other time, Miss Nelson," Aragon said. "I'm reporting in that the documents are ready and I'll have them at the office by late tomorrow afternoon."

"You don't sound very happy about it, considering you might even get a bonus if I play your cards right."

"Ha ha ha. Is that better?"

"What's bugging you, junior?"

"This is a dirty business. The lady is doped up and a little crazy, maybe a lot crazy, and I walked out of there and left her."

"You couldn't very well bring her along. The lifeguard wouldn't like it, would he?"

Aragon didn't respond.

"Junior?"

"I'd rather not discuss it."

"I never figured you for the emotional type. This isn't such a dirty business when you look at other dirty businesses."

"Thanks for helping me see things in a new light, Miss Nelson."

"That's my specialty."

"I can believe it. Goodbye."

"Wait a minute. I haven't finished."

"I have," Aragon said and hung up.

He left a wake-up call with the operator for five-thirty the next morning.

His return to Pasoloma was slowed by fog and by an unexpectedly heavy procession of vehicles heading into Baja, mostly vans and campers and motor homes with California license plates. The fog started to lift when he reached Pasoloma and the clinic was emerging from its shroud. There was activity around the main office and the hospital building, though it wasn't the kind of activity seen around an ordinary hospital or clinic. People seemed to move very slowly, as though they had—courtesy of Dr. Ortiz—all the time in the world.

Aragon drove directly to the cottage shared by Miranda and Grady. The yellow Porsche was missing from the carport. In its place was Pedro, the boy from the café, talking to a stout middle-aged woman with a cartful of cleaning equipment. Pedro nodded good-morning but he didn't smile or speak. As for the woman, she ducked around the side of the building in a surprising show of speed, pushing the cart in front of her. It sounded as if it had a square wheel.

Aragon said, "That cart could use some oil."

The boy shrugged. "It's old. My mother used to push me around in it when I was little."

"How old are you now?"

"Thirteen. Next year me and my brother are going to the U.S. to get a job, make lots of money." He glanced back at Aragon's Chevy. "You don't make lots of money like Mr. Shaw does."

"Not like Mr. Shaw does, no."

"He's pretty important, I bet. He can't waste time taking people for rides. Racing the wind, that's a crazy idea. Nobody can race something they can't see."

"I'm sorry you missed your ride, Pedro."

"I don't care," the boy said. "I never expected nothing anyway."

Aragon knocked on the door of the cottage, softly at first, then more loudly when there was no response. The windows were closed and the blinds shut as if the people inside were trying to avoid the light and noise of morning.

He knocked again. "Mrs. Shaw?"

Another two or three minutes elapsed before Miranda's voice answered, hoarse and sleepy. "Who is it?"

"Tom Aragon."

"Go away."

"I went away. Now I'm back."

She opened the door. She wore a large loose pink-and-orange-striped robe that made her look as though she'd taken shelter in a tent that wasn't quite tall enough and she'd had to cut a hole in the top for her head.

Her eyelids were swollen and blistered by the heat of her tears. She said, almost literally, "I'm not seeing anyone."

"Are you feeling all right, Mrs. Shaw?"

"Close the door. I'm cold."

"Let me order you some breakfast."

"No, thank you. I know you're trying to be kind but it's quite unnecessary. I'm quite—quite fine."

"Where is Grady?"

"Grady is fine too, thank you."

"I asked where."

"Where? Well, I'm not really sure. He took one of the boys from the café for a ride in the Porsche. I wish he wouldn't get so friendly with the hired help, it's not dignified. He must learn to—"

"The boy is still waiting for him, Mrs. Shaw."

She sat down on the edge of the bed, her tent collapsing around her. "So am I," she said in a whisper. "But he won't be back. He left in the middle of the night. I'd been very upset by the news you brought me, so Dr. Ortiz gave me a capsule and I went to sleep. When I woke up Grady was gone. There was a note on the desk."

The note was still there. Though it had been crumpled and partly torn and marked by tears, it remained legible. The letters were large and uneven, the lines slanted downward:

Miranda

Things are beginning to close in on me and I need to get away fast and figure it all out how to do something and be somebody. I thought it was funny at first being called Mr. Shaw but then suddenly it wasn't. Maybe I'll see you in the U.S. after I get established and no more of that Mr. Shaw crap.

Please don't go to pieces over my leaving so sudden. We both agreed it wasn't going to be permanent, nothing is, how can we beat odds like that.

Take care Miranda and maybe I'll see you in the U.S. and we can have fun like we use to.

Your friend
Grady Keaton

P.S. Don't let the doc pump any more of that junk in you. You look OK as is. Why do you want to be young again anyway. Being young is hell.

The note ran true to form. Grady had told no lies, made no promises, expressed no regrets.

126

"Let me take you home, Mrs. Shaw," Aragon said. "We can leave as soon as you're packed."

"Dr. Ortiz won't like it."

"Did you pay in advance?"

"Yes."

"What about refunds?"

"He doesn't give any."

"Then he'll probably be able to absorb the shock of your departure."

"But what if—what if Grady comes back and I'm not here?"

Aragon didn't want to play any what-if games, but he said, "It would serve him right, wouldn't it, to find you gone? Now pull yourself together and we'll head for home."

"No."

"I can't leave you here, Mrs. Shaw. I feel responsible for what happens to you."

"Why? You only met me yesterday afternoon."

"Some people you get to know very fast." *Much too fast, Miranda.*

He waited outside while she packed her bags. Fog still clung to the beach, so he couldn't see the surf. But he heard it, loud and with a slow steady rhythm. Grady claimed every wave was different, every single one, but these sounded exactly alike.

Miranda came out of the cottage in about twenty minutes. She'd put on a white straw hat, oversized sunglasses and a sleeveless blue shift. Her arms were very thin and pale, as though they'd been tucked away in some dark place, unused.

"I'll call a boy to bring out my luggage," she said. "There are two suitcases and a garment bag."

"Don't bother calling anybody. I can do it."

"I hate to put you to any trouble."

"No trouble."

She didn't travel light. The suitcases were the size of

trunks and too heavy to manage more than one at a time. There was no place in the Chevy to hang the garment bag, so he laid it across the back seat. It looked disturbingly human, like someone stuffed, head and all, into a sleeping bag.

She said, "Grady is very strong."

"Is he."

"He can lift almost anything."

Including a Porsche. He almost said it. There was a possibility that she was thinking the same thing and being deliberately ironic, but he couldn't tell for sure. Her expression was hidden by the brim of her hat and the dark glasses and a layer of pride thicker than her makeup.

When he turned the Chevy around he saw the boy, Pedro, watching from the corner of the carport. He waved goodbye. Pedro didn't wave back.

For the first few miles she sat tense and silent, her hands folded tightly in her lap. But gradually she began to relax. She took off her hat and ran her fingers through her hair, she removed her glasses and rubbed her eyes, and now and then she spoke.

"It's awfully hot. Could you turn on the air conditioner?"

"I don't have one."

"I thought all cars came with air conditioners."

In her world they probably did.

Later she talked of Grady. "He left his toothbrush behind. Not that he'll miss it, he's quite careless about personal hygiene. Did you know that?"

"No."

"It didn't seem to matter. Every female in the club had a crush on him anyway, even Ellen, who's a cold fish where men are concerned."

He didn't know that either.

"I wonder what's going to become of me. I can't earn a living. All I ever learned at boarding school was French and ballet and etiquette."

128

She seemed to have forgotten some of the etiquette. While he was explaining the workings of the probate court she went to sleep, her head resting between the doorframe and the back of the seat.

She woke up at the border to answer questions put to her by an immigration official. Yes, she was a United States citizen, born in Chicago, Illinois. She had nothing to declare. She'd gone to Mexico for treatment at a health resort and was now returning home to Santa Felicia.

"That was a lie," she told Aragon afterward. "I'm not going home. I don't have a home any more."

"Certainly you do."

"No. The house is mortgaged, it belongs to strangers."

"Not yet. The law moves very slowly. You can continue living in the place until everything is settled."

"I refuse to accept the charity of strangers."

"The strangers are a couple of banks, they're not in the habit of offering charity."

"It makes no difference. Kindly don't pursue the subject, Mr. Aragon. When I left the house I decided that I would never return to it no matter what happened."

"What will you do?"

"Rent a small apartment, perhaps take a course and learn to perform salaried duties, the kind of thing Ellen does at the club."

"Do you have any cash?"

"A little."

"How long will it keep you going?"

"I don't know. I've never had to keep going on my own before. It should—should be an interesting challenge. Don't you agree?"

"Yes." He agreed about the challenge. Whether it would be interesting, or even possible, would depend on Miranda.

They had a late lunch in San Diego. She ordered a double martini and a green salad with white wine. The combination wasn't as potent as one of Dr. Ortiz's capsules but it had its effect. She lost some more of her boarding-school etiquette.

"He stole my car," she said. "That son of a bitch stole my car."

"I believe he was under the impression that you gave it to him, Mrs. Shaw."

"I gave it to him only if I went with it. It was supposed to be *ours*. Gave it to him, my foot. Do you know how much that thing cost?"

"You can get it back."

"How?"

"Tell the police it's been stolen."

"What police? I don't know what state, even what country he's in by this time."

"Maybe he'll return it voluntarily," Aragon said. "I don't know much about Grady, but I got the impression he's not a bad guy even if he's not the beautiful person you thought he was."

She began to cry, using the paper napkin for a handkerchief. "I thought he was—I thought he was such a beautiful person."

"We all make mistakes."

"Oh, shut up."

He shut up. Back in the car so did she. She went to sleep again, this time with her head pressed against Aragon's shoulder. For a small woman she felt very heavy.

She woke up as he slowed for the off ramp into Santa Felicia. It wasn't a gentle and gradual awakening. She was instantly alert as if an alarm had gone off in her brain.

"Why are you leaving the highway? Where are we?"

"Home."

She shook her head, repudiating the word. "I have an earache and my neck is stiff."

"You look fine." It was true. After her long sleep—plus, or in spite of, the last dose of Dr. Ortiz's goat glands—she seemed oddly young.

"Not really," she said. "You're just being kind."

130

"No. You look great, Miranda."

She checked for herself, staring into a small mirror she took out of her purse, but she didn't indicate who was staring back at her. "Where are you taking me?"

"To your house."

"It's not my house. It never was. Neville paid for it, I only lived there . . . Why did you call me by my first name?"

"I felt like it."

"You really mustn't. It's not proper."

She had remembered her etiquette. Maybe the French and ballet would come later.

Encina Road was only a couple of miles from the freeway, but it was difficult to find and Miranda offered no help. She sat gazing out of the window like a visitor seeing this part of the city for the first time: stone walls covered with ivy and bougainvillaea, ancient oak trees draped with moss, rows of spiked cassias more treacherous than barbed wire, high impenetrable hedges of pittosporum and eugenia.

The ten-foot iron gate at the bottom of the Shaws' driveway was closed, and when Aragon pressed the buzzer of the squawk box connecting it to the main residence, nothing happened. He tried the door of the gatehouse. It was locked and the venetian blinds were closed tight. He waited a minute, almost expecting the old man, Hippollomia, to appear suddenly and explain the situation: *There is no electric . . . Missus forgot to pay.*

He returned to the car.

Miranda looked at him solemnly. "You see? The house will not accept me any more than I will accept it."

"Nonsense. The electricity was turned off because nobody paid the bill."

"That is only the obvious external reason."

"What's the subtle internal one?"

"I already told you. Not that it matters," she added. "I could never stay here again under any circumstances."

"Where will you stay?"

"There must be places for homeless deserted women like me."

"The situation is bad enough without your dramatizing it," he said. "Now let's talk straight. Do you have anyone who can put you up temporarily, relatives, friends, neighbors—"

"No."

"What about members of your club?"

"No. The only person at the club I consider my friend is Ellen. She's been very kind."

"Has she." *If that's the best you can do, you're in trouble, Miranda. Ellen's no friend of yours.*

A gust of wind blew through the canyon, pelting the roof of the car with eucalyptus pods. Miranda winced as if each one of them had been aimed directly at her. "Please take me away from here. There's a santana coming up, I can sense it all over my body. My skin feels tight."

"I thought that's what you went down to the clinic for, tighter skin. You could have stayed here and gotten the same results cheaper."

"That was a boorish remark. What makes you so cranky?"

"I'm tired."

"Why should you be tired? *I'm* the one who's suffered."

"You slept most of the afternoon."

"Surely you don't begrudge me a little sleep after what I've been through."

"No." He didn't begrudge her anything except his time, two days of it so far. Two days of Miranda seemed a lot longer. Three would be more than he could bear. He said, "Suppose we drive to the club and see if Ellen's still there. She might have some advice to offer."

It was a dirty trick to play on Ellen but he couldn't think of anything else to do. At least Ellen was used to her and would know what to expect and maybe even how to deal with it.

•　　•　　•

Walter Henderson, the manager, was in the office but he looked ready to leave. He wore an after-hours outfit, jogging shoes, a striped warm-up suit and a navy-blue yachting cap. A copy of the *Racing Form* was tucked under one arm in case he stopped to rest while jogging or was becalmed while sailing or got caught in a traffic jam on the way to his bookie's.

"Sorry, we're about to close," he told Aragon. "Seven o'clock, you know. That's our winter schedule except on weekends and special occasions. It was clearly stated in our last newsletter. Didn't you read our last newsletter?"

"No."

"Too bad. I had something rather clever in it."

"Drat, I'm always missing clever things," Aragon said. "Is Miss Brewster still here?"

"She's around some place making a last-minute check with the security guard. Two dead stingrays were tossed in the pool last night. We suspect some Mexican boys. These minority goups have become very bold."

"So I've heard. Shocking."

"Today stingrays, tomorrow great white sharks. Well, we'll cross that bridge when we come to it . . . I'm locking the office now. You can wait for Miss Brewster in the corridor. There's a bench to sit on."

He sat on it. Except for a janitor mopping the tiled terrace, no one was in sight. But he could hear voices in the distance, and they sounded angry. After about five minutes he got up and walked around the pool a couple of times to stretch his legs.

There was no trace of the santana that had been blowing in the foothills or the sea winds which almost always began in the afternoon and stopped abruptly at sundown. The water was so smooth that at the far end where it was eighteen feet deep it looked shallow as a reflection pool, mirroring the lifeguard towers, the flagpole, the diving platform and Aragon himself, foreshortened to child size. Along the walls and floor of the pool every mark was clearly defined, the water-depth signs and the racing lanes. He wondered if anyone ever raced here or whether all the winning and losing was done on deck.

The voices were getting louder. It sounded like an argument between two women and a man, but when the trio appeared at the bottom of the steps coming down from the south row of cabanas one of the women turned out to be little Frederic Quinn. He was staggering under the weight of a sleeping bag, a portable television set and a six-pack of 7-Up. Ellen carried the rest of his supplies—a partly eaten pizza, a box of cheese crackers, a package of bologna and another of frankfurters.

Frederic had been planning a big evening, but the security guard caught him in the middle of the pizza and a rerun of *Star Trek*. The security guard, a pear-shaped divinity student working his way toward a pulpit, might have joined the party if Ellen hadn't shown up. For her benefit he put on a show of doing his duty.

"I'm telling you for the last time, young man, you can't spend the night in a cabana."

"Why not?"

"It's against the rules."

"How am I supposed to know the rules? I'm only a kid."

"You are also," Ellen said, "a pain in the neck."

"I can't help it. I didn't ask to be born. Nobody else asked for me to be born either. My father had a vasectomy but it was bungled. He would have sued except he didn't need the money."

"I do not want to talk about your father's vasectomy, Frederic."

"Yeah? What do you want to talk about?"

"Stingrays," the security guard said. "Dead ones. Two of them. In the pool."

"I don't know a thing about stingrays, dead or alive. I can't be expected to know everything, I'm not a genius."

"Any kid that knows about vasectomies must know about stingrays."

"Not necessarily. I specialize, see?"

134

"No, I don't see."

"Don't argue with the child, Sullivan, it's a waste of time. Just be clear and be firm." Ellen looked down at Frederic, who had put the sleeping bag on the floor and was sitting on it drinking a can of 7-Up. "Now, Frederic, let's get this straight. Nobody, absolutely nobody's ever allowed to stay in the cabanas after the club is closed."

"That's what you think. Last week I saw Mr. Redforn making macho with Amy Lou Worthington in the Worthingtons' cabana. He's a real pro."

"You watched them, Frederic?"

"Well, sure. There they were and there was I."

"There you *shouldn't* have been."

"There *they* shouldn't have been either."

"In a minute I'm going to lose my temper with you, Frederic."

"Everybody does. No big deal." It was at this point that Frederic spotted Aragon and let out a whoop of recognition. "There's my lawyer. Hey! Hey, Aragon, come here a minute. Remember me? We made a pact in the parking lot, remember?"

As Aragon approached, the guard watched him suspiciously. "A pact in the parking lot, that sounds like the devil's work to me. And since when do nine-year-old boys have lawyers?"

"Since you cops started pushing us around, that's when," Frederic said. "Tell him, Aragon."

"You do that, Aragon," the guard said. "Tell me."

"What do you want to know?"

"You can start with the pact in the parking lot."

"All right. As I was about to leave the lot a few days ago I ran into Frederic. He gave me some information about a person I was looking for and in return I agreed to act as his attorney when the time came."

"The time has come."

"In that case I'll have to talk to my client alone for a few minutes. If you'll excuse us, Mr. Sullivan—"

"You mean this boy is really your client?"

135

"Yes."

"It sounds like the devil's work, for a certainty."

"Go and finish your rounds, Sullivan," Ellen said. "And leave the theology to us."

As soon as the guard left, Frederic opened another can of 7-Up, switched on the television set and tuned in on a science-fiction movie. Several prehistoric or posthistoric monsters were emerging from a swamp to the sound of some very loud contemporary music.

Ellen spoke above it. "What are you doing here, Mr. Aragon?"

"I found Mrs. Shaw."

"That's fine. It's what you wanted to do, isn't it?"

"Yes."

"Was she alone?"

"Not at first. She is now. In fact, she's out in my car and she'd like to see you."

"Why?"

"You're her friend."

"I'm not. I never was, never will be. I don't see how she can consider me a friend."

"Obviously it's a case of mistaken identity," Aragon said. "So forget it."

"You make it sound as if I'm cruel and unfeeling."

"Are you?"

"I never thought so. I'm kind to animals and I help old ladies across the street. But I don't owe Miranda Shaw anything. She's had the whole bit from the time she was born, money and beauty and being taken care of and cherished."

"All of that's gone now, including Grady. He walked out on her last night. Or rather, he drove out in the Porsche she bought him."

"She bought him a Porsche? My God, what an idiot that woman must be, what a complete—All right, all right, I'll go out and talk to her. Or listen to her, or whatever. I won't be her friend," she added distinctly, "but I'll come as close to it as I can without upchucking."

"You're all heart, Miss Brewster."

On the television screen one of the monsters reared up on its hind legs, bellowing in triumph. Aragon watched for a minute. The limited human imagination which had created a God and a devil in its own image hadn't done much better with monsters. No matter how obviously grotesque they were with their warty skins, pinheads and three eyes, all had four limbs, voices like French horns and 20/20/20 vision.

Aragon went over and turned the set off.

Frederic let out a squawk of protest. "Hey, what'd you do that for? The monsters were just going to take over the world."

"They already have." Aragon said. "It must be a rerun."

"It is. I've seen it before. I've seen everything before."

"You're pretty young for that. How old are you?"

"Nine and seven-twelfths. But when the country switches to the metric system I'm going to add on a couple of years."

"What's the metric system got to do with your age?"

"Nothing. But everybody will be so confused by grams and kilometers and liters they won't notice the difference. In a flash I'll be eleven and seven-twelfths and Bingo Firenze's only eleven, ha ha."

"What if Bingo Firenze has the same idea?"

"He won't. He's too stupid."

"Or too smart."

"No, he's not. His family has to pay extra so the school will keep him. Whose side are you on, anyway? I thought you were *my* lawyer."

"I am," Aragon said. "And indications are that you'll need one."

"The stingray bit, huh? Okay. I found them on the beach where some guy had been practicing spearfishing and I thought I could resuscitate them by throwing them in the pool. It was my good deed for the week—"

"Bad choice of good deed, Frederick. They didn't resuscitate."

"It wasn't my fault. My intentions were pure as snow."

"Have you ever seen snow?"

"No."

"Sometimes it's pretty dirty."

"Well, it starts out clean." Frederic gazed wistfully at the blank television screen as though hoping the monsters would reappear and come charging out to be on his side. "A good lawyer is supposed to trust his client."

"A good client is supposed to tell his lawyer the truth."

"Wheezing Jesus, it was only a joke. I wanted to see the expression on Henderson's face when he walked in the front door and saw creepy crawly things on the bottom of the pool. How was I to know he was going to overreact? Nobody has a sense of humor around this place. When I get old enough I plan to split like Grady, maybe with a chick the way he did, maybe not. Probably not. The only chicks I know are my sister Caroline's friends and they're all fat and hate me."

"I talked to Grady yesterday."

Frederic's face, under the sun scars and freckles and fleabite scabs, turned a mottled pink. "Grady? Honest, no kidding?"

"No kidding."

"Where is he?"

"He was in Mexico when I saw him."

"Isn't he coming home?"

"I don't think so. Not for a while anyway."

"He's on the lam, I bet. I bet the Federales are after him, or the Mexican Mafia. I bet—"

"You'd lose," Aragon said. "Nobody's after him. He's running because that's the way he is. He gets into things and then wants out."

"What kind of things?"

"Relationships."

The boy took a deep breath and held it, preparing himself for a blow. "Relationships like him and me?"

"No, not like him and you. More complicated ones. You—well, he's still your friend."

"How do you know?"

"He asked after you."

"What were his exact words?"

Aragon made some tactful changes in Grady's exact words. "He said, 'How's my weird little pal Frederic?' "

Frederic let out his breath and the color of his face gradually returned to normal. "Yeah, that sounds like Grady, all right. Did he send me any message?"

"Just to stay out of trouble."

"Man, has he got a lot of nerve. Man oh man, look who's talking about trouble. Hey, you know what I'm going to tell Bingo Firenze? I'm going to tell him my best friend is tooling around Mexico with the Federales after him. Bingo will curl up and blow away."

"May I add good riddance."

"Oh, Bingo's not so bad," said the premature convert to the metric system, "for a kid."

It was arranged, via the pay phone in the corridor, that one of Frederic's brothers would come and take him home. Then Frederic settled down to wait under a palm tree, lying on top of his sleeping bag with the television set balanced on his stomach. The monsters returned and took over the world and everybody lived happily ever after.

Aragon went back to his car. Ellen was in the driver's seat talking to Miranda Shaw. When Ellen saw him approaching she got out and came to meet him. She looked cool but the ring of club keys in her hand was clanking a little too vigorously.

"Mrs. Shaw is going to stay with me temporarily until other arrangements can be made." There was a distinct accent on the words *temporarily* and *other*. "Wait till I lock up, and you can follow me to my apartment."

"Thanks, Miss Brewster."

"This is not going to be a long visit. I hope I've made that clear."

"Absolutely. As soon as the office opens in the morning I'll try to get her some emergency funds from my boss. Then you can whisk her to a motel or something."

"*You* can whisk her to a motel or something. I'm going to be working and I don't get whisking breaks . . . I presume she has luggage."

"A couple of suitcases." He didn't mention that together they were heavy enough to contain Grady's dismembered torso.

While Miranda showered, Ellen prepared a light meal of omelette and green salad. Afterward the two women sat at the kitchen table drinking tea. The room which Ellen had always thought of as neat and compact now seemed cluttered and much too small and intimate to be shared with a stranger.

If Miranda felt any similar tension, she didn't show it. She did most of the talking, mixing past and present in her soft high-pitched voice. She spoke of her gratitude to Ellen for her kindness, and to Aragon for his—"Such a nice young man but rather odd because one can't tell for sure what he's thinking"—and of the clinic in Pasoloma, with its tethered goats, pregnant and reproachful. She told of the happy times in her childhood when she was allowed to have supper in the kitchen with the cook—"Cook and I drinking tea just like this and Cook would read our fortunes in the tea leaves, the larger leaves indicating a trip, the specks that meant money and the little twigs that were tall dark strangers who always turned out to be the postman or the plumber or Cook's boyfriend, who was short and fat."

She talked of her first meeting with Grady. "You introduced us, Ellen. Do you remember? It was in the office. I told him there was a child screaming and asked him if he

140

could do anything about it. And he said probably not. That day is so vivid in my mind I could repeat every word, describe every gesture and expression. Grady looked at me very seriously but in a sort of questioning way. You know?"

"Yes." Ellen knew. Grady looked at every woman the same way and it was always the same question and he didn't wait around very long for an answer.

"I keep thinking of him coming back to the clinic—perhaps now, this very minute—and finding me gone and being terribly sorry. Perhaps I should have stayed and waited for him. After all, he was just as upset as I was by the news Mr. Aragon brought us. Once the first shock of it is over he'll see that nothing has changed between us, we can still get married and be happy together."

"I didn't realize you were intending to be married."

"Of course. Of course we were, Ellen. Otherwise I would never have— I mean, I'm not a slut. Grady's the only man I've ever been intimate with except Neville, and that was different. Neville mostly liked to look at me and watch me brush my hair and things like that. He almost never touched me. Grady was different."

"I'm sure he was."

"Oh, I wish Cook were here to read the tea leaves. All of a sudden I feel so hopeful, yes, and determined too, as if I can make everything work out for Grady and me to be together again. I'll start by being realistic. Money is important to him. All right, I'll get some. A lot, I'll get a lot of money and buy him back."

"You're tired. Don't think about it now."

"But I must begin planning right away, right here." She surveyed the room as though she were memorizing every detail of it: the bird prints on the wall, the porcelain kettle on the stove, the bread box and matching canister set on the counter, the bouquet of yellow plastic flowers and the ceramic owl cookie jar on top of the refrigerator. She said solemnly, "I will never forget this room and sitting here like this with you, planning a whole new future for myself. Will you ever forget it, Ellen?"

"No," Ellen said. "Probably not."

She stared into her cup. There were no leaves indicating a trip, no specks that meant money, no twigs that were tall dark strangers. There was only a soggy tea bag.

Part IV

In November, Dr. Laurie MacGregor flew down from San Francisco to spend the Thanksgiving holiday with her husband, Tom Aragon. Considerable time was wasted on the problem of what to do with the live twenty-five-pound turkey which Smedler had sent to each of his employees from his brother-in-law's turkey farm. The turkey, after a tranquilizing meal of grain sprinkled with vodka, was taken to the local children's zoo, having lost no more than a few feathers and two friends.

At the club Mr. Henderson decorated the dining room with life-sized plastic skeletons, thus cutting some of the losses entailed by the Halloween Hoedown. People who questioned the propriety of the decorations were given an explanation which Henderson had cunningly devised to foil his critics. The skeletons were reminders of death and hence of the resurrection, for which everyone should be thankful on Thanksgiving. Little Miss Reach, who was ninety and closer to the subject than most, suggested that it would have been better to wait until Easter. Henderson made a note of this for future reference. There was a chance, however slight, that he and maybe even Miss Reach would still be around by Easter.

For Christmas, Cordelia Young received a new Mercedes from her parents. Her thank-you speech was brief: "Oh, dammit, I wanted a Ferrari."

•   •   •

During the same week Mr. and Mrs. Quinn were sent official notice from Mr. Tolliver, Headmaster, that their son Frederic would not be welcome back for the spring term or any period thereafter. Frederic's speech was also brief: "Hurray!" Mrs. Quinn told Frederic her heart was broken. Mr. Quinn said his was too, but Mrs. Quinn said hers was more broken than his. During the ensuing argument Frederic was forgotten. He went up to his room, retrieved his Hate List from under the desk blotter where it was hidden and crossed off Mr. Tolliver's name. It was silly to waste a lot of good clean Hate.

On New Year's Eve, Charles Van Eyck attended the Regimental Ball to keep alive his contempt for the military in general and his brother-in-law, Admiral Young, in particular. He went through the receiving line three times, audibly noting the amount of gold braid and ornamental hardware and estimating their cost to the taxpayer. His sister Iris struck him on the shin with her cane. The Admiral was more tactful: "My dear Charles, I'm afraid you've had too much to drink. You mustn't make an ass of yourself."

"Why not?" Van Eyck said amiably. "All you fellows are doing it."

Van Eyck was also busy during February.

Amy Lou Worthington received anonymous and somewhat belated acknowledgment of her deflowering in the form of a sympathy card: "Sorry to Hear of Your Loss."

Ellen Brewster found on her desk an old-fashioned lace-and-satin valentine with an old-fashioned message:

> Roses are red
> Violets are blue,
> Sugar is sweet
> And so are you.

Van Eyck had brought it up to date and more in line with his sentiments by penciling out the last line.

Ellen went out to the terrace to thank him in person, but Van Eyck was having one of his sudden and mysterious attacks of deafness. He cupped his right ear and said, "Eh? What's that? Speak up."

"The valentine."

"Eh?"

"Thank you for the valentine."

"Eh?"

"An earthquake has struck Los Angeles and the entire city is in ruins."

"It's about time," Van Eyck said. "I predicted this forty years ago."

At intervals throughout the fall and winter Aragon thought of Miranda Shaw. He'd heard nothing about her at the office, and when he remembered to ask, it was always at an inconvenient time—the middle of the night or over the weekend when the office was closed or during Smedler's and Charity's separate but equal vacations.

It was in April that he saw her on the street, waiting outside the entrance to an underground garage that served a block of stores downtown. Whatever had happened to her during the past months, she had kept up appearances. She was perfectly groomed, her hair in a French twist at the nape of her neck, her dress a flowered silk with a voluminous pleated skirt and scarf. Though she was small, and standing very quietly, she couldn't help being conspicuous among the housewives hurrying to sales and the clerks and secretaries to their jobs. The dress was too fancy and her makeup too theatrical for nine o'clock in the morning.

At closer range he noticed the subtle changes in her. Her red-gold hair seemed a little brassier and there were blue circles under her eyes and lines around her mouth that the makeup didn't hide.

"Good morning, Mrs. Shaw."

"Why, Mr. Aragon. How nice to see you again."

They shook hands. Hers was thin and dry as paper.

"You're looking very well, Mrs. Shaw."

"I'm surviving. One mustn't be greedy." She hesitated, glancing over her shoulder as though checking for eavesdroppers. "I suppose you know my husband's will went through probate in February and the bad news became official. He spent all of his own money and a great deal of other people's."

"How have you been living?"

"Strangely."

"Strangely?"

"I believe that's a fair way to describe it," she said with a faint smile. "I have a job. It's not exactly what I would have chosen but it makes me self-supporting for the first time in my life. I even have a social security number. Yes, it's all quite official, I'm a working woman. Surprised, aren't you?"

"A little."

"The salary isn't much but I get room and board and I won't starve. Do you remember Ellen Brewster at the Penguin Club?"

"Oh yes."

"It was her idea. I never thought I had anything worth teaching anyone, but apparently I do . . . Here they come now. Pretend we're not talking about them."

He didn't have a chance to wonder who "they" were. Cordelia and Juliet were emerging from the underground garage, blinking in the sun like giant moles. They looked at Aragon without recognition or interest. He had no part in their world, there was only room for two.

"Cordelia rammed a concrete pillar," Juliet said. "But it wasn't her fault. There was an arrow pointing left and an arrow pointing right and she couldn't make up her mind, so she hit the pillar which was in the middle."

"An honest mistake," Cordelia admitted cheerfully. "It could happen to anyone."

"But especially you," Juliet said.

"We learned a lesson from it, though."

146

"It's a dumb way to learn a lesson. Which I didn't anyway."

"You did so. You found out a Mercedes is no better than any other car when it comes up against concrete. Crash, bang, crunch, just like an ordinary Cadillac."

"Pops won't care but Mrs. Young will be furious."

"Girls," Miranda said. "Girls, please. Forget the car for a moment and pay attention to your manners. I've told you repeatedly not to refer to Admiral Young as Pops. He is your father. Wouldn't it sound better to call him that?"

Cordelia shook her head. "Father is what you call somebody with his collar on backwards. Or like in our father who art in heaven. That kind of father belongs to everybody."

"Our *personal* father is Pops," Juliet said. "His wife is Mrs. Young."

"Girls, please. I don't want to be harsh with you but I must ask you not to call your mother Mrs. Young."

"Why not? You do."

"She's not my mother."

"She may not be ours either," Cordelia said. "We have no proof. Anyway, she'd just as soon not be."

"She hates us," Juliet explained. "We don't mind. We hate her back. She hates you too, but you can't hate her back because you're a lady and ladies never get to do anything they want to."

Both girls thought this was extremely funny. Cordelia screamed with laughter and Juliet's face turned bright pink and she had to wipe her eyes and nose on the sleeve of her wool sweater, which was very absorbent and ideal for the purpose.

Miranda stood quietly, her only sign of emotion a deepening of the lines around her mouth. "You are attracting attention. I want it stopped immediately or I'll report every word of this conversation to your mother. Now run along and start your shopping and I'll meet you at Peterson's in the shoe department in half an hour. I have to go and check how much damage was done to the car."

Cordelia had the last word. "Not enough."

Miranda watched them walk briskly down the street arm in arm and still laughing. Then she turned back to Aragon. "I told you I've been living strangely. This is it. I'm supposed to teach the girls etiquette and the social graces. As you must have observed, I'm not a very good teacher."

"They're not very good students," Aragon said. "Hang in there anyway."

"I don't have a choice."

"Not now. But perhaps eventually . . ."

"Eventually sounds so far in the future. I'm not sure I can wait."

He didn't ask about Grady and she didn't volunteer any information. Grady seemed as far in the past as "eventually" seemed in the future.

A few weeks later, returning to his office after lunch, he found a message on his desk from Ellen Brewster asking him to drop by the Penguin Club on a personal matter. He went as soon as he'd finished work for the day.

It was five-thirty, cold and overcast, as it often was in May. The club had made the transition from fall to spring with only minor adjustments—a fresh coat of paint on the walls, a change of greenery in the redwood planters, different pads on the chairs and chaises, and a new lifeguard, a short, stocky young man with a blanket draped over his head and shoulders. He appeared ready and willing to save lives, but the pool was unoccupied.

The seasonal changes in Ellen were more obvious. She had shorter hair, curled and frosted at the tips, and she wore oversized sunglasses and lipstick so glossy it made her mouth look like wet vinyl. He wondered about the sunglasses. There hadn't been any sun for a week.

"I'm glad you came," she said, sounding glad. "Would you like some coffee?"

"Fine."

148

"Let's go in the snack bar. No one will be there at this time of day."

She was almost right. The only customer was an old man with a copy of *Fortune* open on the table in front of him. His eyes were closed and his chin rested on his collarbone. He was either asleep or dead; no one seemed interested in finding out which.

A fat pink-cheeked blonde stood behind the counter filing her nails. She gave Ellen a bored look.

"The snack bar's closed. I'm just waiting for my ride."

"Isn't there some coffee left?"

"It's stale."

"We'll take it."

"You'll have to pour it yourself and drink it black. I'm off duty and we're out of cream."

The verbal exchange or the sudden honking of an automobile horn outside the rear door had wakened the old man.

"What's happening around here? Can't a man read in peace?"

"It's time to go home, Mr. Van Eyck," Ellen said. "The snack bar is closed."

"No, it's not. *I'm* here."

"You shouldn't be."

"I don't see any Closed sign posted on the door."

"I'm posting it in a minute."

"What about that fellow with you? Wait till Henderson hears about this, you sneaking young men into the snack bar after hours."

"Mr. Aragon is my lawyer."

"Have you done something illegal?"

"Not yet," Ellen said. "But I'm thinking of committing a murder."

"Think again. You'd never get away with it. You lack the finesse, the savoir-faire, and you have childish fits of temper."

"Please go home, Mr. Van Eyck."

"If you insist. Though I resent being evicted in order

that you may conduct a rendezvous with a young man who doesn't look any more like a lawyer than I do. Where did he go to law school?"

"Hastings," Aragon said.

"Never heard of it." Van Eyck picked up his magazine and left. In spite of his shuffling gait and a pronounced list to starboard he moved with considerable speed.

Aragon tasted the coffee. The fat blonde had been right. It was stale and bitter and lukewarm. He couldn't do anything about the age and temperature but he added a pinch of salt to take away the bitterness.

"I can get you a year's honorary membership in the club," Ellen said.

"Why would you want to do that?"

"I can't afford to pay you and it wouldn't be fair for me to ask your advice for nothing."

"This coffee ought to cover two cents' worth. Ask ahead."

"I had a letter from Grady yesterday."

"Where is he?"

"Las Vegas." She took off her sunglasses and he saw why she'd worn them in the first place. Her eyes were red and slightly swollen. "He wants to come back here."

"It's a free country. He doesn't need your permission or mine."

"No, but he needs money and a job, so it's not all that free, is it . . .? Here, I'd like you to read it."

She tood a small envelope from her pocket and handed it to Aragon. It had been postmarked five days previously in Las Vegas and in the upper left corner was the address of a motel chain that showed porn films. Grady might have worked there, stayed there, or simply borrowed its writing paper.

Dear Ellen

I guess you heard about me and Mrs. Shaw and all that water under the bridge. I hope she's doing OK with no hard feelings etcetra.

I ran into lousy luck which put me in bad with some of the pit bosses and I would like to get out of this freaky place. I feel bad vibes coming at me. What I really wish is I had my old job back. Is there any chance of getting a break from Mr. Henderson. If you think so would you send me an application form to fill out right away. Thanks, you are a real peach.

Best regards from your old friend   Grady Keaton

" 'Mrs. Shaw and all that water under the bridge,' " Aragon repeated. "Grady has such a sensitive nature."

"He feels guilty, I'm sure he does. It's just—he doesn't express himself on paper very well."

"Oh, I don't know. I think that's rather a cute way of saying he ran off in her thirty-thousand-dollar car and left her broke in a foreign country."

She rubbed the sunglasses up and down the lapel of her jacket a few times before putting them back on. It was either a stall or an attempt to clear up the view she had through them.

"That's what I need your advice about. Suppose he comes back to Santa Felicia. Whether or not he gets a job at the club, Miranda is bound to find out about it. Can she prosecute him?"

"Without knowing all the details of the case, I'd say she could at least sue him for the return of the car."

"He probably doesn't have it any more."

"Then she can be a good sport and forgive and forget," Aragon said. "If I were Grady, though, I wouldn't depend on Miranda being a good sport. She's not built for it."

"Could she have him put in jail?"

"Judges and juries decide things like that, lawyers don't."

"If there's any chance he'll be punished, I've got to warn him to stay away."

"Why?"

"You read the letter," she said with a wry little smile.

"He's an old friend and I'm a real peach. Aren't us real peaches expected to do things like that?"

"I guess you are."

"Well?"

"Check with Miranda. She might not want him punished any more than you do. Ask her."

"I can't ask her without letting on that I've heard from him and know where he is."

"Make it a hypothetical question."

"I don't believe I could fool her. We've become pretty well acquainted during the past six months."

"How?"

"Seeing each other here at the club. She isn't a member any more, she can't afford the dues, but she comes in with Admiral Young's daughters. While they swim and have lunch she talks to me in the office. She could swim and have lunch if she wanted to—Mr. Henderson would be glad to bend the rule about employees of members not being allowed the privileges of members. She won't accept any favors, though. Or maybe she just likes to get away from the girls whenever she can . . . Did you know she was working?"

"I met her on the street a couple of weeks ago. She told me you'd gotten her a job."

"Not really. It was my suggestion, that's all. She wasn't trained for anything except being a lady, and there's not much demand for teaching ladyness or ladyship or whatever. Then I thought of Admiral Young's daughters and I suggested to him one day that perhaps Miranda Shaw could teach the girls some of the social graces they lacked. He approved of the idea."

"The girls were with Miranda when I saw her," Aragon said. "I didn't notice much improvement in their ladyship-ness."

"No results were guaranteed. I doubt that the Admiral expected any. He's a wise man, he was probably only trying to help Miranda."

"And you?"

"What do you mean *and me*?"

"What was your motive?"

"I'm a nice girl," she said. "Haven't you noticed?"

"Yes. I also noticed you'd been crying. Why?"

"I went to a sad movie. Or I saw a little dog that looked like one I had when I was a kid. Or I remembered my favorite aunt who died last year. Check one of the above."

"Check none of the above. And you mustn't add your tears to 'all that water under the bridge' Grady mentioned."

"How can I avoid it?"

"Don't answer his letter. Don't tell him to come, don't warn him to stay away. Just stay out of it."

"That's a lot of advice in return for a stale cup of coffee."

"I drank the coffee. Are you going to take the advice?"

"Sorry, it's too late," she said. "I sent him the application form yesterday afternoon."

The girls liked to put on their pajamas and eat dinner in the upstairs sitting room with their cat, Snowball, while watching television. Miranda's arrival had changed all that. She insisted they appear at the table properly dressed, on their best behavior and without the cat. This rule applied especially when guests were expected.

Retired military friends of the Admiral stopped on their way through town now and then, and once a month Charles Van Eyck came to see his sister, Iris, motivated not so much by duty as by expedience. Iris possessed a great deal of money which she would one day have to abandon for more spiritual satisfactions. Though considerably younger than he, she was unwell and unhappy and the combination gave him hopes of outliving her. These hopes changed daily like the stock market, gaining a few points here, losing a few there. As an investment the monthly dinner was becoming more and more speculative. Iris seemed to thrive on adversity. Arthritis and a recent heart attack gave her an excuse to do only what she wanted to do, and unhappiness made her oblivious to the needs and desires of other people and the fact that blood was thicker than water.

By his own standards Van Eyck was not greedy but he liked to think about money and he enjoyed its company. He studied his savings-account books and various senior citizens' publications. He visited his safety-deposit boxes and later he would sit in the lobby eating the free cookies and drinking the free coffee. He knew that the cookies and coffee were not actually free, that he was paying for them one way or another, so he ate and drank as much as he could before bank employees started giving him dirty looks. The dirty looks were free.

Lately Van Eyck had another reason for his regular visits to his sister. He distrusted all women, especially the pretty ones like Miranda Shaw. When she was first hired he wrote an anonymous letter to his sister which began *You have taken a Jezzebel into your home* . . . For several days he carried the letter around in his pocket in a sealed stamped correctly addressed envelope, afraid to post it. Iris with her sharp mind and suspicious nature might trace it back to him, and besides, he had a nagging doubt about the spelling of Jezebel. Jezebelle was more literal, Jezebell had a ring to it, Jezebel looked somehow unfinished. He thought of burning the letter but he hated to waste the stamp and some of the clever descriptive material about Miranda Shaw, so he sent it anyway.

To Miranda herself, who opened the door for him, he was polite, even gallant.

"Ah, my dear, how elegant you look this evening."

"Thank you, Mr. Van Eyck. Mrs. Young and the Admiral will be down shortly. May I pour you a drink?"

"Pour ahead."

"Your usual Scotch on the rocks?"

"One rock. I'm very Scotch."

It was his favorite joke and entirely original, but all Miranda did was smile with one side of her mouth as if she were saving the other side for a later and a better joke. He changed the subject abruptly. There was no use aiming his best shots into a wilderness.

"What are we having for dinner?"

"Beef Wellington."

"Why can't we ever have something tasty like pot roast or chicken stew with dumplings?"

"The housekeeper received a French cookbook for Christmas."

"Wellington was an English duke. Very cheeky of them to name a French dish after him. I intend to pour ketchup all over it."

"I do wish you wouldn't, Mr. Van Eyck. The housekeeper was very perturbed last time."

"I'll go out to the kitchen, find the ketchup wherever she's hidden it and bring it right to the table. Beef Wellington indeed. The poor man is probably turning over in his grave smothered in all that greasy foreign pastry."

"Please reconsider about the ketchup," Miranda said. "It will set a bad example for the girls."

The girls were all ready for a bad example. Inside the confines of their best dresses they squirmed and sighed and made faces. Cordelia's lime-green silk had a sash so tight it divided her in two like an egg-timer, and Juliet wore her tattletale dress, a bouffant taffeta that responded noisily to the most discreet movement, crackling, rustling, complaining, almost as though it had a life of its own.

The girls sat side by side at the mahogany table across from Van Eyck and Miranda, who had done the setting herself—silver bowls floating camellias and miniature candles, and crystal bird vases with sprigs of daphne that scented the whole room. The Admiral at the head of the table complimented Miranda on the decorations, but Iris, opposite him, said she hated candles, flickering lights always gave her a migraine. She asked Cordelia to blow out the candles.

"I can't," Cordelia said.

"Why not?"

"I haven't enough breath. My dress is too tight. I think I'm going to faint."

"So am I," Juliet said loyally.

Their mother didn't seem particularly interested. She had the little poodle, Alouette, on her lap and was feeding it bits of shrimp from her seafood cocktail.

The sight infuriated Cordelia. "I don't see why you can bring that dog to the table and we're not allowed to bring Snowball, who loves shrimp. Shrimp is his very favorite thing."

"What were you saying about your dress, Cordelia?"

"It's too tight. I can't breathe. I'm going to faint."

"Don't be tiresome."

"I mean it. I'm going . . . here I go . . . one, two—"

"Well, hurry up and get it over with so the rest of us can eat. The food will be cold."

"You don't *care.*"

"Of course I do," Iris said. "I'm hungry."

Frustrated, Cordelia turned her wrath on her uncle. "It's all your fault. We had to dress like this just for you."

Van Eyck looked surprised. "Like what?"

"This."

"Up." Juliet said. "We had to dress up like this just for you."

"Really? Whose bizarre idea was that?"

"Hers." Both girls answered simultaneously, scowling at Miranda across the table.

"She said well-bred young ladies always dress up for company," Cordelia explained. "And I said Uncle Charles isn't company, he's only a relative. And Juliet said you wouldn't notice anyway because you'd be three sheets to the wind."

"You said that about me, Juliet?"

"I may have," Juliet said. "But she's a pig to bring it up."

"Unfortunately, my dear nieces, I am not three sheets to

156

the wind. I am not even one sheet or two, let alone three. But I'm certainly working on it . . . Cooper, let's have some of that special stuff you've been hoarding. I understand that when a military man retires he commandeers all the booze he can lay his hands on. Why not share it with us common folk who paid for it in the first place?"

Cooper Young had learned many years ago at Annapolis to eat quietly and quickly whatever was placed in front of him and retained this habit throughout his life. As a consequence, eating was not enjoyable but it was also not unbearable. He could listen without heartburn while Iris and the girls bickered during the salad course, and his brother-in-law, over the beef and asparagus, delivered a lecture on the sinful extravagances of the Pentagon. Cooper did not answer, did not argue. Now and again he glanced at Miranda, who was equally silent, and he noticed how skillfully she pretended to eat while only rearranging the food on her plate and raising an empty fork to her mouth.

Cherries jubilee.

Cordelia was allowed to flame the cherries as a reward for not fainting, and everyone was quiet while they burned. Then it was time for Miranda to provide the evening's entertainment, a report on the girls' progress since the last family dinner.

"This week," Miranda said, "we have been concentrating on attitudes that affect behavior, for example, self-fulfillment as opposed to selfish fulfillment. We made a list of questions to ask ourselves at the end of each day. We gave them a special name, didn't we, Juliet?"

"Yes, but—"

"What was it?"

"Questions for a summer night. But—"

"Can you recite them?"

"*I* can," Cordelia said, still basking in the warmth and glory of the cherries jubilee. "Questions for a summer night. Here they are:

"Have I earned something today?

157

"Have I learned something today?

"Have I helped someone?

"Have I felt glad to be alive?"

"How poetic," Iris said. "And what are the answers for a summer night?"

Juliet and her dress complained in unison. "I didn't know we were expected to have the answers too. Memorizing the questions is hard enough. Anyway, it isn't even summer yet. By the time it comes, maybe I can think of some answers."

"Don't be an ass, there aren't any." Cordelia said crisply. "It's only a game."

"It can't be. A game is where somebody wins and somebody loses. I should know, I'm the one who always loses."

"No, you don't. You only remember the times you lose because you're such a rotten sport. I often let you win to avoid the sight of you bawling and blabbering."

Juliet appealed to Miranda, wistfully, "Is it only a game?"

"No indeed," Miranda said. "I believe they're very important questions."

"But how can I earn anything? I don't work."

"You could earn someone's respect and admiration. Any job well done is worthy of respect. Can you think of a job you did today?"

"I washed the cat, Snowball. He had fleas."

"You see? That's something you earned today, Snowball's gratitude."

"No. He hates being washed and he still has fleas. I got seven more bites on the belly."

"I've got at least twenty-five," Cordelia said.

"Not on the belly."

"I haven't searched there yet. Most of mine are on the wrists and ankles. They itch furiously but I don't dare scratch because Mrs. Young is looking."

Iris was listening as well as looking. "If you girls have fleas, I don't want you coming anywhere near my dog."

"We never do. *He* comes near *us*."

"Then run away from him."

"He can run faster than we can. And also, he cheats by taking shortcuts under tables and things."

"I suggest," Miranda said, "that we consider the second question. Have you learned something today?"

Cordelia related what she'd learned, that the Pentagon was spending billions of dollars each year on uniforms and pensions while the average citizen was being taxed into oblivion. Van Eyck, with his second sheet to the wind and going for three, applauded vigorously and said by God, at least there was one sensible person in the family besides himself.

Juliet couldn't think of anything she'd learned for the first time, though she had learned for the fourteenth or fifteenth time that cats didn't like to be bathed and neither did fleas but it wasn't fatal to either.

In spite of her makeup Miranda was beginning to look pale. "Perhaps we should go on to the third question. Have you helped someone today?"

"They have helped me decide to go to bed," Iris said and slid the little dog off her lap and onto the floor. "Miranda, I'd like to speak to you privately up in my room . . . Cooper, show Charles to his car and don't give him any more to drink . . . Goodnight, Charles. It was good of you to come. Take care of your liver."

She was tired. Her thin yellowing face sagged with fatigue and she had to use the table and her cane to hoist herself to her feet. It was a heavy antique cane she'd brought from Africa, where it had once been part of a tribal chief's ceremonial uniform. Iris continued to think of it like that, as an adjunct to her costume, and she refused even to try the lightweight aluminum crutches prescribed by her doctor. Crutches were for cripples. Her cane was a piece of history and a symbol of command, not dependence.

The procession moved up the staircase, slow and solemn

as a funeral march, Iris leaning on the banister and her cane, taking one step at a time. Miranda walked behind her, then the two girls, and finally the little dog, Alouette. The shrimp and cherries had given Alouette the hiccups and their rhythmic sound accompanied the procession like the beat of a ghostly drum.

The Admiral escorted his brother-in-law to the front door.

"Iris is damned rude," Van Eyck said, straightening his tie and brushing off his coat as if he'd been physically ejected. "*She's* the one who should be taking lessons in the social amenities, though it's about fifty years too late."

"I'm sorry you feel insulted."

"My liver is a very personal thing. I may never return to this house."

"We shall miss you, Charles."

"Don't be in such a hurry to miss me. I haven't left yet. I might change my mind and take that nightcap you offered me."

"I didn't offer you one."

"Why not?"

"Iris told me not to."

"But she's gone to bed. This is between you and me."

"I'm afraid not," the Admiral said. "Now do you think you'll be able to get home all right? If there's any doubt, I can drive you or call a cab."

"Don't worry about me, old boy. Just take care of yourself."

"What do you mean, Charles?"

"She's a sleek little filly, that Miranda, with plenty of mileage left in her. And don't tell me you didn't notice. I saw you staring at her."

"I don't believe we should refer to a lady in terms of horseflesh."

"You didn't stare at her as if she was a lady," Van Eyck said. "You old Navy men never change. Girl in every port, that sort of thing."

"I never had a girl in every port. Hardly any port, as a matter of fact."

"Why not? I understand the military feel that it's their prerogative to—"

"Go home, Charles."

"That's damned rude."

"Yes."

"I'm a taxpayer."

"Yes."

"You'll rue the day."

"I've lost count of the days I'm going to rue," the Admiral said, opening the door. "Probably up in the thousands by this time . . . Goodnight, Charles. Drive carefully. The Pentagon can't afford to lose a taxpayer."

The girls listened at the door of Iris's room on the second floor. They could hear her talking to Miranda in the loud firm voice that was stronger than the rest of her and needed no support from cane or crutches. The words were too fast to be intelligible. They crashed into each other and splintered into sharp angry syllables.

"She's mad," Cordelia said. "Well, for once *we* didn't do anything."

Juliet wasn't so sure. "Maybe we did, unbeknownst."

"We never do anything unbeknownst. It's always spelled right out. She's probably mad at *her*."

"I wonder why."

"Maybe it was those questions for a summer night. The whole thing's pretty silly when you think of it. Why not a winter night? Or autumn?"

"Summer sounds better."

"But it's not sensible. On summer nights people are outside barbecueing steaks or playing tennis. It's on winter nights they have nothing to do but sit around making up dumb questions."

"I hate those questions," Juliet said. "I just hate them. They give me the glooms."

"Don't be an ass. They're only words."

161

"No. She means them. 'Have I earned something today?' How can I earn something when I don't have a job? Maybe we should run away and get jobs, Cordelia. Do you think we could?"

"No."

"Not even a lowly type like washing dishes in a restaurant?"

"They don't wash dishes in restaurants. They toss them into a machine."

"Someone has to toss them. We could be tossers."

"I don't want to be a tosser," Cordelia said. "Now wake up and smell the coffee. We're not good for anything, so we might as well enjoy it."

The heavy oak door of Iris's room opened and Miranda came into the hall with the poodle, Alouette, on a leash beside her. The girls hid behind a bookcase and watched her go down the stairs. She moved very slowly, as if she was tired, while the little dog strained at the leash trying to pull her along.

"We never get to walk the dog any more since *she* came," Cordelia said. "It's not fair."

"We could walk the cat."

"No, we can't. We tried that once and Snowball just sat down and wouldn't budge. We had to drag him around the block and someone reported us to the Humane Society and they sent a man out to investigate."

Juliet's memory was soft and warm as a pillow. She remembered the Humane Society incident as a nice young man stopping his truck to make complimentary remarks about the cat; and the Singapore incident, which Cordelia frequently referred to in a sinister manner, Juliet couldn't remember at all. She took her sister's word that it had happened (whatever it was) because Cordelia had more sophistication and experience than she did, being two years older. By virtue of this age gap, and the phenomenal number of things that must have occurred during it, Cordelia had become an authority who dispensed information and advice like a vending machine.

"In fact," Cordelia said, "we're not allowed to do practically anything since she came. We may have to get rid of her. It shouldn't be too hard if we plan ahead."

"I'm sick of always talking about her. I want to talk about us for a change. You and me."

"What about us."

"Do you think we'll ever get a second chance?"

"To do what?"

"Be born. Will we ever be born again?"

"I hope to Christ not," Cordelia said. "Once was bad enough."

"But it might be different if we had a second chance. We might be good for something. We might even be pretty. And something else. This time *I* might be born first, two years ahead of *you*."

Juliet knew immediately that she'd gone too far. She turned and ran down the hall to her room, locking the door behind her and barricading it with a bureau in case Cordelia decided to pick the lock with one of her credit cards.

She took a shower and before putting on her pajamas she counted her fleabites. Twenty-eight. A record. She scratched them all until they bled. If she bled to death, right then and there, she would speed up her chances of being born again, brilliant, beautiful and two years ahead of Cordelia.

At ten-thirty the Admiral began closing up the house for the night, checking each room for security purposes, making sure that windows were locked and no intruders lurked in closets or behind doors. The job took a long time partly because he enjoyed it and partly because there were so many rooms, some of them never or hardly ever used.

The drawing room, off the foyer, was opened only for formal entertaining. Its elegant little gold chairs looked too fragile to hold a sitter and its Aubusson rugs too exquisite to be stepped on. The walls were hung with gilt-framed family portraits which had, like most of the furniture, been included in the purchase price of the house. For reasons of

163

her own, Iris allowed visitors to think the pictures were of her ancestors, but in fact the amply proportioned ladies and the men with their muttonchop whiskers were as unknown as the artists who painted them. The thrifty Dutchmen who were Iris's real ancestors would have considered such portraits a sinful extravagance.

Next to the living room was the conservatory, which contained an old rosewood grand piano with a broken pedal and ivory keys yellow as saffron. Now and then the Admiral would sit down at the piano and try to pick out melodies he'd learned in his youth: "Shenandoah," "The Blue Bells of Scotland," "Poor Wayfaring Stranger," "Flow Gently, Sweet Afton." But no matter how softly he played, how tightly the doors and windows were closed, Iris always heard and thumped with her cane or sent the housekeeper or the girls to tell him to stop. He opened the lid of the piano, played the first few bars of Brahms' "Lullaby" and replaced the lid almost before any of the notes had a chance to climb the stairs. Then he went on with his job of checking the house.

The solarium, facing south, had an inside wall faucet and a tile floor that slanted down to a screened hole in the middle in order to allow the draining of plants after they were watered. There was only one plant left in the place, a weeping fig which had grown too large to move. The Admiral watered it every night, knowing that at some time, perhaps quite soon, the fig would break out of its clay prison. He usually stayed in this room longer than in any of the others, as though he wanted to be a witness to the plant's exact moment of escape, to hear the noise (big or small? He had no idea) and see a crack in the clay (perhaps a series of cracks, a shattering, an explosion, a room full of shards).

Across the hall the game room had walnut-paneled walls and a billiard table with a rip in it. Year after year the Admiral postponed having the rip repaired. It unnerved the very good players, thus giving the poorer ones like himself a psychological advantage. Beside the library there was a sewing room where no one sewed. Perhaps when the house had been built it was the custom for the women to do petit point or embroidery while the men played billiards. Now the space was a catchall for steamer trunks and suitcases, the housekeeper's reducing machine, a pair of carved teakwood chests Iris had carted halfway around the world, a vacuum cleaner that didn't work, the ski equipment the girls had used at their school in Geneva. Though the equipment was well worn, the boots scuffed, the webs of the poles bent out of shape, he was amazed that the girls had ever skied. Juliet seemed too timid to try, Cordelia too reckless to survive. No matter how hard he attempted to picture them skiing in a nice average way down a nice average slope, he could only imagine Cordelia plunging headlong from Mt. Blanc like an avalanche and Juliet having to be dragged up the smallest knoll and pushed down screaming. Perhaps there never were any nice average slopes in the girls' lives.

The library was in another wing of the house. It had brown leather chairs that smelled of saddle soap. The floor-to-ceiling shelves of books were behind glass and the mantel of the fireplace was decorated with ceramic songbirds. It was a comfortable room, but the Admiral rarely sat there to read or to watch the fire. The bookshelves were locked and he could never remember where he'd put the key; and because of a defective damper the fireplace smoked badly and all the birds had turned gray as if from old age.

The adjoining room was where Iris spent most of her time. Here too there was a fireplace, but its logs were artificial and its flames gas. Iris wasn't strong enough to handle real logs in a real grate. Sometimes she couldn't even light the gas without help from Miranda or the housekeeper. The Admiral turned off the gas and the lamp by Iris's reading chair and the other lamp that lit the table where half a dozen miniature chess sets were laid out, each

165

with a game in progress. These were the games Iris was playing by mail with people in other parts of the world. To the Admiral it seemed a little like war to have unseen opponents in foreign countries planning strategic moves against you. But no blood was shed, nothing was lost but prestige.

The kitchen and the rooms beyond it he left alone. They were the working and living quarters of Mrs. Norgate, the housekeeper, and he depended on her as he would have depended on a chief petty officer to keep her part of the ship tight and tidy.

He returned to the front of the house at the same time as Miranda was coming in the door with the little poodle. She'd put a coat over the formal dress she'd worn at dinner, but it offered little protection from the spring fog. She looked cold and damp and her voice was hoarse.

"Alouette wanted to come home. He acts afraid of the dark lately."

"He might have trouble with his vision," the Admiral said. "I understand poodles often do as they get older. Perhaps I should take him to the vet."

"What happens to their vision?"

"Cataracts, I believe."

"Like people."

"Yes. Like people."

She let the dog off the leash and it bounded up the stairs. "He seems all right now. Maybe he simply wanted to get back to his mistress."

"Miranda—"

"I'd better go upstairs and open the door for him so that Mrs. Young won't be disturbed."

"Miranda, I'm sorry about the dinner tonight."

"*You're* sorry?" she repeated. "That's funny, I was just going to tell you that *I* was sorry. It was my responsibility. I should have made better plans."

"No, no. Your plans were fine. Those 'questions for a summer night,' I thought that was an excellent idea."

"Mrs. Young didn't."

"Mrs. Young's illness makes her hard to please. You mustn't take her opinions too seriously. She doesn't mean to disparage your abilities."

"She means to and she's right. I'm not qualified for a position like this, I'm not qualified for anything. It's useless for me to keep on pretending."

"Sit down, Miranda. I'll get you a drink to warm you up."

There was a bench along one wall that looked as if it had once been a pew in a small church. She sat down, shivering, pulling the coat around her. It was several sizes too large. The poodle had been in such a hurry to go out that she'd grabbed the coat out of the hall closet without knowing or caring whom it belonged to.

"A drink won't change how I feel," she said.

"It might. Let me—"

"Those questions for a summer night, what a joke. Hundreds of summer nights have passed, and fall and winter and spring, and I couldn't answer one of those questions positively. I haven't earned or learned or helped or felt glad to be alive."

"You've made me feel glad to be alive."

"You mustn't say nice things like that. You'll make me cry."

"Please don't. I insist you don't, Miranda."

Her face was hidden in the collar of the coat, her voice barely audible. "All right."

"You won't cry."

"No."

"Promise?"

"I promise."

"Thank you." He cleared his throat as if it were his voice, not hers, being muffled in the folds of the coat. "Actually you're the best thing that's happened to this household for a long time and we're all grateful to you. I hope you're not planning to leave."

"I'm not accomplishing anything here."

"But you are. There's a definite improvement in the girls' behavior. They're less self-centered, more responsive to other people. At dinner, for instance, they talked directly to their Uncle Charles instead of around him to each other. Did you notice that?"

"Everyone noticed," she said. "Especially Uncle Charles."

"It was a step up from ignoring him, as they're in the habit of doing. But I'm not only thinking of the girls when I ask you to stay with us. I'm being quite selfish. In fact— well, you must be aware of how happy I am in your presence, Miranda."

"No." She'd hardly been aware of him at all except as a figure in the background, like one of Iris's ivory and wooden chess pieces. Now suddenly he was stepping off the board alive, making sounds, having feelings, being happy and unhappy. It frightened her. She wanted him to step back on the chessboard where he belonged.

The girls, reconciled by this time, were hiding behind the railing at the top of the stairs.

"He said he was happy with her presents," Juliet whispered. "I've never seen her give him any presents. I wonder what kind they are."

"Use your imagination, stupid."

"You mean hanky-panky? Surely they wouldn't commit hanky-panky with Mrs. Young right in the house."

"They wouldn't have to. Pops has tons of room in the back seat of the Rolls."

"Do you think we should tell Mrs. Young?"

"My God, no," Cordelia said. "She'd probably blame us. Let her find out for herself."

Miranda stayed for two months.

During this time the weather remained cold and Van Eyck blamed it on the environmentalist members of the municipal government, accusing them of trying to limit the city's growth by controlling the weather. He wasn't sure how this was being done, but he wrote letters to alert the daily newspaper, the Chamber of Commerce and, in case more inspired revelations and clout were necessary, the bishop of the Episcopalian diocese.

At the beginning of June, Frederic Quinn was released from the high-priced detention facility Sophrosune School, and before being transported to the high-priced detention facility Camp Sierra Williwaw, he had a whole month of freedom. He intended to make the most of it.

He collected a dozen starfish from the wharf pilings and put them in the ovens at the club to dry out. The ensuing stench permeated the ballroom, drifted through the corridors into the cabanas, hung over the pool and terrace. The entire staff was pressed into service to track down the source, but no one thought of opening the ovens until it was time to start cooking for the Saturday-night banquet.

Mr. Henderson immediately blamed Frederic, who had made the common criminal mistake of hanging around to see how things turned out.

"By God, this time you've gone too far, you bastard."

"I didn't do it, I didn't, I didn't!"

He swore his innocence on the small Bible which he carried around in his pocket for this very purpose. It was one of the more useful things he had learned at Sophrosune School.

Some of his exploits were more or less in the interests of science. He jumped off the thirty-three-foot diving platform holding a beach umbrella to see if it could be used as a parachute. It couldn't. After that, the cast on his left wrist curtailed his activities to a certain extent but he was still able to let the air out of Mr. Henderson's tires and to put red dye into the Jacuzzi when little Miss Reach was dozing. She woke up, assumed she was bleeding and began to scream to the full capacity of her ninety-year-old lungs. When a stem to stern, inch by inch examination by a number of bystanders proved that she wasn't bleeding, she was rather disappointed. Her whole life had been passing before her eyes and she was just coming to an interesting part.

That same week Charity Nelson reached retirement age. She didn't tell her boss, Smedler, or anyone else at the office, since she had no intention of retiring. Instead she celebrated by herself with two bottles of Cold Duck. Halfway through the second bottle she became quite sentimental and decided to phone her first husband, who lived somewhere in New Jersey. By the time she'd tracked him down to Hackensack and learned his phone number she couldn't remember why she was calling him.

"Hello, George. How are you?"

"It's three o'clock in the morning, that's how I am."

"Your clock must be wrong. Mine says twelve."

"Who is this?"

"Oh, George, how could you forget our anniversary?"

"I'm not having an anniversary. You sound stinko."

"George, I *am* stinko."

"Who the hell is this, anyway?"

"This is me," Charity said. "*Me.*"

She hung up. Men were beasts.

In mid-June, Grady Keaton returned to work at the Penguin Club. The girls brought the news home as their contribution to the dinner entertainment that night, but the Admiral was dining out and Iris was confined to her room, so they had only Miranda to contribute it to.

"That lifeguard is back again," Cordelia said. "The one who locked Frederic Quinn in the first-aid room. Remember, Miranda?"

"No." Miranda raised an empty fork to her mouth, chewed air, swallowed. "No."

"You were there."

"I don't remember."

"*I* do," Juliet said. "All hell broke loose. And afterwards Frederic threw up all over your dress and everybody could see what he'd been eating, ugh."

"This isn't a very appetizing subject for the dinner table, Juliet."

"It doesn't bother me."

"Or me," Cordelia agreed. "I don't see why it's all right to talk about food while you're eating it but not when you throw it up."

"Stop it, girls, this very minute . . . Now let's start over on a more civilized level. Tell me what you did today that was interesting."

"We already told you about seeing the lifeguard who's back working at the club. We forget his name."

"Grady," Miranda said. "I think that was his name— Grady."

She went down to the club the next afternoon while the girls were at a movie. She stood outside looking in at the pool through the glass door. Grady was leaning against the steel frame of the lifeguard tower, his arms crossed on his chest, an orange-colored visor shading his face. He seemed smaller than she remembered, as though someone had located a vital plug and let some of the air out of him. He had shaved off his mustache—some girl probably asked him to or asked him not to. She wondered how many girls there'd been in the eight months and three days since Pasoloma.

She wanted to leave, to go back to the Admiral's house and hide in her room, but she couldn't force her limbs to move. She stood there for such a long time that one of the porters came out of the club and asked her if she needed help. He was a young Mexican who spoke the Spanglish of the barrio.

She said, "No, I'm fine. I was just about to leave."

"Okay?"

"Yes. Thank you. *Muchas gracias.*"

"*Por nada.*"

He reminded her of the boy in the dining room of the clinic, Pedro. Grady had promised him a ride in the Porsche, but Grady wasn't very successful at keeping promises. The instant they rolled off his tongue they rolled out of his head and heart. *"I never said anything about marriage or commitment or forever . . . Jeez, I'm not a for-ever-type guy, Miranda."*

Poor Grady, he didn't recognize what was good for him, he would have to be forced into doing the right thing.

As soon as she returned home she called Ellen. She used the kitchen phone because it was the only one in the house not connected to any of the others and nobody could listen in.

Ellen answered. "Penguin Club."

"Ellen?"

"Yes."

"Why didn't you tell me Grady is back?"

"I wasn't sure how you'd take it."

"I'm taking it very well, thank you. How long has he been here?"

"A week."

"A whole week and you never said a word to me."

"I intended to, but—"

"Are you trying to keep us apart?"

"You are apart, Miranda. You've been apart for a long time."

"No," Miranda said. "Not for a minute. Perhaps Grady doesn't realize it yet, but I do. He came back here to see me."

"He needed a job and Mr. Henderson agreed to rehire him."

"That's simply a cover-up."

"Miranda, please—"

"Oh, I won't rush him. I'll give him a little time to adjust and then I'll arrange a meeting. I've saved enough money to buy a whole new outfit. Grady likes soft silky things."

"Stop it, Miranda. He hasn't even asked after you."

"Of course not. He's too subtle for that. He wouldn't ask you anyway. It's been obvious from the beginning that you've had a hopeless crush on him."

"You just won't listen to reason, will you?"

"Not yours," Miranda said. "You're not my friend any more."

To celebrate the July Fourth holiday Mr. Henderson planned a special event for the club. It was his most inspired idea since the Easter Egos costume ball where everybody came dressed as the person they would most like to be resurrected as. (Toward the end of the evening two of the resurrectees, Héloïse and Abélard, staged a knockdown dragout fight. This didn't spoil the party, since it was generally viewed as part of the entertainment, especially the choking scene. A number of volunteers gave Héloïse artificial respiration, but she survived anyway and a good time was had by nearly all.)

The July celebration, which Henderson called a Wing Ding, was given the theme Unidentified Flying Objects. Denied a special permit for a fireworks display on the beach in front of the club—fireworks were illegal throughout the state—Henderson rented a barge and had it anchored offshore as a base for the *fuegos artificiales* he'd brought across the border from Tijuana. The display was a great success until the Coast Guard literally cast a damper on it by dousing the barge with a firehose.

Henderson wasn't the only miscreant. The police and sheriff's deputies were busy all over town trying to enforce the ban on fireworks. From the barrio along the railroad tracks to the elegant old streets which zigzagged up through the foothills the night was alive with the explosions and flashes of homemade bombs and mail-order or under-the-counter shooting stars and Roman candles and whiz-bangs.

An extra loud explosion at 1220 Camino Grande attracted no special attention until a passing motorist saw flames shooting out of a window and called the fire department. By the time the flames were extinguished Iris Young was dead.

Part V

Iris's sitting room was officially sealed off and both the damaged wall and the door were boarded up to prevent further collapse.

Police poked around in the rubble, carrying away boxes of ashes and shattered glass, burned sections of tables and window frames and splinters of lamps, the disemboweled chair where Iris normally sat, her record albums melted now into masses of black glue, the charred remnant of the cane she always used, her mutilated chess pieces blown around the room like men in war.

The people living in the house were questioned and re-questioned, separately and together, and bit by bit the circumstances of Iris's final hours emerged. During the afternoon she listened to a new album of *Tosca* while paying some bills and balancing her checkbook. She did some typing. She finished a mystery story she'd been reading. She executed her next moves in the chess game she was playing by mail with the professor in Tokyo and the medical missionary in Jakarta and gave both letters to Miranda to mail.

In the evening she was alone in the house. At her urging the Admiral took the girls to the fireworks display at the club. The housekeeper, Mrs. Norgate, went to baby-sit her infant grandson. And Miranda was out walking the dog, who had suffered a digestive upset after eating a chocolate éclair.

It was a warm night, but Iris's poor circulation made her

175

susceptible to cold and even in summer she frequently used the gas log in her sitting room downstairs. Miranda offered to light it for her before she left the house. Iris refused. She was in a bad mood as well as in pain. She had appeared at dinner only long enough to complain that the vegetables were overcooked, the beef roast tough and the candles gave her a migraine.

Miranda took the dog to Featherstone Park, half a mile down the hill toward the sea. He seemed to feel better out in the open air, so they stayed for quite a while, the dog lying beside her while she sat on a bench listening to the night explode around her. When she returned to the house the driveway was blocked by police cars and fire engines and a small crowd of curiosity seekers being held back by men in uniform.

"What's happened? Let me past. I live here. Mrs. Young . . . I've got to see if Mrs. Young is all right."

As in all cases of violent death under unusual circumstances, an autopsy was performed. Though the body was severely burned, enough blood and tissue samples were recovered to confirm that the actual cause of death was smoke inhalation. The evidence indicated that while Iris was attempting to light the gas log she'd lost her balance and fallen. A frontal head injury rendered her unconscious and unable to escape the subsequent explosion and fire.

When the body was finally released for burial a memorial service was held in the chapel of the mortuary. The Admiral kept his head bowed throughout the proceedings. Charles Van Eyck, lulled by the minister's voice and three double martinis, drifted into sleep. Now and then Miranda dabbed at her eyes with a lace handkerchief very carefully to avoid smudging her mascara. The girls kept staring at the closed coffin as though they half expected it might open and out would pop Iris, having decided she didn't like being dead.

Cordelia was openly critical of the nature and length of the service. "It's so silly, the minister yapping away about

176

God and heaven when Mrs. Young didn't believe a word of that stuff."

"It's better to be on the safe side," Juliet said. "Just in case."

"In case what?"

"In case it's all true. Besides, it's not hurting anyone."

"It's hurting me. I'm hungry."

"Shut up. I want to hear about heaven."

Even after Iris's burial the damaged door of her sitting room remained boarded up and no workmen were allowed in to start cleaning up and rebuilding. A guard was kept in the hall to enforce the rule.

The girls, perturbed not so much by the death of their mother as by the disruption of their normal routine, hung around the hall trying to get answers and assurances, especially from the day guard, a red-haired young man named Grella.

"We thought the investigation was over and done with," Cordelia said. "Why are you still here?"

"Orders."

"That's not a real answer."

"Best I can do," Grella said. "The fact is, the reports haven't come back from Sacramento yet, and until then—"

"Why Sacramento?"

"That's where the crime lab is."

"What do they do there?"

"Analyze evidence to try and find out exactly what happened."

"It's perfectly clear what happened. Mrs. Young fell while she was lighting the gas log and hit her head. I'm not a bit surprised. She was always bumping into things and getting mad about it and cussing to beat hell."

"We're Navy, you know," Juliet explained, "we learned all the cuss words years ago. But we're not allowed to use them except in the privacy of our own rooms, like chewing gum. You're chewing gum right now, aren't you?"

"Yeah, I guess I am."

"Are you allowed?"

"I think so. I never asked."

"You'd better ask."

"Let's stick to the subject," Cordelia said sharply. "Why is the lab in Sacramento taking such a long time?"

"They're busy. They test evidence sent to them from every place in California."

"That's just physical evidence. Somebody should test the other more important kind of evidence, like what such and such a person said to so-and-so. We know plenty of that stuff."

"No kidding."

"Only nobody will listen."

"I'll listen," Grella said. He didn't have much else to do anyway except, as Juliet had observed, chew gum.

The girls conferred in whispers behind cupped hands, Juliet frowning and looking worried. She would rather have limited the conversation to nice friendly things like gum and the weather and the Navy, which wouldn't offend anyone, with the possible exception of Uncle Charles, who didn't care very much for the Navy. But Cordelia wasn't passing up her chance at an audience.

"Well, first of all," she said, "Mrs. Young had a terrible temper. And every year it got worse. When she went on a rampage she yelled and screamed and threw things. One day she even hit Miranda on the arm with her cane and Pops had to raise Miranda's salary two hundred dollars a month so she wouldn't quit."

"No kidding," Grella said. "Who's Miranda?"

"Oh, you've seen her floating and fluttering around the house. Mrs. Shaw. She's supposed to be teaching us etiquette, which is really dumb because we never go any place we can use it."

"What happened after she got the two-hundred-a-month raise?"

"She stayed. And she used the extra money to buy him presents."

178

"Mrs. Shaw bought your father presents?"

"Yes."

"Like what?"

"We don't know."

"You didn't see them?"

"No. But we heard him thank her for them. It was one night after Uncle Charles had been here for dinner. Miranda and Pops were standing right in this very hall."

"And where were you?"

Cordelia indicated the railing at the top of the stairs. "Up there. It's our favorite place for finding out what's going on when nobody will tell us."

"So what went on?"

"It was a kind of a mushy scene, with her playing the little woman and him apologizing for the way Mrs. Young treated her and saying don't cry, please don't cry. Sickening. Nobody ever asks *me* not to cry, let alone tacking a please onto it."

"Then what?"

"He thanked her for the presents, said he was very happy with them."

"Your father and Mrs. Shaw, were they chummy? That is, did they . . . ?"

"We think so," Juliet said a little sadly. "Probably in the back seat of the Rolls-Royce."

Blushing, Grella looked down at his feet, which were still there, and then at the door of Iris's sitting room, which wasn't. "Did you witness this—ah, this—"

"Hanky-panky," Cordelia said. "That's what we call it. Everyone knows what we're talking about but it's not vulgar. No, we didn't actually witness it. There were signs though, plenty of them, smiles and stares, touchings that might have looked accidental but weren't."

"Did your mother suspect what was going on?"

"Maybe. She couldn't hear very well but she had eyes like a hawk. Of course, *we* didn't say a word to her about it. She'd have gotten mad at *us*."

"Why?"

"Everyone does."

"This is a very interesting development," Grella said. "I'm not sure what I ought to do about it."

"You ought to tell that lab up in Sacramento there are lots of things they won't find out in test tubes."

Grella didn't tell the lab but he told his sergeant and the sergeant told his lieutenant. There was general agreement that the hanky-panky in the Rolls-Royce put a different light on the case.

On a morning in mid-July, Aragon was summoned to Smedler's office.

Charity was waiting for him when he stepped out of Smedler's private elevator. She had just finished misting her plants and the room was as hot and wet as an equatorial jungle. Beads of moisture clung to her red wig, which was draped over a life-sized bust of President Kennedy.

Charity saw him staring at it. "A work of art, isn't it? I got it at a swap meet over the weekend in exchange for my old muskrat jacket. I was passionately in love with Jack Kennedy, still am after all these years."

"It might cool your ardor if you turned on the air conditioning."

"My plants wouldn't like it."

"Don't tell them."

She wiped some of the moisture off the wig with a piece of Kleenex. "Better not come on funny today, junior. Boss man had another bash with his wife and now he's feeling guilty because he won. Guilt always gives him a migraine."

"What's he want from me?"

"How should I know? Maybe he wants to give you something."

"Like what?"

"His migraine."

Smedler was sitting behind his desk reading the morning mail. The bash with his wife had resulted in no visible scars, but even now his face was flushed and his hands had a very slight tremor.

He wasted only two words—"Sit down"—before coming to the point. "I saw in the newspaper a couple of weeks ago that Admiral Young's wife was killed in a fire. Know anything about it?"

"Only what I read in the newspaper account."

"Sketchy. Very sketchy. Makes me wonder . . . You aren't privy to any off-the-record stuff, are you?"

"No."

Smedler rubbed the left side of his neck and the area behind his left ear, which was a deeper color than the other ear. "I've played golf with the Admiral a couple of times. Nice quiet chap, hardly the type you'd suspect of fooling around."

"Who suspects him of fooling around?"

"My wife heard it on the grapevine at the country club. The rumor is that Miranda Shaw has been working at the Admiral's house in some capacity, and one capacity led to another capacity. I've instructed my wife not to repeat a story like that unless she's sure of the facts. It would be damned embarrassing for a man in my position to be sued for slander. Women don't realize the possible consequences of this gossip. Of course, it may not be gossip. Give me your personal opinion, Aragon. Does a relationship between the two of them seem feasible, considering his age, et cetera, et cetera?"

"The feasibility of a relationship depends on the number of et ceteras."

"Oh, for God's sake, don't talk like a lawyer. Are they sleeping together?"

"I don't know."

"Find out."

"How?"

"Miranda's a friend of yours."

"I spent a day and a half with her," Aragon said. "Most of the time I was driving and she was unconscious. That hardly adds up to a friendship."

"It's possible."

"It didn't happen. What's more, I don't consider it part of my job to pry into the love affairs of admirals."

"It's one admiral, not the whole U.S. Navy, and one love affair, not a history of Hollywood. All I'm asking is that you and Miranda should have a nice cozy talk over a couple of drinks. If she indicates no personal interest in the Admiral, I'll muzzle my wife and that'll be the end of that . . . It's funny she was left alone in the house that night."

"Who?"

"Iris Young. As I understand it she was crippled. A wealthy woman like that would surely have someone around to look after her or at least to keep her company."

"She had Miranda."

"Yes," Smedler said dryly. "She had Miranda."

The death of Iris had dealt a fatal blow to Charles Van Eyck's social life. Her house was the last place in town where he was more or less welcome for dinner, and in spite of the mediocrity of the food, drink and conversation, he missed the invitations. To his surprise he also missed Iris. She'd been his last surviving relative—if he didn't count the girls, and he didn't—and he felt quite depressed at the idea of being the final Van Eyck, with nothing to leave behind as a memorial except his correspondence. Since most of this was unsigned, it didn't constitute much of a memorial.

Iris had found out about the anonymous letters when he made the mistake of writing one to her about Miranda, and the even worse mistake of not checking the spelling of the word Jezebel. She wasn't taken in by his denials. "People who live in glass houses," Iris had said, "should learn to spell. I can only guess you've been scattering these around the landscape like confetti. Do try not to get caught, Charles. It would embarrass the family."

He had not been caught. Concerned Citizen, One Who Knows, a Word to the Wise, Irate Taxpayer, Member of

Loyal Opposition, Awake and Aware, Cassandra and Pentagon Pauper continued their correspondence.

It was a warm sunny afternoon. At the club Van Eyck sat in a deck chair under the twisted old cypress tree. He wore his writing costume: flowered Hawaiian shirt, walking shorts, a tennis visor and bifocals. He had a new refill in his pen and plenty of paper, which he'd snatched from the office while Ellen was on a coffee break. The tide was high but the waves gentle, so there was minimal noise to distract him. Still he was distracted. The pain in his left hip worried him. He thought of a mare he'd ridden as a child which had to be shot when she broke her leg. He wondered where he was going to spend Christmas Day now that Iris was dead. Finally he dozed off for an hour or so, and when he woke up he felt refreshed and the mare and the hip pain and Christmas were going out with the tide. Charles Van Eyck went with them and Seeker of Truth got down to business.

To the District Attorney of Santa Felicia County:—

Are the police deaf to the voice of a woman crying out from her grave for Justice?

The fire which killed Iris Young was no ordinary fire, her husband no ordinary man, his employee, Miranda Shaw, no ordinary servant. One of these 3 people is dead.

$3 - 1 = 2$

$2 = $ a pair

Is this what the anguished voice from the grave is trying to tell you?

Listen! Heed!

This alert comes from:-

A Seeker of Truth

As a precaution Seeker inked out the club name and address at the top of the page and the lefthand corner of the envelope. Truth didn't necessarily mean the Whole Truth.

Switching identities, Fair Play wrote a short note to the Admiral advising him to reject further pension payments now that he was a wealthy man, and to consider reimbursing the taxpayers for previous payments.

He lay back in the chair and closed his eyes. Righteousness flowed through his system like a spring tonic. The pain in his hip had disappeared, the broken-legged mare had been old anyway, and he would go to Waikiki for Christmas and eat poi and drink mai tais.

When Aragon phoned the Admiral's house a woman with an English accent told him Mrs. Shaw had taken the girls to the Penguin Club for lunch and a swim and would probably be gone all day. He called the club and talked to Ellen.

"She's here," Ellen said. "She's been showing up with the girls every day lately. The Ingersolls are letting her use their cabana while they're in South America and she just sits in it by herself."

"Why?"

"She wants to avoid people. Most people."

"Who's the exception?"

"Grady. He came back to work about a month ago."

"You don't sound very happy about it. Isn't that what you wanted?"

"Not like this." There was a short silence. "She's still crazy about him, sick-crazy. She sits up in that cabana posing and preening and staring down at him. He can't stand to look at her and she never takes her eyes off him."

"I heard it different. The rumors going the rounds of the country club are about her and the Admiral. What do you think of that?"

"Nothing. He's an old man."

"A rich old man."

"Forget it. I see her every day and I'm telling you the way she watches Grady is—How rich?"

"A whole bunch rich, you should know that."

"I knew his wife was rich, which isn't necessarily the same thing."

"There's no reason to believe he won't inherit a large part of her estate."

"But suppose—Oh, never mind. It was just a thought. I have to hang up now anyway. Henderson has an errand for me in town."

"I'd like to come down and talk to Miranda. Is that okay?"

"With me it is. With her maybe not."

"I can try."

"Try ahead," Ellen said. "If I'm not here, go right on up to cabana number twenty-one."

He left his car in the club parking lot. As he was walking across the street to the front door he saw Grady about fifty yards away heading for the employees' entrance at the back. Aragon waved at him but got no response. Either Grady didn't recognize him or didn't want to.

A wide thickly carpeted staircase led to the row of cabanas on the second floor. The impression of opulence ended abruptly at the top. The corridor was a kind of long dark tunnel dimly lit at each end by a sixty-watt bulb suspended from the ceiling. The brown wooden floor was strewn with swimmers' towels like mounds of dirty snow on a mud road.

He knocked on the door of 21 and Miranda's voice responded immediately.

"Who's there?"

"Tom Aragon."

"Aragon?" She opened the door. "My goodness, this *is* a surprise."

She sounded as though it was a pleasant one. Too pleasant. It made him vaguely uncomfortable.

She wore a pink and yellow silk caftan and her long hair hung loose over her shoulders. It was a couple of shades lighter than when he'd last seen her on the street with the two girls in April. Her hair wasn't the only change. In April she'd been a little depressed, resigned to her fate and

185

not expecting any change for the better. Now she seemed in high spirits. Her eyes sparkled and she had an almost feverish color in her cheeks.

"Come in, Mr. Aragon, come in."

"Thank you."

"How did you find me? Oh—Ellen, of course. Dear little Ellen, she knows everybody's secrets, doesn't she?"

He considered the reference to Ellen inaccurate on all counts but he didn't challenge it.

The cabana was a small three-sided room furnished with webbed plastic chairs and chaise and a glass-topped table. The fourth side had a half-railing which showed the pool below, and beyond it the sea, and twenty miles to the southwest the hazy blue offshore island, a piece of mountain caught and held. Between the island and the shore were the oil platforms like isolated steel prisons built for incorrigibles.

After a few amenities—she was fine, he was fine, the weather was fine—she changed the subject abruptly.

"Grady's back," she said. "Did you know that?"

"I had a glimpse of him outside."

"Doesn't he look beautiful?"

"I—well, he was pretty far away. I'll take your word for it."

"You're probably laughing at me because men aren't supposed to be described as beautiful. Only what if they *are*? You might as well admit the truth."

"All right, I admit the truth," Aragon said. "Grady is a beautiful man."

She smiled. "That's better. He really *is*, believe me. You didn't see him at his best when you came down to Pasoloma with those papers for me to sign. He was in shock."

"I can understand why. Has he gotten over it?"

"Of course. He needed a little time to think, that's all. The instant we met again when he came back here to work I knew nothing had changed between us, that we were as much in love as ever. Naturally, he can't be obvious about it, but I catch him watching me out of the corner of his eye. It's so cute . . . Glance over the railing and see if he's down there now on the lifeguard tower."

"Yes."

"Is he staring up here?"

"No."

"He's very good at pretending to ignore me."

"Is that how you want it?"

"Of course it is. We can't afford to be seen together just yet. The police are everywhere. Fortunately Grady understands, he's being extremely tactful about the situation. He disappears the minute I enter the club and stays out of sight until I'm settled up here in the cabana. But it will be nice when we can act natural again."

"You claim the police are everywhere," Aragon said. "What are they doing?"

"Asking questions about Iris Young, every conceivable sort of question. And I'm sure they're getting every conceivable sort of answer, especially from the girls. Juliet and Cordelia are like children, they'll say anything to draw attention to themselves. I expect some of their statements will be critical of me. They've never liked me, they're not used to anyone giving them orders or even advice, but that's what I'm paid to do and I do it."

"According to the newspaper report, Iris Young was alone in the house the night she died."

"Yes."

"Why?"

"She wanted to be."

"I understand she was crippled."

"She wasn't helpless. She could walk with the aid of a cane, and God knows she could talk, or rather scream. When she got mad you could hear her for miles. Believe me, whatever happened in the house happened because she wanted it to, whether it was being left alone or being waited on hand and foot."

"What was her state of mind that night?"

"The same as it always was—selfish, mean, arrogant."

He hoped, for her sake, that this wasn't an example of her conversations with the police. "Did she seem depressed?"

"Why should she be depressed, with all that money and power? *I'm* the one who should be depressed."

"And are you?"

She gazed at him somberly for a minute, then one corner of her mouth twitched in a demure smile. "What do you think? How do I look?"

"You look very pretty." *And a little wacky.*

"I'm deliriously happy, if you want the truth. Everything's working out the way I planned. May I tell you something in confidence?"

"Yes, but I'd prefer—"

"Absolute confidence, like between lawyer and client, I forget the legal term for it."

"Privileged information."

"Let's call this privileged information."

She was smiling fully now, as if something was turning out to be a great joke. He hoped he wasn't it.

"I'd ask you to cross your heart," she said, "except I've always been told lawyers don't have one."

"I hear beating inside my chest. Maybe I'm an exception."

"Then cross your heart."

He did. Miranda liked games and he didn't mind as long as they were as innocent as this one.

It didn't remain innocent very long. She said. "I'm going to be married within two or three months. Surprised?"

"Yes. I didn't peg Grady as the marrying type."

"I'm not marrying Grady, I'm marrying Cooper."

"Cooper?"

"The Admiral. I expect him to set the date when this business about his wife is all settled. Oh, it will be nice having money again, being able to afford things."

"Things like what?"

"Like Grady."

He knew then why she looked a little wacky. She was. He said, "You can't buy people, Mrs. Shaw."

"Most people you can't, some you can. Grady's one of the some. Of course, it will take a lot of money and I could never manage it on my own. Cooper is going to help me."

"Is he aware of this?"

"No."

"Is Grady?"

"No. Just you and I. And you can't tell because it's privileged information and you crossed your heart."

Behind the boiler room, which contained the heating and filtering tanks for the pool, there was a small toolshed with a padlock on the door. The lock had been broken so often that no one bothered replacing it any more and employees had access to the shed for whatever purpose they had in mind. Grady's purpose was lunch. He'd purchased it at a taco stand a couple of blocks up the street, and he sat now on a wooden chest among the rakes and shovels and hedge clippers, the ants and pill bugs, the lengths of piping and coils of rope.

The shed smelled of paint thinner and fertilizer and the cooking fumes from the snack-bar grill, but it was peaceful and quiet except for the sound of the waves. Grady liked to listen to them, trying to estimate their size and shape and whether the tide was coming in or going out. Usually he checked his tide book as soon as he reported to work and then chalked the numbers up on the blackboard beside the pool. High 10:25 p.m. 5.7 Low 5:41 p.m. −0.5. He hadn't done this yet today because he'd seen Miranda arriving with the girls and he wanted to stay out of sight until she went up to the cabana. Avoiding Miranda was easy. Avoiding certain other people wasn't.

"So there you are," little Frederic said. He carried a skateboard and was wearing protective equipment—knee and elbow pads and a red plastic helmet. In spite of these precautions he was plastered with an assortment of grimy bandages on his hands, nose and legs. "I've been looking all over the place for you."

"Now you found me," Grady said. "Bug off."

"What are you hiding in here for?"

"Who says I'm hiding?"

Frederic fitted his skinny little rump snugly into the center of a coil of rope. Then he removed his lunch, a package of bologna, from underneath his helmet. "What's it worth to you if I don't tell?"

"Nothing."

"Take your time. Think it over."

"There's no one to tell."

"Sure there is. You don't happen to have a dill pickle on you, do you? There's this kid at school who wraps a piece of bologna around a dill pickle and he calls it—"

"I don't give a goddamn if he calls it mother. Who is there to tell?"

"The chick you went to Mexico with." Since no dill pickle was available, Frederic didn't bother separating the slices of bologna. He took a bite out of all eight at once. "She's always asking people where you are—the porters, Henderson, Ellen, even me. How come you don't want her to find you?"

"Listen, Frederic. Let's talk this over man to man."

"Hell no. That palsy-walsy stuff just means you're not going to pay me."

"I can't, I don't have the money. Anyway, you're my friend. Aren't you?"

"What gives you a dumb idea like that? I don't have friends. I get shut up in some crazy school that teaches Greek—and who rescues me? Nobody. And where am I going to spend the rest of the summer? A prison camp in the boonies, only they call it an outdoor learning experience in the Sierra wilderness."

"Stop it, kid. I cry easy."

"You might."

"What does that mean?"

Frederic ate the last chunk of bologna, then he tucked the empty container under one of his knee pads beside a gum wrapper and a soggy piece of Kleenex. He disapproved of littering. "You want to know what she's doing up in the cabana right this minute? Wow, you'll throw a fit when I tell you."

"Try me."

"She's talking to her lawyer. His name's Aragon. The reason I'm sure is he's my lawyer too. Him and me, we're going to sue people together when I grow up, maybe sooner. I'm keeping a list."

Grady didn't throw a fit but he drew in a quick breath and held it as though he'd been knocked over by a wave he didn't see coming. "What are they talking about?"

"Search me."

"I'm searching you."

"I don't know what they're talking about, man. I stood in the hall and listened but I couldn't hear a thing."

"Suppose you got in the cabana next door," Grady said. "You might be able to hear something from there."

"Might. How do I get in?"

"Ellen has a set of master keys."

"She wouldn't give them to me for a million dollars."

"She might give them to me."

Frederic's eyes widened. "Oh, now you're going to turn on the old macho, right? Can I come along and watch?"

"No."

"I haven't seen you in action since—"

"No. Stay here and I'll be back soon."

"If you change your mind, send me some kind of signal, like whistling three times."

"Sure, kid. Sure."

After Grady's departure Frederic amused himself by catching a spider that had spun a web between two of the crooked rust-stained teeth of a rake. For a while he had hopes that it was a black widow and he could train it to bite people to death, a reasonable alternative to suing them, but the creature didn't have the black widow's distinguishing red hourglass on its abdomen. Nor did it seem to want to bite anything, not the ant Frederic offered it, or the scab from his thumb, or a shred of the bandage dangling from his left wrist. He replaced the spider in the teeth of the rake.

During these maneuvers he kept listening hard, but nobody whistled three times or even once and Grady was still missing. Frederic waited another five minutes, then he picked up his skateboard and went back into the boiler room. He kicked a couple of pipes and tried to turn a wheel marked Do Not Touch and to remove a High Voltage sign from the fuse box. But everything was sealed, padlocked, clamped, welded.

Through the kitchen (Private, Keep Out) he left the club by the rear door (Employees Only), where he had a view of the parking lot. Grady and Aragon were standing beside Aragon's old Chevy, right in the very center of the lot without any trees or shrubbery around to provide coverage. There was no possible way of approaching them without being seen. They were out of reach, twenty years and a thousand miles away, and he could never catch up with them.

He had made a secret pact with his best friend, Henry, not to cry under any circumstances. But Henry was in Philadelphia visiting his parents and Frederic was here and now, hurting inside and outside.

Tears rolled down his cheeks like leaden bubbles.

"You got it all wrong," Grady said. He had pulled a pair of jeans on over his trunks because it was against the rules for any employee to enter or leave the club wearing only swimming attire. Aragon noticed that the jeans were too tight around the waist—Grady was eating regularly again.

"I swear to God, Aragon, I haven't even spoken to her since I came back."

"Why not?"

"I tried to, I wanted to be friendly, but she avoided me. I thought she was sore at me and I didn't blame her. I just felt grateful she hadn't put the cops on me about the Porsche. So while she was avoiding me I was avoiding her and it was working out fine. Then suddenly zap, I get this letter."

He handed Aragon a piece of pale blue paper that had obviously been unfolded and refolded a number of times. It was soiled at the crease lines and damp from moisture seeping from his swim trunks into the pockets of his jeans but the ink hadn't smudged. The writing, neat boarding-school backhand, was embellished with a few touches of Miranda's own, extra-large capitals and circles over the i's instead of dots.

> Beloved:
> I want to write that word over and over again because it is beautiful like you. Beloved, beloved, beloved.
> Oh, how hard this masquerade has been on both of us, acting like strangers when all we can think about is lying in each other's arms. But be patient, my dearest. I have made my plans very carefully, and though they may seem strange to you at first, please trust me. We must *live* as well as *love* . This is the only way we can do both.
>
> Your own
> Miranda

"I couldn't believe it at first," Grady said. "I thought she was putting me on. But she's not the type, she's deadly serious about everything." He read the note again before he replaced it in his pocket. "That's a lot of crap how all we can think about is lying in each other's arms. Jeez, I never even thought about it when I was doing it, and that was a year ago."

"Eight months."

"Close enough. I don't sit around staring at calendars."

"In the note she refers to plans," Aragon said. "What plans?"

"You're the one who talked to her, not me. I told you before, I haven't even spoken to her since I got back. Now suddenly she's writing stuff about lying in each other's arms. For all I know, she's got a church and preacher lined up. I feel trapped, man. Trapped." He thumped the hood of the car with his fist. It left an imprint in the dust like an animal track.

"Why did you come back here, Grady?"

"I needed the job and the surfing's good. I never dreamed Miranda would be waiting for me with a bunch of crazy ideas. Maybe I should run away. What do you think?"

"You're pretty good at it," Aragon said. "Maybe you should."

"I mean it. She might be really far out. She might try something wild, like taking a shot at me or sticking a knife in my back, especially if she finds out I'm interested in someone else."

"Are you?"

"Sort of."

"Explain 'sort of.'"

"Well, Ellen and me, we got something going. She's a nice girl with class and a steady job. It might work out okay. I could do worse."

"Could she?"

Grady thumped the hood of the car again but there was no force behind it. It was like a gesture he'd seen done in a movie by someone he identified with. "Stop coming down hard on me because of that business in Mexico. It wasn't my fault. None of it was my idea in the first place, not her and me, not the trip, not even the Porsche, which never did me any good anyway. You know what happened to it?"

"You sold it and lost the money in a crap game."

"I parked it in a garage in Phoenix and it got ripped off," Grady said. "How's that for a laugh?"

"Fair."

"You still think I'm a louse, huh?"

"Close enough. I don't sit around staring at dictionaries."

"Well, I'm not so crazy about you either, you self-righteous bastard. You probably never had to do a day's work in your life, everything handed to you on a platter, college, law school, the whole bit. Me, I ran away from home when I was thirteen, they were going to kick me out anyway. Want to know why? I stole a car. How's that for laugh number two?"

"About as funny as laugh number one."

"It was my uncle's car and I didn't mean to steal it, I only wanted to go for a ride. But once I started driving I couldn't stop. I kept right on going until the gas tank was empty. I ended up near a ball park in Visalia. I watched the game for a while, then I hitchhiked home and got the hell beat out of me. I left again the next day, this time with the money my aunt kept hidden under her mattress . . . So there you have it, the story of my life, chapter one."

"The lady, the mattress, the money," Aragon said. "You started early and learned fast."

"I found out where it's at and how to get there. Sure. Why not?"

"Is the word out about you and Ellen?"

"We haven't done any advertising, but I guess Mr. Henderson has caught on and some of Ellen's neighbors in the apartment building, people like that. Ellen's got a lot of friends, and friends talk."

"Are you living in her apartment?"

"Not technically, no. I rent a room on Quinientos Street."

"Does Miranda know about it?"

"I don't see how, unless she followed me home from work one night, and she wouldn't do that. She's always got those two crazies with her. They tag along after her like she's their mother."

195

"Or stepmother."

From Grady's lack of reaction to the word, Aragon was certain that he wasn't aware of Miranda's plans for his future and her own, via the Admiral.

"What do you think I should do?" Grady said.

"What do you want to do?"

"Sit tight, keep things alive with Ellen, pretend I never got the letter."

"When did you get it?"

"Three days ago. It was slipped under the door of the guard shack with my name on the envelope."

"So you can't very well pretend you didn't get it."

"I guess not."

"Have you showed it to Ellen?"

"No."

"Do you intend to?"

"No. It's strictly between Miranda and me, or rather between Miranda and Miranda. I can't be held responsible for what's cooking inside her head."

Frederic slalomed across the parking lot on his skateboard between parked cars and lampposts and concrete markers. When he reached Aragon's Chevy he came to a stop by jumping off the skateboard. The board kept right on going, under a BMW and a Lincoln and ending up against the front tire of a Ford van. Frederic retrieved it, spun the wheels to make sure they weren't damaged and approached the two men. His recent tears had cleared little paths through the dirt on his cheeks.

"Bug off," Grady said.

Frederic shook his head. "Can't."

"Try."

"Can't. Your girl friend sent me here on an errand."

"What girl friend?"

"Don't rush me, man." Frederic took off his plastic helmet, releasing a squashed yogurt carton and two sticks of gum now soft as putty and molded to the shape of his head.

He looked up at Grady, red-eyed and reproachful. "I waited a long time in that stinky shed for you to come back with the keys."

"The situation changed," Grady said.

"You never meant to come back."

"Sure I did."

"No, you didn't."

"Have it your way. What's the errand and who sent you?"

"Maybe I won't tell you."

Grady put his hands on the boy's shoulders and squeezed. "Then again, maybe you will, right?"

"Sure. Right. Lay off the rough stuff. I was only kidding. Can't you take a joke? Ellen sent me to tell Mr. Aragon to come back to the club and call his office. A lady wants to talk to him."

"Thanks, Frederic," Aragon said.

"You don't have to thank me," Frederic said. "A small tip will be enough."

"I've only got two dimes. You can have one."

"One skinny little dime. There ought to be a minimum-tip law like the minimum-wage law. Say, how's that for a new political idea?"

"Great. In another twelve years you can run for Congress." It was a sobering thought.

Aragon used the other dime on the public telephone in the corridor. Only one lady was likely to know where he was, and the switchboard transferred the call to her office.

"Miss Nelson? It's me."

"Who's me?"

"Tom."

"Tom who?"

"Aragon."

Charity tapped the phone sharply with a pencil by way of reprimand. "I'm beginning to wonder if you'll ever make the big time in this business, junior. An attorney headed for the larger life doesn't say it's me. He says this is Tomas Aragon of Smedler, Downs, Castleberg, McFee and Powell."

"You already know that."

"It won't kill you to practice a little."

"All right. This is Tomas Aragon of Smedler, Downs, Castleberg, McFee and Powell. So what's new?"

"Plenty. Smedler just came from the courthouse and the whole place was buzzing with rumors. The report in Iris Young's death arrived from the crime lab last night by special messenger and the word is she was murdered."

"Whose word?"

"There's an old babe in the D.A.'s office who has a crush on Smedler—he's fairly attractive if you squint a little and the light's not too good—and she's always getting him in a corner and feeding him goodies to arouse his interest. Verbal goodies, I mean. He's on a diet. Anyway, she told him that the D.A.'s in seventh heaven."

"What does it take to put a D.A. in seventh heaven, or even fifth or sixth?"

"Evidence for a case that will make him look good to the voters in the next election," Charity said. "You saw Iris Young once, didn't you?"

"Briefly."

"Was she using a cane?"

"Yes. It was burned in the fire."

"Wrong. There was a lot of intricate metalwork on the head of it which didn't burn. Where the metal joined the wood some blood seeped into the cracks. It matched the blood taken from Mrs. Young's body, but there was a difference in the two samples that's supposed to be very significant."

"In what way?"

"Smedler's snitch didn't know."

"Why are you telling me all this, Miss Nelson?"

"Smedler asked me to clue you in. He thought maybe you could find out more by sort of hanging around the sheriff's department."

"If I sort of hang around the sheriff's department, somebody's going to sort of wonder why."

"Tell them you work for Smedler, Downs, Castleberg, McFee and Powell. After all, Miranda Shaw is one of our clients, or used to be, and she was living in the Youngs' house when the murder occurred and we have a right to— Oh my God, you don't suppose she's actually *involved*. Yes, you do. I can tell by your silence."

"I—"

"And so does Smedler. And that's why he's so curious about the report from the crime lab. Well, if he really wants to find things out, I wish he'd pick somebody more competent than you."

"So do I," Aragon said and hung up.

Ellen Brewster was standing outside the door of her office waiting for him. She wore a short sleeveless white dress which showed off her newly acquired tan but made her look as if she was trying too hard to be like one of the teenagers herded in flocks on the beach and in the snack bar and around the lifeguard towers.

Her voice was strained. "Do you have time to come in for a minute, Mr. Aragon?"

"I think so."

He went in and she closed the door behind him. The room was still noisy. There was shouting and laughing from the pool area, and outside by the roadway some men were pruning a eucalyptus tree with a power saw.

She said, "Did you talk to Miranda?"

"Yes."

"It wouldn't be fair for me to ask what she told you, would it?"

"No."

"I can't help it, I have to ask one question anyway. Does she know that Grady and I—that we—"

"No."

"I was pretty sure she didn't but I had to be positive."

"Why?"

"I guess I'm afraid of her."

"She's not exactly formidable—twice your age, about half your size and a little nuts."

"She isn't a little nuts," Ellen said. "Where Grady's concerned she's totally irrational. She hasn't changed since the night you dumped her on me when you drove her here from that clinic in Mexico. She told me then that she'd do anything to make it possible for her and Grady to be together again. She said if he needed money to be happy, no matter how much money, she'd get it somehow and buy him back. Can you believe it?"

"Yes." They were the same words Miranda had used in the cabana half an hour ago. "So what are you afraid of, that he can be bought?"

"I don't know whether he can or not. I just don't want her to try. It's not fair."

"Don't worry. She hasn't a nickel."

He sounded more confident than he felt.

"Nothing," he told Charity when he returned to the office later in the day.

"Nothing?" she repeated. "You've been gone all afternoon, and *nothing*?"

"Nothing definite. I did what you told me to—hung around here and there, kept my ears open, asked subtle questions like how are you, got subtle answers like fine. There are the usual rumors which a case of this kind inspires. But one of them may possibly be worth something."

"What is it?"

"That the D.A. has enough evidence to ask the grand jury for an indictment."

"An indictment against whom?"

"I don't know."

"Probably the husband," Charity said. "It usually is in this day and age. Nobody keeps a butler any more."

Part VI

Let the record show that all nineteen members of the grand jury are present and have been sworn and the District Attorney is ready to continue the presentation of his case.

"Mr. Foreman and ladies and gentlemen of the grand jury. During the morning session I outlined the general procedure I would follow, since this is the first homicide brought before you. In the course of the afternoon I will deal more with specifics. But first I would like to state that I am aware, as you must be, that the grand jury system has recently been criticized in the media on several grounds: the manner in which jurors are selected, the secrecy of the proceedings, the absence of any attorney to represent the defense and of a judge to rule on what is or isn't permissible, and the fact that only twelve votes are required to issue an indictment, which allows for seven dissenters if the full jury of nineteen is present, as it is now. It is not my business to answer these criticisms. The system exists and we must operate within it. I have complete faith in your ability to reach a fair and impartial decision and I believe it will be a unanimous one."

The District Attorney stopped to wipe his forehead with a handkerchief. The courthouse air conditioning was on the blink again and the chamber, in spite of its size and high ceiling, was ʜ ᴏt. ᴀll the windows had to be closed to shut out traffic noises. A fan droned at the back of the room, pushing the air around without cooling it.

The District Attorney's name was Zachary Tilford and he was in his early thirties, an age considered by many to be too young for the job. He knew this and in order to counteract it he spoke in an aggressively sharp staccato voice. His words bounced off the walls like Ping-Pong balls.

"The house at 1220 Camino Grande is a mansion by today's standards. Purchased about a dozen years ago by Vice-Admiral Cooper Young, USN, Retired, and his wife, Iris Van Eyck Young, it has been occupied since then by the Admiral and his wife and their two unmarried daughters, Cordelia and Juliet. A housekeeper, Mrs. Paulette Norgate, joined the household a short time later, and last year Miranda Shaw, a well-bred attractive widow, then fifty-two, was hired to act as a kind of social governess for the daughters. These five people lived in the house. During the day other employees came to assist with the cleaning and cooking and general household chores, but for purposes of this hearing we will not concern ourselves with the latter group.

"Iris Young was sixty-two and in poor health. A chronic arthritic, she had suffered two heart attacks. She lived the life of a semi-recluse, spending most of her waking hours in her sitting room on the main floor, occupied with her business interests—she was a wealthy woman—as well as her books and music. For a hobby she played chess by mail with various people around the world. This was among her activities on the afternoon of July the fourth. We know that because she gave Mrs. Shaw two letters to post, one addressed to a professor at the University of Tokyo, the other to a missionary in Jakarta. The rest of the time she spent finishing a book she'd been reading and listening to an opera. For Mrs. Young it was a typical afternoon, except for one thing. It was her last.

"Shortly after nine o'clock that night Iris Young died. Preliminary reports indicated that she was attempting to light the gas log in the fireplace when she fell forward, struck her head and lost consciousness. The escaping gas exploded and set fire to the room and everything in it, but an autopsy proved that Mrs. Young's death was actually due to smoke inhalation. I want to bring to your attention at this point that the official temperature reading in Santa Felicia at nine o'clock on the night of July the fourth was seventy-two degrees after a daytime high of eighty-one. The temperature in Iris Young's sitting room must have been somewhere between those two extremes, probably about seventy-six degrees, warm even for someone who was an invalid. Yet she allegedly tried to light the gas log. I call this curious circumstance number one.

"Curious circumstance number two: Mrs. Young was alone in the house. As I promised this morning, I will not waste the jury's time and the taxpayers' money bringing in witnesses to testify to evidence already well-documented in the investigative reports which are included in the exhibits.

"Where was her family and the other people who lived in the house? The Admiral had escorted his two daughters to a fireworks display at the Penguin Club; Miranda Shaw was out walking the dog; and the housekeeper, Mrs. Norgate, had gone to baby-sit her grandson. The last person to see Mrs. Young alive was Miranda Shaw. I want to bring to your attention at this point that it was Mrs. Shaw's habit to walk the dog before she retired between ten-thirty and eleven o'clock. On the night in question she left the house at eight-thirty, claiming the dog suffered a digestive upset. This may be true. Certainly, neither Iris Young nor the dog is in a position to deny it.

"At any rate, our list of curious circumstances continues to grow. Number three: Miranda Shaw left the house with the dog a couple of hours earlier than usual. Number four: she was the last person to see Iris Young alive."

The District Attorney paused again to wipe the sweat off his forehead and take a drink of water from the pitcher on the table in front of him. He was suffering from a sudden attack of nerves in addition to the heat. Although he'd reminded the grand jury—somewhat unnecessarily—that this was the first case of homicide to be brought before them, he had neglected to inform them that it was also his first. Since grand jury proceedings were always secret, and the transcripts often sealed afterward by order of a judge, he was more or less flying blind. It was small consolation that the jurors were in the same plane.

"Most of you, if you have heard at all of the crime lab in Sacramento, may think of it as a remote place where obscure research is carried on which has no connection with you personally. Well, it is no longer remote and its work no longer obscure. The lab, in fact, has moved right into your lives in the form of the document I am now holding in my hand. It contains the results of the tests made on the material taken from the scene of Iris Young's death. This covered a wide range of things, the most important being the blood and tissue samples from Iris Young's body. Among the items salvaged from the ruins—the wood splinters and pieces of glass and other rubble—two specific items stand out, a cane and a candlestick.

"Each of you has been furnished with a list of exhibits I will offer you in support of my case. The first is the document I'm now holding in my hand. Many people, scientists and lab technicians, contributed to it, but it's signed by Dr. Gustave Wilhelm, acting head of the arson division. Dr. Wilhelm cannot be here to testify until later in the week, so I will take the liberty of presenting to you an outline of his report in order to answer the first of the three significant questions in this case: Was a murder committed? What were the reasons behind it? Who had these reasons? It would be illogical to proceed with the last two questions until we've established a definite answer to the first. Was a murder committed? Yes. This document in my hand is, in fact, the story of a murder, written in the language of science instead of literature and having as its leading character not a person but a cane.

"The cane belonged to Iris Young. According to a statement by her husband, she purchased it merely as an artifact used by an African chieftain in certain tribal rites. Later it became her constant companion. It is made of zebrawood with an ornamental head of copper and the remnants of it are on the table to your left wrapped in plastic and identified by a red tag. Even without my unwrapping it you can see that it's been badly burned. What you can't see is that at the head, where the copper has been hammered into the wood, there are bloodstains. The fact that any of Iris Young's blood was found on this cane is enough to suggest foul play. Microscopic tests have made the suggestion a fact. Let me clarify.

"A by-product of any fire is carbon monoxide, a colorless, odorless gas which has a strong affinity for the red blood cells of the body. Its presence is easily detected not only in the bloodstream but in the respiration passages and the lungs, where small granules of carbon can be found if a person has breathed in smoke. Tissues taken from Iris Young's nasal and bronchial passages and lungs contained such granules. Also, samples of her blood indicate that carbon monoxide had forced the vital oxygen out of her red cells and caused death by asphyxiation. So what she died of is clear. How it happened is another matter.

"It was at first believed that Iris Young while leaning over in the act of lighting the gas log lost her balance and fell, that she struck the upper area of her face hard enough to cause bleeding and to render her unconscious. But now let's ask some basic questions:

"Was blood found on the gas log? No.

"Anywhere near it? No.

"Any place in the room at all? Yes. On the head of the cane.

"What type of blood was it? AB negative.

"Did it, in fact, come from Iris Young's body? Yes.

"Did it contain evidence of carbon monoxide? No. I repeat, no. The blood on the cane came from a woman who had not breathed in any smoke at all.

"Is it possible that Iris Young's head wound was the

result of her falling on her own cane? No. The force of such a fall would not have been enough to cause the kind of injury she sustained.

"How, then, did she die? She was struck. She did not fall and strike anything, she was struck with her own cane.

"Could this blow have been an act of impulse and the fire a desperate attempt to cover up the attack? No. I believe that the fire was, in fact, the main event, premeditated, carefully planned even down to the date, July Fourth, when the sound of an explosion would be nothing unusual. The holiday also made it easier to get the other people out of the house—Admiral Young to watch a fireworks display with his daughters, and the housekeeper to baby-sit her grandson while his parents went out celebrating. Oh yes, it was carefully planned, all right, except that explosions and fires are not predictable whether they're arranged by an amateur or a professional. As many prisoners are painfully aware, arson doesn't necessarily burn up evidence of itself.

"Iris Young was meant to be cremated in that fire. Perhaps that would have happened if she'd been fatter, since body fat acts as a fuel, but Iris Young was a thin woman. Her cane was meant to be destroyed and it was, but only partially. The part that was left provided the blood samples to compare with those taken from her body.

"There is still another object which was intended for destruction, or at least for damage enough to render it useless as evidence."

He walked over to the table where the exhibits were displayed and picked up a candlestick wrapped, like the cane, in transparent plastic.

"Here it is. An antique silver candlestick, ten inches high, bent, as you can see, by the force of the explosion and somewhat discolored by smoke. According to the housekeeper and the members of the family, it's one of a set of four always kept on the buffet in the dining room. How did it get from the buffet in the dining room to the floor of Iris Young's sitting room? The obvious explanation is that she

206

took it there herself. But let me read a couple of sentences from a statement given to one of my deputies by the housekeeper, Mrs. Norgate:

" 'Miranda Shaw liked to use candles on the dinner table because she thought they made her look more youthful. But lately Mrs. Young had gotten so she couldn't stand them. She said flickering lights gave her a headache.' There's no reason to doubt Mrs. Norgate's word. Moreover, the same observation has been made by other members of the household, that Mrs. Young hated candles. Yet this candlestick was found in her room. Without her fingerprints on it, without, in fact, any fingerprints on it at all. I have lost count of the curious facts in this case but this must be number five or six. Or ten. Or fifteen. More questions arise:

"What was the candlestick doing in Iris Young's room? It was doing what came naturally, holding a candle.

"And what was the candle doing? Committing a murder.

"And what does all this add up to? The following sequence of events: Iris Young was struck with her own cane, the candle was lit and its holder wiped clean, the gas was turned on and the murderer left the house."

The District Attorney paused again, not for effect but because one of the jurors, a retired librarian, had raised her hand.

"Yes, Mrs. Zimmerman?"

"Why don't you bring in some witnesses?"

"I will, of course. But in order to save both time and the taxpayers' money—two important advantages of the grand jury system—I'm calling only enough witnesses to present my case without the kind of detail and repetition necessary in a criminal trial."

"I'm sorry. I didn't—"

The foreman intervened. "The calling of witnesses—who, when, how many—is up to the District Attorney, Mrs. Zimmerman."

"But he's just standing there telling me what to think."

"He's giving you material for thought. That's an entirely different matter . . . Please continue, Mr. District Attorney."

"Thank you, Mr. Foreman. I would like to go back for a minute to the results of the autopsy performed on Iris Young. Tissue removed from her air sacs and breathing passages showed carbon particles which indicated that she died of asphyxiation caused by the inhalation of smoke. Tissue removed from other areas, especially the abdominal cavity, showed traces of other chemicals, in particular flurazepam hydrochloride. This is a crystalline compound readily soluble in either alcohol or water and rapidly absorbed and metabolized by the body. It's a commonly used sedative sold, by prescription only, under the name Dalmane. That Iris Young, a semi-invalid, should have taken something to induce sleep is not surprising. But the circumstances are peculiar. Dalmane is a very quick-acting drug meant to be administered only after the patient has retired or is about to retire. Iris Young was in her sitting room, fully clothed. So we have another curious fact to add to our growing list.

"And on the heels of that one we come to still another. Dalmane, as I said before, is available by prescription only in fifteen-milligram orange and ivory capsules or thirty-milligram red and ivory. Dr. Albert Varick, Mrs. Young's personal physician, is attending a medical conference in Puerto Rico this week but we have his sworn statement available for you to read. The gist is as follows: From time to time Dr. Varick has prescribed various medications for Iris Young, mainly Indocin, to alleviate the pain of her chronic arthritis. But according to his records and Iris Young's medical file, Dr. Varick never issued her a prescription for Dalmane. Yet there was such a prescription in that house. A police sergeant will give you the details about it later.

"Now, before calling my first witness, Admiral Cooper Young, I feel you should be told in advance that Admiral

Young did not wish to testify and so stated when he was served with a subpoena. He cannot by any means be called a hostile witness, but he is a reluctant one, agreeing to testify only because he believes it's his duty to assist in the enforcement of the law. Please bear this in mind as you listen to him."

The Admiral moved to the witness stand with the brisk no-nonsense walk he'd learned at Annapolis fifty years previously. He gave the appearance of wearing a uniform, though it was only a dark gray suit with a white cuff-linked shirt and black tie and shoes. His face had the slightly jaundiced color that accompanies a fading suntan.

His reluctance to testify would have been apparent to the jury without any previous warning. He glanced at them with obvious distaste before responding to the District Attorney's first question.

"Will you state your name and address for the record, please?"

"Cooper Randolph Young, 1220 Camino Grande, Santa Felicia."

"And your occupation?"

"Vice-Admiral, United States Navy, Retired."

"What was the nature and duration of your relationship with Iris Van Eyck Young?"

"She was my wife for thirty-five years."

"Was it a happy relationship?"

"Yes."

"Would you say that your household was, by and large, a congenial one?"

"Yes."

"I realize this must be a painful experience for you. I wouldn't have asked you to go through it if it weren't necessary. Do you understand that?"

"I hear you talking."

"I can't very well apologize for doing my duty, Admiral."

"No. Such an apology would not be accepted anyway."

"Very well, let's proceed. Would you tell the jury where you were in the late afternoon and early evening of July the Fourth of this year?"

"At home with my family—my wife and my two daughters."

"Anyone else in the house?"

"Mrs. Norgate, our housekeeper, who was cooking dinner."

"And Mrs. Shaw?"

"Yes."

"What was Mrs. Shaw doing?"

"I'm not sure, but she was probably fixing the table for dinner, arranging the centerpiece, the flowers, and so on."

"And candles?"

"And candles, yes."

"Were your dinners usually formal?"

"Yes, as part of my daughters' social education."

"Was there anything different about the dinner that night?"

"It was quite a bit earlier than usual because Mrs. Norgate had an engagement and I had promised my daughters to take them to a display of fireworks at the club. Mrs. Shaw was invited to go along but she refused."

"She refused on what grounds?"

"She didn't want to leave Mrs. Young alone."

"But she *did* leave her alone."

"Only to walk the dog."

"That was long enough, wasn't it?" The D.A. glanced pointedly at the table of exhibits. "Wasn't it?"

"Mrs. Shaw is not responsible for what happened. She was always very gentle and kind to my wife."

"And vice versa?"

"And vice versa, yes."

The District Attorney had been sitting back in his chair until this point in the questioning. Now he leaned forward and wrote on the legal pad in front of him *And vice versa?!*

"Did you know Mrs. Shaw before you hired her, Admiral?"

"Yes. She and her husband were members of the same beach club my wife and I belonged to. All four of us knew each other, though not very well."

"What was the name of the club?"

"The Penguin Club."

"That's pretty well restricted to people in the upper financial brackets, isn't it?"

"Yes."

"Was Mrs. Shaw still a member when she came to you seeking employment?"

"She was not a member and she didn't come to me seeking employment. The possibility of such a job was suggested to her by Miss Brewster, the club secretary, who then spoke to me about Mrs. Shaw's predicament."

"Predicament?"

"Her husband had died leaving a great many debts."

"And so you took her into your house, like a good Samaritan?"

"No, not like that at all. My wife and I needed help with our daughters."

"Would you care to elaborate on that?"

"No."

"All right. Now—"

"Am I permitted to make a statement?"

"Go ahead."

"I want to protest my two daughters' being given subpoenas to testify."

"Do you have any reason to *object* to their testimony, Admiral?"

"I simply feel they're not equipped to deal with stressful situations like this."

"They're of legal age, are they not?"

"Yes."

"And represented by legal counsel?"

"Yes, but they won't listen to his advice."

"I talked personally with both your daughters and they exhibited no signs of stress and no aversion to testifying. Your paternal concern is admirable but perhaps not justified in this instance."

"I have registered my protest."

"It will be on the record, Admiral . . . Now, when did Mrs. Shaw start working for you?"

"Sometime in January."

"Did she fit in well with the other members of your household?"

"Yes."

"Right from the start?"

"There was the usual period of adjustment under such circumstances."

"What was your own relationship with Mrs. Shaw?"

"Relationship?"

"Was it strictly one of employer and employee?"

"She was an employee certainly but I considered her more like a friend. And vice versa, I believe."

"You were friends?"

"Yes."

"More than casual friends?"

"We were friends."

"Close friends?"

"No, I wouldn't say we were—Look, she lived in my house, we saw each other every day, we talked, we ate at the same table. What does that make us?"

"A good question, Admiral."

Once again the District Attorney leaned forward to write on the yellow pad in front of him *What does that make us?* He didn't hurry. He wanted to be sure the jury had plenty of time to supply their own answer to the Admiral's question.

"Tell me, Admiral, did Mrs. Shaw go out socially?"

"What exactly do you mean?"

"Did she have dates?"

"I don't know."

"What percentage of her evenings would you say she spent at home? Fifty percent?"

"I didn't keep track."

"Seventy-five percent? Ninety percent?"

"She spent most of her evenings in the house with the family. Dinners usually lasted until quite late because they were, as I said before, part of my daughters' social education."

"You and your wife, your two daughters and Mrs. Shaw, was this a happy group?"

"Happy is a pretty strong word."

"I agree, happy is a pretty strong word. I'll amend the question. Did the five of you get along in a reasonably civilized manner?"

"Yes."

"That will be all, Admiral."

"I beg your pardon?"

"I have no more questions. You're free to leave."

The old man didn't move.

"Admiral? You may step down now."

"Before I do I would like to make another statement."

"Go ahead."

"If this is all you wanted from me, you might have spared me the embarrassment of a subpoena. I haven't told you anything you didn't already know and I haven't cast any new light on the situation . . ."

"Perhaps you have, Admiral. Thank you very much."

"You didn't even ask me about my wife's death, how it must have happened."

"We know how it happened, Admiral. Please step down."

It was the second most important occasion in Cordelia's life—the first being the Singapore incident—and she had prepared for it by buying a new outfit, a red and white polka-dot pantsuit and genuine red snakeskin shoes. ("Whoever heard of a genuine red snake?" Juliet said.

"You were *had*.") She put on her best wristwatch, three rings, a bracelet made of carved ivory elephants and as a last-minute addition the ruby necklace, formerly Miranda's, which she'd bought from Mr. Tannenbaum a year ago. She hadn't worn it since Miranda moved into the house and she didn't know why she suddenly decided to wear it today, keeping it hidden under the collar of her jacket until she got into her car and on her way to the courthouse.

No one had clearly explained to Cordelia the actual function of the grand jury, but she wasn't nervous. She had, in fact, the pleasant feeling that she was doing her duty, and she spoke in a loud distinct voice, giving her name, Cordelia Catherine Young, and her address, 1220 Camino Grande, and her occupation, none.

"Miss Young, have you discussed the testimony you're about to give with any members of your family?"

"You asked me not to."

"I'm asking you now whether you did."

"Maybe I exchanged a few words with Juliet. I couldn't very well *not*. The subpoenas arrived at the same time and there she was and there I was. We could hardly pretend nothing was happening."

"Did you discuss with her in detail what you were going to say before this jury?"

"No." Cordelia kept her hands in the pockets of her jacket, fingers crossed to protect her from a perjury charge, but in case crossed fingers had no legal significance she added, "Not really."

"Do you know Miranda Shaw, Miss Young?"

"Naturally. She lives in the same house, day and night."

"What is her job?"

"She's supposed to teach me and Juliet things like etiquette, which we already know and anyway we're never invited any place where we can use it. Mrs. Young just couldn't get that through her head."

"Mrs. Young is—was—your mother?"

"I assume she was. That's what it says on my passport."

"Did you get along well with your mother?"

"Nobody got along well with her. She was too hard to please and she had a terrible temper."

The District Attorney stood up and walked around the table, partly to stretch his legs, partly to give the jury a chance to examine this new picture of Iris Young, considerably different from the one presented by the Admiral.

He returned to face the witness chair. "Miss Young— may I call you Cordelia?"

"I don't mind if you think it's etiquette."

"We make our own rules of etiquette in this courtroom. Now, you said a moment ago, Cordelia, that nobody got along well with your mother."

"It's true."

"If Mrs. Shaw, for instance, didn't have a fairly pleasant relationship with her, what made her stay in the house?"

"Money."

"Will you explain that?"

"Mrs. Shaw intended to leave after Mrs. Young hit her with the cane but Pops gave her a raise so she'd stay."

"How much of a raise?"

"Two hundred dollars a month."

"Do you know how Mrs. Shaw received the extra money? Was it added to her salary?"

"Good lord, no. That way Mrs. Young would have found out about it because she paid all the bills and salaries and stuff."

"Then where did this extra two hundred a month come from?"

"Pops gave it to her. It worked out fine because she gave some of it right back."

"How?"

"She bought him presents."

"Mrs. Shaw bought your father presents?"

"Yes."

"Did you ever see any of them?"

215

"No. But Juliet and I heard him thanking her one night in the hall. He said her presents had made him very happy."

"What did you think when you heard this?"

"Exactly what you're thinking," Cordelia said. "Hanky-panky."

"Hanky-panky?"

"That's Juliet's expression for it. She hates to say dirty words when she doesn't have to. Of course, I can spell it out for you if you—"

"No, no. Hanky-panky is fine." The District Attorney sat down again, heavily, as though the pressure of gravity on him had suddenly increased. "I'd like you now to go back to the early evening of July the Fourth. Where were you and Cordelia?"

"Home."

"Doing what?"

"Helping Miranda get the table ready for dinner. The sun was still shining but she made me pull the drapes so we could eat by candlelight. It's supposed to be more civilized, that's what *she* says."

"Did your mother come to the table for dinner?"

"Long enough to gripe about the food and take her medicine. The doctor made her take a capsule for her arthritis at every meal."

"And you distinctly recall her doing so?"

"Yes. She took one of the same capsules she always did."

"What color was it?"

"One end was white and the other end blue."

"The colored end couldn't have been orange?"

"No."

"Or red?"

"No. I was sitting right beside her. She took one of her ordinary blue and white capsules and after that she got up and left without finishing her food."

"Where did she go?"

"Where she always went to escape from the rest of us,

her sitting room. She even had a lock put on it to keep us out."

"When?"

"About a month before she died. It worried the doctor because he was afraid something might happen to her and nobody would be able to get in to help her. But I told him not to fret, I could always pick the lock with one of my credit cards."

"You could pick the lock?"

"It's easy. Even Juliet can do it."

"Getting back to dinner on the night of July the fourth, why did your mother leave the table before finishing her food?"

"She said the meat was tough and the candles had given her a migraine. Even though Miranda took the candles off the table right away, she left anyway."

"Evidently she didn't share Mrs. Shaw's feeling that eating by candlelight was more civilized?"

"She never liked anything Miranda did."

"Why didn't she fire her?"

"Because Miranda took us off her hands, out of the house. Mrs. Young hated having us around but she worried about us when we weren't. We spent a lot of time down at the beach club. I swam a lot but Juliet mostly ate because she had a crush on one of the waiters. It wasn't very romantic. She got fat as a pig and then she found out he was married and had five children. It was a shattering blow plus having to go on a diet."

"I'm sure it was. Thank you, Cordelia. I have no more questions."

Cordelia stepped down from the stand with some reluctance. The second biggest occasion of her life was over and she didn't know for sure what it was all about. In addition, the red snakeskin shoes were beginning to pinch and the ruby necklace felt quite heavy around her neck, as if Miranda herself had somehow become entangled in the silver clasp.

217

· · ·

In comparison with her sister, Juliet was conspicuously dowdy. She'd inherited the frugal nature of her mother's Dutch ancestors, and all her clothes came from Salvation Army and Humane Society thrift stores, and out-of-the-way little shops with names like New to You or Practically Perfect or Born Again Bargains.

The beige chiffon dress she wore had a pleated bodice which moved in and out like an accordion with every breath she took. She took a great many because ever since breakfast she'd been having an attack of nerves. People had urged her to tell the truth but nobody had defined what the truth was except Uncle Charles Van Eyck, and his advice was diluted with alcohol: "Truth is a matter of opinion. So opine, Juliet. Opine."

She wished that Cordelia could be on the stand beside her encouraging her to opine, but the District Attorney explained that this was against the rules of a grand jury hearing, and like it or not, she was on her own. It gave her a creepy feeling having no Cordelia to watch for guidance, a frown, a nod, a shrug. When she walked to the front of the room her knees shook and the accordion pleats kept going in and out very rapidly. She could feel her lips quivering in the anxious little smile Cordelia hated—"You look like an idiot when you do that"—and her mind was an absolute blank—"Opine, Juliet, opine."

She knew the grand jury was supposed to consist of nineteen people, but there seemed to be at least fifty and she noticed that the District Attorney, who previously seemed rather nice, had very cruel eyebrows. She gave her name and address in a whisper, as if the information were top secret being dragged out of her under duress: Juliet Ariel Young, 1220 Camino Grande.

The District Attorney's eyebrows jumped at her. "I must ask you to speak louder, Miss Young."

"I . . . can't."

"Please try. Would you like a glass of water?"

Even the mention of water made her want to go to the bathroom, and she said "No" quite firmly.

"That's better, Miss Young. Perhaps you'd feel more at ease if I called you Juliet. Let's give it a try anyway . . . Now tell me, Juliet, were you living at 1220 Camino Grande the first week of June, approximately a month before your mother died?"

"Yes."

"On the afternoon of June the sixth was a package delivered to the house for Miranda Shaw?"

"Yes. She wasn't home, so the deliveryman asked me to sign for it."

"And did you?"

"Yes."

"Would you describe the package?"

"It was a huge silver box tied with white satin ribbon. There was a fancy label on it, The Ultimate in Intimate, which is the name of a bridal boutique downtown."

"What did you do with the box?"

"Left it on the hall table. Miranda got very excited when she came and saw it. She took it right up to her room and locked the door."

"Did she mention it to anyone?"

"No."

"Were you curious?"

"I guess I must have been."

"Please speak up, Juliet. Did your curiosity prompt you to take any action?"

"You know it did. I told you all about it."

"Now tell the jury."

"It was Cordelia's turn to help Miranda fix the table for dinner, so while they were busy downstairs I went upstairs and sort of let myself into Miranda's room."

"You picked the lock?"

"I guess you could call it that."

"Did you find the box?"

"I didn't have to find it. It was in plain sight on the floor, empty."

"What about its contents?"

"There was an expensive-looking nightgown made of some white filmy material trimmed with lace and little pink rosebuds. A robe made of the same material was draped over a chair."

"Where was the nightgown?"

"On the bed, lengthwise, as if someone invisible was lying inside it. The wig made it worse."

"Wig?"

"She had put one of her wigs on the pillow. It made me feel qualmsy. I got out of there in a hurry."

"Did you talk to anyone about it?"

"No."

"Not even your sister?"

"Expecially not her. She would have wanted to go and see it for herself and drag me along and I was scared we'd be . . . that Miranda would catch us and . . . well, you know."

"I don't know. Tell me."

"I was scared if Miranda caught us she'd take steps. That was the way she threatened us, saying she'd take steps if we didn't listen to her and obey her. She never explained what she meant, but she meant something not very nice. If my father marries her it'll be murder. She can twist him around her little finger."

"Wait. Hold on a minute, Juliet. You said if your father *marries* her?"

"Yes."

"Let's put things in perspective here. The clothes which Mrs. Shaw bought at the bridal boutique were delivered on June the sixth, is that right?"

"Yes."

"That was a month before your mother died."

"Yes."

"Do you think there's something peculiar about this order of events?"

"I don't . . . can't think anything."

"Why not?"

"I live in the same house with her."

"Are you afraid, Juliet?"

Juliet didn't answer. She had her hands clasped together very tightly, as though someone had threatened to separate them by force.

"Let the record show," the District Attorney said, "that the witness is nodding her head affirmatively."

From the moment Charles Van Eyck walked into the courtroom it was obvious to the District Attorney that the old man had primed himself for the occasion with alcohol. He thanked the bailiff effusively for escorting him to the witness stand, bowed to the members of the jury, shook hands with the District Attorney and swore to tell the truth, the whole truth and nothing but the truth.

"Are you feeling all right, Mr. Van Eyck?"

"Yes, indeed. Never better. And yourself?"

"Please sit down, if you don't mind."

"Oh, I don't mind. Not at all. A pleasure to be here. Didn't have anything else to do anyway."

"Will you state your name and address for the record?"

"Charles Maas Van Eyck, 840 Camino Azur, the azur referring to the jacaranda trees planted along the road, though the blossoms are actually more purplish than bluish, wouldn't you say so?"

"You're retired, are you not, Mr. Van Eyck?"

"Dear me, no. I'm a monitor of government waste. Can't afford to retire from a job like that when there are so few of us and millions of them. Even *you* are one of *them* because you're a county employee."

"Then I suggest we get down to business immediately and avoid further waste. You were related to the deceased woman, Iris Young?"

"She was my sister."

"Was it a close relationship?"

"Close as either of us could stand."

221

"When was the last time you saw her?"

"Towards the end of June, shortly before she died. She called and asked me to come over, she had something important to talk to me about while the Admiral and the girls were out of the house. Very odd. We never had much to say to each other."

"Did you go?"

"Hard to say no to Iris. She's always been a forceful woman. Kicked and screamed when she was a baby and much the same sort of thing when she got older."

"Who let you into the house?"

"Miranda Shaw. She was on her way to the garden to cut some flowers."

"Did you exchange any words?"

"I asked her about the possibility of a small drink before I talked to Iris. But she said no because Iris had seen my car coming up the driveway and was waiting. In fact, the music was already playing."

"Music?"

"People like Iris who are getting deaf often use the trick of playing loud background music so that other people will have to shout above it. Most irritating. An ordinary conversation turns into a shouting match."

"Do you remember what the weather was like?"

"It's always pretty much the same at that time of year, warm, sunny, rather monotonous."

"Were the windows open in your sister's room?"

"Yes, I distinctly recall sitting beside one to get away from the music. Never cared much for Mozart, same damn thing over and over. He probably started too young, should have been booted out to play cricket like the rest of the boys."

"Can you give me the gist of the conversation you had with your sister, Mr. Van Eyck?"

"She was in the process of drawing up a new will and she wanted to warn me not to expect anything, since I already had an adequate income. I objected to the idea of being cut off without a penny—the principle of the thing, her own flesh and blood and all that—so she said very well, she would leave me a penny. Iris had a rather crude sense of humor."

"Did she tell you anything else about the will?"

"Its main purpose was to set up trusts for the two girls so they'd be well provided for during their lifetime but unable to throw money around. The capital would eventually go to various institutions and foundations."

"What did she intend to leave to Admiral Young, her husband?"

"The house."

"Just the house?"

"Probably its contents too."

"No cash, stocks, bonds?"

"He has a sizable pension. Iris thought anything more would simply make him a target for some predatory woman."

"Did she mention anyone in particular?"

"She didn't have to. Cooper never got much chance to meet other women, predatory or not, and Miranda was right there in the house all the time. I said, 'Cooper's too old for Miranda.' And she said, 'He's also going to be too poor.' "

"Let's recapitulate for a minute, Mr. Van Eyck. This discussion about your sister's new will took place in a room with the windows open and music playing so loud that you had to shout in order to be heard."

"Yes."

"Did the possibility of an eavesdropper occur to you?"

"Certainly. I'm sure it occurred to her too. I'd say she probably depended on it to get her message across."

"By that you mean she expected and wanted to be over-heard?"

"I think so."

"You may step down now, Mr. Van Eyck. Thank you very much."

"It was no trouble, not a bit. I didn't have anything else to do anyway."

Once again Van Eyck shook hands with the District Attorney and bowed to the members of the jury. Then the District Attorney sat back in his chair and watched the members while they watched the old man leave. They looked a little uneasy, as though they'd just caught the first real scent of blood in the air.

It was time to call in the police.

Sergeant Reuben Orr of the sheriff's department testified that in the early hours of July the fifth—"as soon as we could wake up the judge"—he had obtained a search warrant to enter the premises at 1220 Camino Grande.

"And did you search the premises, Sergeant?"

"Yes, sir. I and my partner, Ernesto Salazar, spent the next two days going through the house room by room except for the burned area, which was left to an arson specialist."

"Did you find anything which has a particular bearing on this case?"

"Yes, sir, several items."

"Are they in this courtroom now?"

"Yes, sir, on the table with the other exhibits. They've been marked 15 A, 15 B, 15 C, and 16."

"Let's consider 15 A first. Would you go over and pick it up and show it to the jury?"

"Yes, sir."

"Now describe it, please."

"It's a piece of pale blue notepaper which has been crumpled and then straightened out and placed between sheets of heavy plastic for safekeeping. The paper is of good quality, made of rags instead of wood pulp, and there are words on it written with a felt-tipped black pen."

"Where did you find it?"

"In a trash bin outside the door of the main kitchen."

"What condition was it in at that time?"

"Crumpled."

"What is it?"

"A letter or note, at least the beginning of one."

"We'll return to that in a moment. I direct your attention to exhibit 15 B. What is it, Sergeant?"

"A half-empty box of pale blue stationery."

"Could the sheet of paper marked 15 A have come from this box?"

"Not only could, it did."

"Where was the box found?"

"In the room occupied by Mrs. Miranda Shaw."

"What about exhibit 15 C?"

"I found that in the same place, on the desk in her room. It's an address book bound in blue leather which has faded and turned greenish from overexposure to light. There are gold initials on the front, M.W.S."

"What does the book contain?"

"Names, addresses and phone numbers, dates of anniversaries and birthdays, and a Christmas card list going back several years."

"All in what appears to be the same handwriting?"

"Yes, sir, even though the entries were made at different times with different writing instruments—pencil, metal nib and ballpoint pens, and in the case of the most recent entries, a black felt-tipped pen."

"Was this handwriting similar in any way to that of the unfinished letter or note found in the trash bin?"

"It was similar in all ways, including the instrument used, a black felt-tipped pen."

"So 15 A was written on a sheet of paper from 15 B, the box of stationery found in Miranda Shaw's room, in the same handwriting as in 15 C, Miranda Shaw's address book."

"Yes, sir."

"Would you read to the jury the words written on 15 A?"

"Yes, sir . . . 'Dearly Beloved: I don't expect you to

approve of my plan. It must seem drastic to you but please please realise that it is the only way we can be together. This is the important thing, being together, you and I, now and always . . .' The word realise, spelled with an s, has been stroked out and realize, spelled with a z, written above it. Possibly on this account the note was crumpled up and thrown away."

"Does the phrase 'dearly beloved' have any connotation in your mind?"

"Those are the words that usually begin a marriage ceremony."

"A marriage ceremony?"

"Yes, sir."

At the back of the room the fan, as if it had been waiting for the right moment, made a few gasping noises and expired. The District Attorney poured himself another glass of water.

"Sergeant Orr, which of the exhibits 15 A, B and C did you find first?"

"We started our search on the ground floor, so we found the note in the trash bin first, 15 A. It sounded peculiar in view of what had happened, so I was on the lookout for any clue as to who wrote it. When I found the box of stationery and then the address book containing the same handwriting, I became interested in everything else in Mrs. Shaw's room which might possibly have some bearing on the case."

"Such as exhibit 16?"

"Yes, sir."

"Show it to the jury and explain what it is and where you found it."

"Yes, sir. It's a bottle of red and ivory capsules prescribed by Dr. Michael Lane for Mrs. Miranda Shaw on June the twentieth of this year. I found it in the medicine cabinet of Mrs. Shaw's bathroom. Each capsule contains thirty milligrams of Dalmane, which is a fast-acting sedative. The dosage on the bottle is given as one capsule at bedtime for sleep."

"How many capsules are left in this bottle?"

"Six."

"How many were in it originally?"

"According to the pharmacist's label, thirty."

"Now, if Mrs. Shaw took one every night as prescribed, beginning June the twentieth until July the fourth when you picked this up in her medicine cabinet, how many should there be left in the bottle?"

"Fifteen."

"Are there fifteen left?"

"No, sir. As I said before, there are six."

"So nine are unaccounted for."

"They're missing, yes, sir."

"Thank you, Sergeant. That will be all."

It was enough.

On October the fourteenth the grand jury of the county of Santa Felicia returned an indictment of willful homicide against Miranda Waring Shaw in the death of Iris Van Eyck Young, a human being.

Part VII

Shortly after Miranda Shaw was arrested Aragon went out to the county jail to see her. He was escorted to one of the consulting rooms, which was the size of a shoebox and smelled of disinfectant flowing in through the air conditioner along with cold dry air and the inescapable noises of an institution.

A policewoman brought Miranda as far as the door and then left, or appeared to leave. Aragon had the feeling she was standing just outside in the corridor.

He said, "Hello, Mrs. Shaw," but she didn't answer or even glance at him.

She had changed during the weeks since he'd talked to her in the cabana at the Penguin Club. The makeup around her eyes only emphasized their dullness and her face seemed frozen under its layers of pink and ivory. She'd been allowed to wear her own clothes instead of the cotton dress which was the women's uniform. She had on a blue faille suit that made her look as if she were on her way to a cocktail party and had just dropped in at the jail for a visit with some erring relative.

"I'm sorry," he said. "I'm very sorry."

"Are you. Well, that doesn't change a thing, does it?"

"I thought you'd like to be told anyway."

"Thanks."

They sat down on steel and plastic chairs riveted to the floor.

"Smedler sent me," he said. "He wanted you to know

that Admiral Young is arranging bail for you. It's taking time because of the amount of money involved, a hundred thousand dollars. Though that's much too high under the circumstances, there's nothing we can do about it, the judge has an ulcer and quotes Scripture. However, you should be out of here by tomorrow morning."

"Then what?"

"A trial date will be set, which won't be definite because there'll probably be a number of postponements. You can figure on three or four months minimum."

"And where do I spend these three or four months?"

"Not here, that's the important thing."

"I have nowhere to go. I can't very well return to the Admiral's house. It wouldn't look right and I wouldn't feel right with those girls following me around, spying on me. They'd enjoy that, it would be like a new game to them."

"Or not so new."

She clutched the steel arms of the chair. He noticed that most of the coral polish on her nails had been chipped or peeled off and the nails themselves bitten. "Did they say evil things about me to the grand jury?"

"Evil? No."

"Why does Cooper want to bail me out?"

"He thinks you're innocent. A lot of people do."

"It's too bad some of them weren't on the grand jury."

"Some of them were," Aragon said. "The vote of four-teen to five means that five people were against the indict-ment. After going over the transcript, Smedler agrees with them and so do I. Not only is the D.A.'s case weak, he broke half the rules of evidence in presenting it. He won't be able to get away with that kind of stuff when the actual trial comes up . . . Do you feel like answering some ques-tions?"

"I'm not sure."

"Suppose we find out."

"Go ahead."

"Did you ever buy the Admiral any presents?"

230

"Of course not."

"Both the girls claim they overheard him thanking you."

"They're mistaken. Surely nobody believed them. Why should I, living on a pitifully small salary, buy presents for Cooper with all his money? It's ridiculous."

"People do ridiculous things."

"In this case two people *heard* ridiculous things. Surely nobody believed them," she said again.

"The fact that both girls claim to have overheard it may make it twice as believable."

"But the two of them are always in cahoots about everything."

"I think we can find ways to establish that when the time comes." He consulted the page of notes Smedler had made when he read the transcript of the hearing. "One of the points brought up was that you refused an invitation to go to a fireworks display at the club on the grounds that you didn't want to leave Mrs. Young alone. Yet you left her alone anyway."

"I walked the dog."

"A couple of hours earlier than usual."

"Yes. She asked me to. She said Alouette was acting sick. Heaven knows, that was nothing unusual. She fed the poor creature absurd things like chocolate éclairs and cheesecake."

"At dinner that night you removed the candlesticks from the table because the flickering lights were giving Mrs. Young a migraine. Where did you put them?"

"On the buffet."

"Then at that time both candlesticks would have had your fingerprints on them. Did you handle either of them again?"

"No. I had no reason to."

Aragon felt encouraged. Though she couldn't under the circumstances have been enjoying herself, at least she was coming to life. Her eyes were getting brighter and a trace of animation showed on her face.

He said, "A bottle of Dalmane was found in your medicine cabinet. Do you take it regularly?"

"No. Hardly ever. I've been afraid of drugs ever since that clinic in Mexico."

"There were only six capsules left."

"Six? That's impossible. The bottle was nearly full the last time I noticed it."

"And you don't know what happened to the rest?"

"No."

"Did anyone have access to your room?"

"It was cleaned twice a week by one of the day staff. Otherwise I kept it locked. I'm not positive, but I suspect the girls had learned some method of unlocking it. Occasionally items would be in a slightly different place from where I'd left them, or a drawer would be partly open."

"They picked the lock with a credit card," he said. "That's how they knew about the lingerie from the bridal shop."

"I see."

"You bought it on June the sixth."

"Around then, yes."

"Why?"

"For my marriage to Cooper. I had to have a decent trousseau."

"Mrs. Young was still alive at the time."

"Yes, but she didn't *stay* alive. Wasn't it a nice coincidence that she—"

"Be quiet. I mean, for God's sake, don't say things like that. It wasn't nice and a lot of people think it wasn't a coincidence."

"Well, you don't have to be so mean about it. I see things from my standpoint and you see them from yours."

"For the next few months we're going to be sharing a standpoint. Mine." In spite of the air conditioning he had begun to sweat. He loosened his tie and opened the top button of his shirt. "In fact, from now on you've got to consider yourself on trial. Watch what you say, what you do. Be careful where you go and with whom."

"It would be simpler if I just stayed here in jail," she said bitterly. "I might as well if I have no rights left, if I can't even see the people I want to."

"That depends on what people you want to see."

"I won't tell you. You'll only get mean again if I do."

"Grady Keaton. Is he one of them?"

"Yes."

"Why?"

"*Why*? Because we love each other. And I must explain to him that whatever I did was for the two of us, so we could be together."

"I think we should avoid bringing Grady into the case if we can," Aragon said.

"What difference does it make?"

"It may seem peculiar in this day and age, but juries are more likely to vote for a conviction if sexual misconduct is involved. The events leading up to and down from Pasoloma—or down to and up from if you want to be geographical—can do you a lot of harm."

"I want to see Grady."

"I'm advising you not to, for the time being anyway. If you have a message for him, let me deliver it."

She was silent for a long time, staring at the blank gray wall as though it were her window on the world.

"I love him," she said finally. "Tell him I love him and when all this silly fuss is over we'll be together again."

The front doors of the club were propped open with rubber wedges and taped with Fresh Paint signs. There was no one in the office. Aragon walked in unchallenged.

Under a shroud of late-summer fog the terrace was deserted and in the pool only one swimmer was visible, a large woman moving slowly through the water like an overloaded barge.

In the corridor Walter Henderson, the manager, was occupied at the bulletin board tacking up some of the pictures from the last party, a backgammon and bingo tournament. By Henderson's standards it had been a dull affair, with a great deal of confusion about who was playing what, and he was trying to plan something more dynamic for the next theme party, which would fall on Halloween. Since the social-events committee had vetoed any more money for decorations, he was working on a clever way to use the life-sized plastic skeletons from the previous Halloween. A Gallows Gala might be effective, with each of the skeletons dressed as a famous murderer or murderee and strategically placed throughout the club and its grounds, hanging from the diving tower and from a limb of the cypress tree (very effective if there was a decent wind), peeking into the ballroom windows from the oleander hedge, even sitting on one of the toilets in the ladies' powder room. (What delicious screams, he could hear them now: *Help, help!*)

". . . could help me," Aragon said.

Henderson was jolted back to reality as the skeletons fell from the diving tower and out of the tree and off the toilet. "Oh, damn. What do you want?"

"I'm looking for Ellen Brewster."

"She's in the office."

"No."

"Well, she's *supposed* to be in the office. But of course, that doesn't mean a thing around here. Try the snack bar. She's been drinking coffee by the gallon lately."

"Thanks."

Aragon went down the corridor to the snack bar. A couple of the tables were occupied by boys and girls in tennis costume. Little Frederic Quinn was among them, his tennis racket stuck in the back of his sweater in order to leave his hands free for shooting straws out of their paper sheaths. He acknowledged Aragon's presence by shooting a straw at him. It missed.

Ellen was sitting at a corner table with a pot of tea in front of her and a doughnut with a bite taken out of it. She looked cold.

He said, "May I sit down?"

234

"I guess."

"Anything the matter?"

"I hate the summer fogs. They depress me. Winter fogs are natural, you expect them and you're depressed anyway and—Oh hell, the fog has nothing to do with it. I feel lousy, that's all."

"Sorry."

"Why did you come here?"

"To see Grady," Aragon said. "I have a message for him."

"Really? Well, you're about forty-eight hours too late. He took off as soon as he heard the news about Miranda. Oh, I think he wanted to leave anyway, I could see him getting restless, bored. Miranda's arrest simply brought it to a head. He was afraid she'd drag him into it and the whole business about the Porsche would come out and maybe a lot of other stuff as well."

"Do you know where he went?"

"He didn't leave a forwarding address. He just patted me on the head, told me I was a nice girl and packed his bags." She had begun crumbling the doughnut and rolling the pieces into greasy little pills. "Want to hear something funny? I lent him fifty dollars."

Frederic aimed a straw in her direction. It hit her on the side of the head but she paid no attention.

"Tell Miranda," she said, "tell her he wanted to say goodbye to her but he had to leave right away because a chance for a decent job came up very suddenly. In Oklahoma."

"A chance for a job came up very suddenly in Oklahoma."

"Yes."

"She won't believe it."

"Why not?" Ellen said. "I did."

The indictment and arrest of Miranda also led to some less predictable events.

In early fall Cordelia, free of the restraint of her mother and to a large extent of the Admiral, who was preoccupied, bought an Aston-Martin guaranteed by the dealer to go one hundred and thirty miles an hour. Anxious to determine the accuracy of this claim, Cordelia chose for the test a side road that was practically deserted. When she floored the accelerator, only one other car was in sight, but unfortunately it belonged to an off-duty patrolman.

Cordelia's defense was that nearly everything in the Aston-Martin was computerized and something must have gone wrong with the circuits controlling the speedometer. Her driver's license was revoked anyway and she took up bicycling. Clad in matching jogging suits and plastic helmets the girls pedaled around town on a bright red tandem equipped with a horn on the main handlebars for Cordelia and a bell at the rear for Juliet.

Juliet had some criticism of this arrangement, which pretty well limited her view: "Your behind is enormous."

"What do I care," Cordelia said. "I'm in front."

In late September, Frederic Quinn was, for a price, reinstated at Sophrosune School. For his first report in Social Studies class he chose a black widow spider. After spending two days (and a hundred and fifty demerits) in the search he found a specimen underneath a gopher trap in the garage and brought it to school in his sister April's Lucite earring box. By this time the spider had lost a couple of legs and considerable *joie de vivre* as well as *joie de tuer*. However, the red hourglass on its abdomen was still visible, identifying it as dangerous.

"Get that damn thing out of here," the teacher said. "You're supposed to be making your report on a current event from the newspaper."

"I am. It was in all the newspapers how a woman I know personally was arrested for murder just like a black widow spider stinging her mate to death, only it wasn't her mate—"

"Put it in the wastebasket."

"This is my sister's best earring box. She'll kill me."

"You have a choice," the teacher said. "Her or me."

It was in mid-November, after Miranda's trial had been postponed for a third time, that Charles Van Eyck received the letter from Tokyo. He didn't know anyone in Tokyo, and those of his acquaintances financially able to travel in the Orient were no longer physically able.

There was no doubt, however, that the letter was meant for him. The envelope was neatly typed Charles Maas Van Eyck, 840 Camino Azur, Santa Felicia, California, and even the zip code was correct. Still he hesitated to open it. At his age bad news outnumbered good by a considerable margin and he felt it would be wise to prepare himself for the worst with a glass of the best. He poured himself half a tumbler of Scotch from the decanter in his den.

It was a cold drizzly day, exactly the kind he remembered from his trips to Scotland—hardly any wonder the natives had invented Scotch, it was a simple matter of survival—so he lit the logs laid tepee style in the grate, avocado prunings, gray and smooth and no bigger than a child's arm. Then, using his thumbnail as a paper knife, he slit open the envelope.

Dear Charles:

I don't know when or if you will receive this. I am enclosing it in my chess move to Professor Sukimoto in Tokyo, asking him to stamp and post it for me. I have addressed the outside envelope to his office at the university as usual but this time I marked it *Hold for Return*. I know he is on a research leave in Paris and won't be back for several months. This fits in perfectly with the plans I've made for Miranda.

It won't surprise you to learn that I've worked things out as carefully as my limited mobility allowed. What will surprise you is that you were actually present when the idea took shape in my mind. It was the last time you came to this house for dinner. Miranda, acting out her role of governess, had given the girls some questions to answer, questions for a summer night she called them. Juliet protested that it wasn't summer yet, so she didn't have the answers. But I had mine, right away, then and there.

Do you remember those questions? I can never forget them:

Have I earned something today?

Have I learned something today?

Have I helped someone?

Have I felt glad to be alive?

In my case the answers were easy: no, no, no and no. I added one more question. Did I have a reason to go on living? No.

You were right, Charles, in that anonymous letter you wrote warning me about taking a Jezebel into my home. She is exactly what you claimed, a Jezebel. And Cooper is what he always has been, a nice gullible fool. And the girls, my daughters, they will be the victims unless I act to stop it.

I must protect my girls. They will never marry, never create, never be employed. (What happened? Why are they like this? I've blamed myself a thousand times and Cooper a thousand more, though the blame game is useless.) But within their limits they can be quite happy if they aren't criticized or ridiculed, if they're not at the mercy of a woman like Miranda.

So I have made my plans and I think they'll work. Even some of the things I didn't really plan may implicate her in my death. The Dalmane is an example. I took a dozen or so capsules from her medicine chest—I learned from watching Cordelia how easily a lock can be picked—to alleviate some of the suffering which is inevitable. I have endured a great deal of suffering and I can endure more, but I hope the Dalmane capsules will help. I will swallow them after the candle is lit and before I turn on the gas and strike myself on the head with my cane, not hard, just enough to cause bleeding. Heads bleed easily, more easily than hearts, perhaps.

I expect the handle of the cane and the candlestick, both being metal, to survive the fire to some extent. There will be blood on the cane, which should start the police wondering, and no fingerprints on the candlestick because I will have wiped it clean, and that will keep them wondering. Probably none of them will even think of suicide because the whole thing is too bizarre. That's why I planned it the way I did.

I intend to get Miranda to mail this to Professor Sukimoto, a grotesque little touch I can't resist. I'll also see that she walks the dog early. She's bound to tell the police I asked her to, but will they believe her? Will anyone believe anything she says? Cooper, perhaps. No one else.

Poor Cooper. I feel sorry for him, but he'll get over my death pretty quickly even without Miranda around to help him. And she won't be around. She won't be marrying my husband, spending my money, managing my daughters.

I have unloaded all this on you, Charles, because I have a notion you'd rather not think of me as a victim. I have been a victim of some cruel things in my life but I am in full charge of my own death.

It's a victory of sorts.

Iris

The receptionist in the District Attorney's office wore a uniform of a mustard color which made Van Eyck quite nauseated.

He said faintly, "Some time ago, July, I believe it was, I wrote the D.A. a letter about the Iris Young case."

"What is the name, please?"

"My name or the name on the letter?"

"I thought you said you wrote it."

"I did. But I didn't sign it. I never do. I mean, there are so many things one can express better without signing a name."

"I'm sure one can," the woman said. "But when you do sign a name, what do you sign?"

"I believe in this case it was Fair Play. That's not important, however. I mentioned my letter to the D.A. merely to introduce—or rather to let it be known that my interest in the case is—"

"Wait here a moment, Mr. Play."

"No, no. I'm not Mr. Play."

"But you just said—"

"Forget about the name. The important thing is that I've just had a revelation, a most astonishing revelation."

"We don't have time for revelations in this department, expecially those induced by alcohol. And you have been drinking, haven't you, Mr. Play?"

"I told you I'm *not* Mr. Play. I don't even *know* anybody called Mr. Play."

"Then why did you sign his name to a letter?"

"Oh God," Van Eyck said and turned and ran.

Back home he poured himself another tumbler of Scotch. Then he threw some more avocado logs in the grate and put the letter from Tokyo on top of them.

It flamed briefly, turned black, turned gray, and rode the updraft into the chimney.

Dear me, he thought with a little twinge of surprise. *I believe I've just murdered Miranda.*

About the Author

Born and educated in Canada, MARGARET MILLAR lives in Santa Barbara, California, with her husband, writer Ross Macdonald, three dogs and an assortment of wildlife. Her vocation and avocation are the same—books. In 1956 she received the Edgar Allan Poe award from the Mystery Writers of America and was a *Los Angeles Times* Woman of the Year in 1965. She and her husband are active environmentalists.